"You c[...] isn't whole.

"I won't let you throw yourself away like that."

Maggie blinked at the vehemence of Garrick's words.

"You've seen me. You've seen my leg," he went on, before she could deny his self-description. "I'll be blunt, Maggie—can you really bear to think of *that* in your bed? Because that's what it would mean, sooner or later, if we go on kissing and touching. I'm not a boy to be fobbed off with a few kisses and caresses in the moonlight, Maggie—I'm a man. And I'll be damned if I'll open my heart to another woman who's going to run screaming from my bed."

"I'm far from perfect myself, Garrick. And you are not your *leg*, Garrick. That is a part of you, yes, but when one loves, one loves the *whole* person. And there is much in you to love...."

Dear Reader,

Entertainment. Escape. Fantasy. These three words describe the heart of Harlequin Historical novels. If you want compelling, emotional stories by some of the best writers in the field, look no further.

Award-winning author and native Texan Laurie Grant has really hit her stride with *Maggie and the Maverick*, the last of her DEVLIN BROTHERS books. Garrick Devlin mistrusts women—with good reason: his wife left him when he came home wounded from the Civil War *and* she never told him she was pregnant. Now, trying to put a life together for his three-year-old boy, he hires a newsman to help him start a paper. Only, M. L. Harper is really Maggie—a dainty Texas Yankee!—who wins his respect and shows him how to love again.

The Unlikely Wife by Cassandra Austin is a sparkling Western about a flirty, truly *unlikely* wife and the officer and gentleman who shows her what the love of a good man can do. Margaret Moore returns with *The Welshman's Bride*, part of her WARRIOR SERIES, about a roguish nobleman and the shy lady he takes to wife, who prove that opposites do attract!

Be sure to look for *Hunter of My Heart* by talented newcomer Janet Kendall. In this fascinating, multilayered Regency, two Scottish nobles are bribed into marrying in an effort to protect their past secrets. Intrigue and passion abound from start to finish!

Whatever your tastes in reading, you'll be sure to find a romantic journey back to the past between the covers of a Harlequin Historical® novel.

Sincerely,

Tracy Farrell
Senior Editor

Please address questions and book requests to:
Harlequin Reader Service
U.S.: 3010 Walden Ave., P.O. Box 1325, Buffalo, NY 14269
Canadian: P.O. Box 609, Fort Erie, Ont. L2A 5X3

MAGGIE AND THE MAVERICK

Laurie Grant

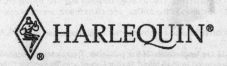

HARLEQUIN®

TORONTO • NEW YORK • LONDON
AMSTERDAM • PARIS • SYDNEY • HAMBURG
STOCKHOLM • ATHENS • TOKYO • MILAN • MADRID
PRAGUE • WARSAW • BUDAPEST • AUCKLAND

ISBN 0-373-29061-6

MAGGIE AND THE MAVERICK

Copyright © 1999 by Laurie A. Miller

This edition published by arrangement with Harlequin Books S.A.

® and TM are trademarks of the publisher. Trademarks indicated with ® are registered in the United States Patent and Trademark Office, the Canadian Trade Marks Office and in other countries.

Look us up on-line at: http://www.romance.net

Printed in U.S.A.

Books by Laurie Grant

Harlequin Historicals

Beloved Deceiver #170
The Raven and the Swan #205
Lord Liar #257
Devil's Dare #300
My Lady Midnight #340
Lawman #367
The Duchess and the Desperado #421
Maggie and the Maverick #461

LAURIE GRANT

combines a career as a trauma center emergency room nurse with that of historical romance author; she says living in two worlds keeps her sane. Passionately enthusiastic about the history of both England and Texas, she divides her travel time between these two spots. She is married to her own real-life hero, and has two teenage daughters, two dogs and a cat.

Laurie loves to hear from her readers. You can write to her at P.O. Box 307272, Gahana, OH 43230.

To Ann Bouricius and Carol McFarland, who between
them coerced me into writing this book,
To Deborah Simmons, fellow Harlequin Hussy, who
gave me the title,
To the determined and inspiring folk who make up the
Amputee Coalition of America,
And to my own personal curmudgeon and hero, Michael.

ACKNOWLEDGMENT

I would like to thank Dale Starr, who works in the Print
Shop at the Ohio Village, Ohio Historical Society, for his
guidance in researching the newspaper industry in
general and printing presses as they existed in frontier
America in the 1800s.

I would also like to thank Alvin C. Pike, certified
prosthetist, President and Clinical Director of Amputee
Rehabilitation Services in Hopkins, Minn., and
Ian Gregson, editor of *Amputation Online Magazine,* for
their invaluable assistance in researching the history of
leg prosthetics and in understanding the adjustments,
both physical and psychological, that amputees
must make.

Prologue

"It's been very enjoyable, Maggie mine," Captain Richard Burke told her, smiling regretfully as he rose from the horsehair sofa in front of the hearth. "But I'm afraid marriage is out of the question. You see...I have a wife back East."

Even as her mind tried to process the words, Margaret Harper automatically noticed how handsome he looked in his uniform, his captain's bars gleaming against the crisp dark blue. Richard Burke was an attractive man. And even now, as she began to comprehend the full horror of what he had just said, she still couldn't rid her mind of the thought that he looked the very picture of a soldier.

"Y-you're *married?*" Her lips, which still felt the taste of his passionate kiss, grew numb, and she could hardly form the words. "But you...but we've been courting— we've been *lovers!* How could you make me think... How could you say you *loved* me—when you...belonged to another?"

Richard sighed, smiled at her again and started to cup her chin in his hand, a gesture she had always found charming. Now she shrank from his touch. He had betrayed her!

How could he think she would let him put his hands on her *now?*

"Ah, Maggie, who wouldn't love you? Who could resist you? You're an unusual woman, you know. Why, I've never met a female like you—a reporter, no less! And I wasn't lying when I said I loved you. I do—in a way I'll never love Beatrice, my wife. You understand me as she never could. And you're so honest—"

"That's certainly a virtue you can't claim, isn't it, Richard?" she snapped, ignoring the pain that sliced through her like a cavalry saber. She slapped his still-extended hand away and jumped to her feet. "Don't you dare touch me, you—you cur! Get out!"

But Richard Burke gave her another of his coaxing smiles. "Now, Maggie, let's not be so hasty. Boston is hundreds of miles away, and what you and I found together was very…special to me. I believe it was to you, too. Surely we can just go on as we've been? You'd miss my loving, wouldn't you? I know I'd miss touching you, kissing you—"

"You *bastard,*" she hissed. "I'd feel contaminated if your shadow ever again so much as crossed mine. I told you once to leave, and I meant it. Now *get out,* or I'll call my father."

"Margaret, I wouldn't do that if I were you," Burke retorted silkily. "Would you really like him to know why you're upset? Do you really want your dear papa to know his innocent daughter is innocent no more? You know, I never expected you to be a…to be untouched, the way you smiled at me."

"*Damn you,* Richard Burke," she said between clenched teeth, feeling her hands curl into claws and fighting the urge to launch herself at him and rake that handsome face. "Damn you to hell!"

"Now, now, I've always admired your fiery temperament, m'dear—it goes with that red hair—but a *lady* doesn't curse. But then, a lady doesn't soil her hands in printer's ink, either, does she? Can you wonder that I thought you a woman of the world?''

She wasn't aware of her hand closing around the delicate little figurine on the end table beside the couch; she didn't know she had picked it up until it shattered against the wall just an inch or two above Burke's head.

He flinched as shards of porcelain rained around him, and after one last reproachful look, beat a hasty retreat out the door.

From above, Maggie heard her father call, ''Is anything amiss, Margaret? I thought I heard a noise. Did something break?''

''Everything's all right, Papa,'' she called back, hoping he did not hear the shakiness of her voice. ''Mr. Burke was just leaving, and I'm afraid I accidentally knocked the little china ballerina to the floor and broke it.''

''Oh, is that all? Too bad, but I thought you were hurt. Tell Mr. Burke goodbye for me—and why not invite him to Sunday dinner?''

The only place I'll invite him to go is straight to hell, Papa. Then she realized she'd better clean up the damage before she had to explain why the remains of the figurine were lying scattered on the braided rug next to the parlor door rather than next to the end table. She knelt and, holding up her skirt to form a pocket, began dropping the broken pieces into it.

How could she have been so foolish? she wondered, as tears began to blind her eyes to the task. How could she have trusted Richard Burke so completely when he said he loved her, in spite of the still, small voice inside her that said it was too soon, that words of admiration and love came too easily to the Yankee captain's mouth? *This is what you get for ignoring that warning, whether you call it conscience or an angel's voice,* she told herself fiercely. *You deserve this heartache, because your instincts told you Richard Burke was too good to be true, and you didn't believe them.*

He'd sworn they'd be married just as soon as they could arrange it, but he'd begged to be allowed to make love to her sooner. He was on fire for her, he'd claimed that night about a month ago, when he'd come calling. Her father had been working late at the newspaper office, and she'd known better than to let Richard in, but he'd coaxed her and teased her until she'd done so.

He'd begun his seduction as soon as the door had closed behind him. She'd surrendered to him that night, and he'd kissed away her tears from the pain of losing her virginity. He'd told her she was magnificent, that he loved her, and he'd renewed his promise that they'd soon be married.

She had passed the next weeks in a sensual haze, stealing out to meet him several times a week. She'd neglected her duties as one of her father's chief reporters for the newspaper that served both the occupying troops and the horde of profiteers that had descended on conquered Texas.

Richard had tutored her in the ways of sexual pleasure— always calling it love, of course. He hadn't mentioned marriage again, and whenever she tried to, he'd adroitly distracted her.

Tonight she'd been determined that they should settle on a date and, after a few kisses, had told him smilingly but firmly that she wanted to plan their wedding.

Then he had told her about the wife in Boston. He had never meant to marry Maggie, of course. She had just been a pleasurable distraction to him while he served with the federal occupation troops in Austin.

And now she was ruined. It was entirely possible she could be carrying his child. And even if she escaped that disastrous consequence, there was nothing to stop Richard from boasting of his conquest to the entire regiment.

Fool! her brain screamed as tears began to flood down her cheeks. Blindly, she reached for a piece of the porcelain ballerina's arm and gasped as a needle-sharp sliver of china slid into the tender flesh of her fingertip.

The pain was the last straw. Collapsing against the wall, the pieces of porcelain still cradled in her skirt, she began to sob in earnest.

Chapter One

Bryan, Texas, January 1869

The stage was late. That was nothing new—it was always late—so the fact that it hadn't arrived by noon, as scheduled, wasn't what had Garrick Devlin fidgeting on the bench seat outside the Bryan Hotel, where the stagecoach always unloaded its passengers and their baggage. No, it was the thought of *who* was on the stage that had him checking his pocket watch every few minutes, raking a hand through his hair, then reaching into his pocket for his comb to repair the damage his fingers had done.

She had given him that carved-ivory comb, he remembered, for their first Christmas together as husband and wife. It was during the middle of the war, when finding money to spare for gifts and celebrations had been difficult. He had been home on leave from his regiment, so glad to be away from the sounds of shelling and the constant threat of death that he was sure his little corner of Texas was heaven itself. Of course, that leave had been two years before the minié ball had shattered his right leg just below the knee. When he had awakened in the field hospital to find out the army surgeon had amputated what was left of his lower leg, Garrick knew that heaven was just a fable. It didn't exist.

And now she was coming back, according to the letter she'd sent. Cecilia, the wife who had once loved him enough to save her scarce pennies to buy him that comb for Christmas. The same woman who had fled in horror the morning after he had come home from the war, hobbling on crutches, his right trouser leg pinned up so it wouldn't flap in the breeze.

Hell, he wished he was a whole man so he could get up and pace. But he was damned if he'd give the old gray-beards loitering across the street in front of the saloon a show. He despised his awkward, dragging gait, even now that he'd gotten the wooden leg made by the Hanger Company and he'd been able to abandon the hated crutches in favor of a cane.

It seemed he was not to escape their attentions, however, for a moment later one of them came shuffling across the street and hailed him.

"Howdy, Garrick. Mighty fine day fer January, ain't it?"

"I suppose so," he muttered, wishing the old man would take the hint and go away.

"Yore gittin' around mighty fine, mighty fine indeed, yessir," the old man said approvingly, nodding in the direction of Garrick's wooden leg. "Y'kin be right proud."

Right proud that a seventy-year-old man walked with more grace than he did? Garrick purposely leveled a look at the old man that would have frozen a Texas lake in mid-July. "I'm afraid you'll have to excuse me, sir," he said. Maybe if he disappeared into the hotel for a few minutes the old man would go back across the street to rejoin his cronies.

However, just then the distant sound of galloping horses and creaking wheels announced the coming of the stage.

"Yore meetin' the stage?" inquired the old man, apparently unaffected by Garrick's glare. "Who's comin' t'visit? Anyone I know?"

There was no way Garrick wanted the likes of this elderly busybody present in the first moments of his reunion with Cecilia. He prayed for the ground to open up and swallow the garrulous old fool, but it seemed God wasn't listening to such mundane requests today.

He shoved a hand in his pocket and came out with a coin. "Here's two bits," he growled. "Go and buy yourself a drink, okay?"

The old man cackled, acknowledging that he was being bought off, then retreated to other side of the street just before the stagecoach rounded the corner.

This was it, Garrick thought, as the stagecoach driver reined in his team in a cloud of dust in front of the hotel. In a moment or two he'd be face-to-face with his wife, the woman who had once fled his home and his bed. What had caused her to write him and say she was coming home again now, after being gone more than three years?

Lord, he wanted to believe it was because Cecilia had discovered she loved him—loved him enough to realize she'd done wrong by running away, loved him enough to come back and be a wife to him. He knew it was hard to look at him—a man who was not whole anymore, whose right leg ended in a clumsily closed stump right above the knee—but if they truly loved one another, they could work their way past that, couldn't they?

Then the stagecoach door was being thrown open and Garrick's heart seemed to surge into his throat, choking him with its runaway rhythm. A man stepped out and turned to assist a lady behind him.

Cecilia? No, the woman was black haired, not blond like Cecilia, and from the tender look she and the man exchanged, it was probable they were married. Then another man exited, a drummer by the looks of him, and then, finally, a woman appeared.

It was not Cecilia. The woman was elderly, with gray hair and a lined, pinched face, and she was holding the hand of a small boy.

Alarmed, Garrick looked behind her, hoping that the cramped, shadowy interior of the coach miraculously held one more passenger. There was no one there. Had Cecilia missed the stage? Would there be a telegram coming, explaining that circumstances had held her up for a day or two?

The woman had stepped down into the street, and was now picking up the boy and assisting him to the ground. Then she turned around and squinted at the crowd. Garrick saw her fasten her eyes on his cane and then step decisively forward.

"You must be Garrick Devlin," the woman informed him, her gaze piercing as it rose to his face.

Apprehension had turned his spine into a rod of ice, and the foot that was no longer there throbbed like a toothache. "Yes," he admitted uneasily. "Who might you be? And where's Cecilia, my wife?"

The old woman shielded her eyes against the bright winter sunlight. "I'm Martha Purdy, Cecilia's neighbor. She couldn't come. She sent this little feller instead."

Garrick's eyes lowered to the boy, who was standing in the street gazing up to where Garrick stood on the plank walkway in front of the hotel. The boy looked absolutely terrified and was clinging to the old woman with both hands.

"I—I don't understand...." Garrick felt a cold sweat breaking out on his forehead. "Why couldn't Cecilia come? And who's the boy?"

The woman snorted again, then shrugged her shoulders. "It's kind of a long story, mister. Better if you read it in this here letter she sent," she added, pulling a wrinkled and much-folded piece of paper from her reticule and holding it out to him. "You *can* read, cain't ya?" she asked, squinting up at him.

"Of *course* I can read," Garrick snapped.

"No need to take offense, mister—I cain't read," she said equitably, then looked about her as if searching for something. "Johnny, lookit that puppy over yonder," she said, pointing to where a small mongrel dog lounged in the shade of the bank awning several yards away. The dog had spotted the boy and was thumping its tail against the wood planking. "He looks like he likes little boys. Why don't you go say howdy to him for a minute?"

She waited, hands on her hips, until the boy had gone over to pat the dog and was out of earshot, then she turned back to Garrick. "I dunno what Cecilia wrote, exactly, but I kin tell ya this here boy is yore son—yores and Cecilia's."

Her last sentence hit Garrick like an blow to his gut.

"My…s-son? But that's impossible! He couldn't be!" He felt his face burning as the woman stared at him while he sputtered. "It's one of her tricks! That boy is no son of mine! Whose bastard is she trying to pass off as mine?"

The old woman drew herself up. "Mr. Devlin, I'll thank ya to soften yore tongue a bit. Don't you call that sweet little innocent boy no nasty names."

He lowered his voice. "I mean to say, she left—we didn't…" He stopped, thunderstruck. "Oh, Lord, there was just that one time…it isn't possible, *is it?*"

He didn't know he had spoken aloud until the old woman chuckled at his discomfiture. "Well, sir, I'm a widow, so I guess I'm qualified t'tell you it only takes the once."

Garrick froze, remembering the day he'd come home from the war, just before Lee surrendered at the Appomattox courthouse. His brothers weren't home yet, but his mother and his sister had put together a family celebration out of the meager food supplies they had. Cecilia just kept staring at him—at his pinned-up trouser leg—her eyes wide with fright in her pale face.

Later that night, when they'd gone up to the bedroom they shared in the Devlin family home, he'd tried to tell her how much he had missed her, how hers had been the name on his lips when the doctor, after giving him a little whiskey for an anesthetic, had hacked off the shattered lower portion of his leg. Shyly, he'd kissed her and asked if he could make love to her.

He had never had to ask before. She'd always been eager to participate in the marital act—almost too much so by Victorian standards, but he'd always loved her for it.

She'd told him to blow out the lamp—she who had always been excited to see the passion in his face. And then she'd just lain there, still as a marble statue and just as cold, and let him exercise his husbandly rights.

He'd been careful to be gentle and had tried not to touch her leg with the bandaged stump, but as he was withdrawing from her and preparing to lie on his back, the foreshortened leg had brushed her shin.

Cecilia had gasped as if revolted, and had then begun to cry, turning away from him and hugging the far side of the bed. He'd tried to comfort her, to apologize, but she'd just ordered him, in a tight little whisper, not to touch her again.

Garrick hadn't slept until dawn was paling the skies, and he was pretty sure Cecilia hadn't, either. When he'd finally awoke midmorning, Cecilia had gone. Later he learned she had not only left the farm, but had taken a stage heading south.

And over there, petting the friendly dog, was the result of that night, he realized. He stared at the boy, whose face he could see in profile.

His son. But suspicion remained. "When was he born?"

"I dunno the exact date," the woman admitted with a shrug. "You read this here letter. She probably told you in it."

He accepted the wrinkled, folded piece of paper as one might accept a dozing rattlesnake. But before he unfolded it, he paused. "All right, supposing he *is* my son...why now? He's what—three years old? Why is she sendin' him to me now?"

"Read the letter," the old woman said. "There's more to this here tale, but she said ya was to read it first."

Realizing that the old woman wasn't going to make it any easier, he gave up and unfolded the letter, holding it so that the bright noon sunlight made it easier to read.

Dear Garrick,
I know I hurt you when I ran away. It was awful of me to treat you that way, after all you had been through in the war, but I just couldn't help it. I guess I wasn't strong enough and good enough to be the wife you deserved, and I'm sorry about that, but I just couldn't be someone I'm not. I'm trying to make it up to you now by sending our boy. I know you won't believe he's yours, and I don't reckon I blame you, but his birthday is New Year's Day, 1866—which, if you count back, is nine months after you came home. I named him John Garrick. I know you hate me now, Garrick, and you have a right. But if you ever loved me, I hope you'll be good to our son. I know he'll be better off with you.

Cecilia

He read it through twice before lifting his eyes from the paper.

"It tells me his name and his birthdate, but it doesn't tell me what I asked you. Why now? She's had him for three years.... Why is she sending him to me *now?* What's she up to?"

The woman looked uneasily at the boy, then back at Garrick. "Bigamy, that's what. I'm sorry to be the one t'tell ya that, but it's the truth."

"*Bigamy?* She's *married* to someone else?"

"That's what bigamy means, don't it?" the old woman responded, adding a regretful *tsk, tsk.* "Yup, she's Miz Cecilia *Prentice*—has been ever since soon after she showed up in Houston in '65 and started workin' at the hotel. Pretty as a picture, she was. Men flocked 'round her like flies around a picnic. It warn't a week afore Will Prentice up and married her and cut out the competition."

"But she was—*is*," Garrick corrected, "my wife! We were never divorced! How did she explain, uh, being in the family way to her new 'husband'?" He felt his face flush; one didn't discuss such delicate issues as pregnancy with a lady, even one who had brought him the news that his wife had committed bigamy.

The old woman chuckled again, a sound Garrick was growing to heartily detest. Nothing they were talking about was funny.

"Who knows? It's the oldest trick in the book, fobbin' off some other man's child on a husband, ain't it? You'd think a feller wouldn't be dumb enough to think that big healthy baby was his, come early, but I reckon he was, 'cause he used to be proud as a banty rooster of him," she said, nodding toward the boy.

"'Used to be?'" Garrick echoed. "What happened?"

"There was an accident...they was comin' home from a barbecue one night. I was keepin' the child for 'em. A storm blew up and lightnin' was flashin', and the horse got skeered and run away with them. The shay overturned and Mr. Prentice was thrown clear, but Miz Cecilia, she was trapped under a wheel. She was hurt bad, and it looked like she might die on the spot. Anyway, I reckon she was afeered for her immortal soul, 'cause she confessed to Will Prentice that that boy wasn't his.''

"Did she...did she...?" Garrick couldn't bring himself to say the words.

"Did she die?" Martha Purdy finished the question for him. "No, but she's been bedridden ever since. I take care o'her every day, her an' the boy. Prentice told her he wouldn't keep the boy under his roof any longer, not now that he knew the brat wasn't his."

Garrick felt his jaw drop as nausea churned in his stomach. He could no longer feel the burning hostility that had flamed up only moments ago toward Cecilia. Now he could only think of the cruelty Prentice had shown to the boy and his injured mother.

"I'll keep the boy until his mother—" he couldn't bring himself to name Cecilia just now "—recovers. Then I imagine she's going to want to leave that sorry excuse for a husband, who won't even keep the child he *thought* was his ever since he was born. And you can tell her that if she's willing—" He was about to say that he'd take her back.

"Mr. Devlin," the old woman interrupted, "you don't understand. Cecilia ain't *gonna* recover. Her back was crushed in the accident. She's paralyzed—cain't move from her waist down. She don't hardly eat, and she gets weaker every day. She ain't gonna make old bones, Mr. Devlin. The only way she's gonna leave Prentice—" she glanced around, to make sure the boy was still entranced with the dog "—is by dyin'. And I don't reckon it's gonna be too long. She jest seemed t'lose what little will to live she had left when Prentice said the boy had to go."

Garrick felt as if he were in the middle of a nightmare. This couldn't be happening!

"But she wrote me that she was coming herself!" he protested. "She didn't say anything about a child!"

The old woman sighed. "Mebbe she thought you wouldn't take the boy iffen you'd knowed he was comin', an' mebbe she thought you wouldn't turn him away once you seen your son's face."

Just this morning Garrick had been full of nervous but happy anticipation at seeing Cecilia again—and now she was *dying?*

"I—I've got to go to her—see her," he mumbled, looking wildly about for the stagecoach driver, hoping the stage was going directly back to Houston. He'd be on it if it was, never mind that he'd be leaving without a word to his family and with nothing more than the shirt on his back.

Martha Purdy reached out a hand, as if she knew he wanted to go find the driver.

"She don't want you to come, Mr. Devlin. She told me to tell you that, iffen you was to say somethin' about comin'. She don't want you to see her like that."

He stared at her, and she looked him right in the eye. "I'm tellin' the truth, Mr. Devlin. Please don't go all that way fer nothin'."

He nodded, feeling cold all over despite the bright sunlight. "You'll stay...for a while? Just till the boy gets...accustomed to me?"

"I can stay for a coupla days, and that's only 'cos the stage won't be back this way till then," the old woman told him. "Sooner I get back, the better. Prentice said he'd take care a' Cecilia till I got back, but that man don't know nothin' about nursin'. He'll forget to turn her, to make her eat...."

The image her words engendered, of Cecilia lying helpless on her bed, made Garrick close his eyes in horror. And she didn't even want him to help her. "All right. I—I'll get the wagon."

Again the woman laid a restraining hand on his wrist,
studying Garrick. "Ya know, he *does* kinda favor you, Mr.
Devlin. His hair's lighter'n yourn, but the eyes—oh, yes,
he's your boy, all right. Just look at him."

She bent over and called, "Johnny, tell the doggie bye-
bye and come say hello to Mr. Devlin."

Garrick watched as the boy gave the dog a last caress
and obediently came back to the old woman. He was thin
as smoke. Garrick knew his mother would say he needed
"feedin' up."

"Johnny, this is Mr. Devlin. Turns out he's yore real
papa, and he wants to meet you. Don't worry, he don't
bite."

The child jerked around, visibly trembling. "How kin he
be my papa if my papa's at home?" he piped in a childish
treble.

It was possible. The boy *could* be his son, Garrick realized, staring at eyes that were as blue as his own. The
lad's hair was lighter, but then, his mother was a blonde,
so maybe that affected such things. But it was the mouth
that made Garrick think maybe the letter hadn't been a pack
of lies, after all. The boy had sensed he couldn't be sure
of his welcome, and to Garrick, the stubborn set of his lips
was like looking at his own mouth in the mirror.

Garrick knew he should kneel down, so that he wasn't
staring at the child from such an intimidating height, but
although kneeling was possible with his Hanger leg, it was
awkward at best. And he'd just as soon not frighten the
boy any more than he already was.

"There was a mistake, Johnny. Everyone thought Wil-
liam Prentice was your papa, but this letter tells me *I* am,"
he said slowly, nodding toward the refolded paper. "Your
mama wrote it, and in it she asks me to look after you for
a while, till she's feelin' better. I didn't know I had a little
boy till I read that letter, you know."

"You didn't?" The boy's eyes grew rounder. "Why?"

Lord, what was he to say to that? "I don't know, Johnny," he said. "But I'm happy to meet you, and I'll take good care of you, all right?"

Transferring his cane to his other hand, he extended his right hand to the boy.

The boy seemed to see the cane for the first time. He stared at it, then up into Garrick's face, and seemed to come to a decision.

He dived into the old woman's skirts. "I want my *mama!*"

Garrick felt his face flame. He hadn't yet decided if he believed the boy was his son, but it was clear Johnny wanted nothing to do with him. Yet he could hardly turn away and leave him and the old woman to their own devices!

"Aw, don't pay that no mind," the old woman said calmly. "He'll get over it. He's plumb wore out from th' long trip in that rattletrap box," she added, nodding her head toward the stagecoach. "We've had our bones about shook outa our body. A good meal and a good night's sleep and he'll be right as rain in th' mornin'."

Garrick sighed. "We'd best be getting on out to the farm, then. My wagon's just down the street."

But the old woman wasn't moving. "Mister, that little boy is hungry and thirsty. He'd do a lot better if he had some dinner *now,*" she added, with a meaningful glance at the hotel. "It's been a long time since we et breakfast."

Garrick lifted his eyes from the child's back, suspecting Martha Purdy was thinking of her own stomach rather than the boy's. Fortunately, he had been planning to take Cecilia into the hotel for dinner, so he had some money with him. He hoped he had enough left to pay for the woman's ticket home, if Prentice hadn't given her return fare.

"All right, ma'am, we'll eat in there," he said, gesturing toward the hotel door.

Chapter Two

"She sent *your son* all the way from Houston with that woman, instead of coming herself?" Sarah Devlin cried. She watched out the window as the boy, accompanied by Garrick's sister, Annie, his sister-in-law Mercy and Martha Purdy, discovered the cat's latest litter of kittens. "Why the nerve of that...that—"

"Hold on, Mother. I haven't told you everything yet," Garrick said, rubbing his eyes wearily. He hadn't slept well last night, tormented by phantom pains from his leg and the buzzing questions that refused to leave his brain. Then, just as he'd finally dropped off, the boy had awoken screaming in his room down the hall. Garrick had heard the old woman soothe him, and in a few moments, the crying had stopped.

Quickly he told Sarah Devlin about Cecilia's bigamous marriage in Houston, and the carriage accident that had left her paralyzed and likely to die of her injuries soon. He also told her about Cecilia's wish that he not come to see her.

"Lord Jesus, have mercy," Sarah Devlin breathed, her hand to her mouth. "That poor, misguided girl...your poor little boy..."

"Mama, I'm not at all sure he's my son," Garrick warned.

Sarah Devlin's jaw dropped. "Why, Garrick, of course he is—anyone with eyes can see he is. He looks just like you when you were his age. Are you saying that you and Cecilia…that night you came home…" She turned away in a flurry of embarrassment.

Garrick was no less embarrassed. "Well…yes, Mama. But she ran off the very next day and married the first man who'd have her, apparently. How am I to trust the word of a woman like that?"

"He's yours, I'm tellin' you. And you can't turn your own son away," Sarah Devlin said.

Garrick sighed. His suspicion that Cecilia had lied to him about Johnny's paternity had already begun to waver as he'd observed the boy closely over the past twenty-four hours. It wasn't just the color of his eyes, but things he did—little things, like the way he walked, or the way he slept with the pillow turned lengthwise against his face and chest—that convinced Garrick; they were pure Devlin, and nothing like Cecilia. And now, in the face of his mother's certainty, he began to think that Johnny *was* indeed his.

He sighed. "No, I didn't intend to. But the boy's scared of me. I can't get him to come within three feet. And who could blame him?" he added, glaring down at his artificial leg, which, covered by his trousers and shoe, looked identical to the other. "I walk like a drunken sailor."

"Son, just give it some time," suggested his mother. "He'll warm up to you. He won't think about your wooden leg if *you* act as if it's nothing unusual."

Easy for you to say, Garrick thought, but just then his mother, standing by the window, said, "Look yonder. Here comes little Johnny carryin' a kitten. You tell him he can keep it if he wants to—it's old enough to be weaned."

Sure enough, flanked by Mercy, Annie and Martha, Johnny was coming toward the house, carrying a black ball of fur with all the care a three-year-old was capable of. As the trio came through the door, Garrick could plainly hear the kitten's mews.

He saw the child look uncertainly at Annie and then at Mercy.

"Johnny, remember, you have something to ask your papa," Mercy murmured, nodding toward Garrick.

Johnny looked pale but determined. "P-Papa, I want this kitty. Please?"

Garrick found he had been holding his breath and had to catch it again before replying. The boy—*his son*—had called him Papa. He felt as if the sun had just come out from behind the clouds after years of gloomy days. He felt tears sting his eyes, and blinked, sure it would only confuse the boy to see him cry. He certainly didn't want the other adults to see it.

"I reckon so, Johnny," he said. The boy smiled shyly. Moved even more by the gift of that smile, Garrick felt his own lips curve upward. Smiling felt almost foreign to him, as if it had been years since he'd last done it. He added, "What're you gonna name it?"

"I don't know how those Conservative Republicans can even claim to be Southerners," Garrick muttered, crumpling the week-old Austin newspaper in disgust. Then, belatedly remembering the presence of his son, he looked around, but Johnny had just chased his kitten out of the room. "They're Unionists and always have been, even during the war! Tarnation, they might as well burn Texas to the ground now, 'cause there's not going to be anything left to bury once the carpetbaggers and scalawags are done plundering."

"*If* we elect a Republican government, maybe Texas will get readmitted to the Union that much quicker," his brother Cal remarked. It was a week after little Johnny had arrived, and Cal and his bride, Olivia, had come for an overnight visit before leaving on a delayed wedding trip to Galveston. Garrick, Cal and the youngest Devlin brother, Sam, were arranged on chairs in the parlor while the women talked and did dishes in the kitchen.

"Good! Maybe that'll mean all those bluebellies occupying us like we were a conquered foreign country can go back to the rocks they crawled out from under," Garrick growled. "Ahem! Beggin' your pardon, brother," he said, turning to Cal. "I imagine *you'll* be sorry to see them go."

Cal raised an eyebrow. "Even those of us who served with the Union army aren't happy when we see federal troops helpin' Northern swindlers get by with wholesale robbery," he said mildly.

Garrick realized he'd gone a little far, and looked back at the crumpled newspaper, saying nothing for a moment. Then he changed the subject. "So there's nothing much going on in Gillespie Springs?" he asked, looking at Cal again. "It must be pretty calm if you're fixin' to go away for a while."

Cal tipped his chair back until it rested against the wall. "Yeah, my deputy's going to watch over things while I'm gone. I'm happy to leave that tin star at home— I've been looking forward to a little time at the seashore with my bride."

"Well, I hope you two have a fine time," Garrick said, still feeling awkward about the way he'd talked to Cal a moment ago.

"Whoa! Can this be *our* brother, Garrick the cantankerous, speaking?" teased Sam, who was sitting just beyond Cal, his long, booted legs stretched out before him.

"Sounds like the little feller's been good for you, Garrick," he added, nodding toward Johnny, who was now trotting from room to room, pulling a strand of yarn for his kitten to chase.

Sam always knew just how to rile him. "If 'the little feller' weren't within earshot," Garrick growled, "I'd tell you what particularly hot place you could go to, little brother. I've never been without family feeling."

Sam just grinned.

"He's a good-looking boy, that Johnny," Cal said, before Sam could tease any more. "I believe he favors you, Garrick."

Garrick couldn't help his pleased smile. "You think so?" Then he grew more serious, and noting the boy had followed the kitten into the kitchen, out of earshot, added, "He's a good boy. I wish I hadn't missed his first three years. I—I want to make it up to him, somehow.... You know what I mean?"

His brothers nodded. "You'll do a fine job bein' a father, Garrick," Cal assured him, and Sam murmured in agreement.

Garrick frowned, feeling the old familiar despair. "What kind of an example can *I* be, a cripple? How can he learn what a *man* is from watchin' me clump around this farm? Oh, I can teach him to cipher and spell and read, but so could Annie or Mama. How's he gonna ever look up to *me*, unless I make somethin' of myself?" Despite the difficulty of moving around, he grabbed for his cane and hobbled over to the window, then stood staring out into the darkness.

Behind him, his brothers were silent, waiting.

"I think maybe it's time I did somethin' more than clump around the farm," Garrick mused, then raised his hand when Sam started to interrupt. "Now don't tell me that what I'm doin' here keeps this household runnin'. You know very well Mama leaves writin' and figurin' chores to me so I'll feel useful," he said. "Cal, didn't you tell me that banker fellow Gillespie that used to run Gillespie Springs had been just about to start a newspaper before he got put in jail?"

"Yep, sure did," Caleb said. "In fact, the printing press was delivered by freight wagon just the other day. It's just sittin' there in that vacant building across from the hotel, where Gillespie was gonna have the newspaper office. Mayor Long sure was disappointed. He was lookin' forward to havin' a newspaper to read. He said he reckoned that printing press belonged to the town by rights, after all that swindler Gillespie had done, so he said he'd donate it to anyone who'd start up a paper in Gillespie Springs."

"Any reason I couldn't be the one?" Garrick said, still staring out the window so that he wouldn't see the expressions of doubt he was sure were painted all over his brothers' faces.

Now Sam spoke up. "You? You talkin' about bein' the editor? I don't know why not, big brother. You're smart as a treeful of owls. You can argue circles around me about politics and such."

"Shucks, Sam, anyone can talk circles around *you*," joked Cal, but he grinned to show it was all in fun. "But Sam's right, Garrick. You've got a fine mind and you don't use it for much but keepin' the farm's accounts paid up and writin' letters to the editor of that paper about how the carpetbaggers are ruinin' Texas...." His voice trailed off for a moment. "And you could come home on the weekends and see your son, of course. Mama and Annie'd keep him taken care of during the week."

"Why would I leave the boy here? I'm his papa, by thunder, and the boy belongs with me."

His brothers exchanged glances, saying nothing.

"Mama isn't gonna be happy about lettin' Johnny go away," Sam said at last. "She's awful fond a' the little feller already."

"So am I," Garrick said, and realized it was true. "But I'll bring him home to visit often enough. Once Mercy has her baby, Ma won't mind so much."

"Sure, why not? If you can write those fiery letters to the editor, you can write newspaper articles," Cal said, obviously warming to the idea. "And just think, every week you could write an editorial and criticize—or praise—any ol' thing you wanted."

Garrick thought getting to express his opinion in print, in his official capacity as editor, sounded very fine indeed. Then he had a disturbing thought. "But I don't know anything about running a printing press."

"Well, you could learn, I reckon," Caleb assured him. "You could hire someone who's worked on a paper, and get 'em to teach you. You'd be the editor and write the articles, and he'd run the press."

"But what about Johnny? I have a responsibility now," Garrick reminded himself aloud.

"Shoot, I imagine Livy'd be willing to lend you her housekeeper," Cal said. "Señora Mendez is always complaining we don't give her enough to do, and asking us to have a baby real quick so she'll have somethin' to keep her busy."

"You *are* tryin' to comply with *that* command, aren't you, brother?" Sam inquired, his face the picture of innocence.

Cal grinned. "Maybe."

Garrick watched his brothers, suddenly envious of their happiness. Both of them had found a good woman to marry. That avenue seemed closed to him, however. Even if Cecilia had entered a bigamous marriage, *he* wasn't free to marry again—and even if he were, what woman would marry a man with a wooden leg?

Resolutely he shut his mind to the idea of a woman's love and focused on the rising excitement he felt about the idea of starting a newspaper. He was ready for a change. He'd been sitting around the farm for too long as it was. If he didn't try something new, he'd just become an old man before his time, and Johnny would grow up smothered by his grandmother and his aunt, who, with the best intentions in the world, cossetted the boy too much.

"All right, ask that Mendez woman if she'll be my housekeeper. I'm going to do it, boys. I'm going to start a newspaper in Gillespie Springs. You reckon you could find a house for me there?"

Sam let out a rebel yell that had the women running from the kitchen to see what was the matter, and Cal clapped him on the back. "I'm sure of it, brother," Cal said.

"Gillespie Springs!" the stagecoach driver sang out, as he reined in his team in front of the Gillespie Springs Hotel.

Maggie Harper sighed with relief. The jolting, swaying ride, which was supposed to have taken only a couple of days, had taken three and a half, thanks to the spring rains. The roads between Austin and Gillespie Springs were a quagmire. Torrential downpours had delayed their start two mornings out of the three, and at least twice each day the driver and the men in the coach had had to push the coach out of muddy ruts.

Once, a flash of lightning had struck a nearby tree, which terrified the team and caused them to gallop on in a runaway panic. They had gone a full two miles before the driver could rein them in, and Maggie had been sure that at any moment the coach would hit a bump, tilt and crash onto its side, crushing its hapless occupants.

Afterward, to amuse herself as the tedious, muddy miles rolled by, she'd composed a newspaper article in her head as if the worst had happened. The headline read: Stagecoach Overturns—Famous Female Journalist Tragically Perishes Before Her Time.

The red-faced woman in black bombazine sitting across from her glared in her direction. Belatedly, Maggie realized she had been smiling. The journey hadn't been enjoyable, but the rain had finally stopped, the sun was shining and they had at last arrived in Gillespie Springs.

Mrs. Red Face was just one of the fellow travelers Maggie wouldn't be sorry to bid farewell to. The coach was filled to capacity with two rotund drummers who had a fondness for foul-smelling cigars, an anxious mother holding a teething, fretful baby, and Maggie—and of course Mrs. Red Face, who had surely uttered a complaint for every mile that passed.

Every fifteen miles the coach had stopped to change teams, but it was usually raining too hard for Maggie to get out and stretch her legs. Every fifty miles they'd halted for a longer time, so the passengers could eat, drink and relieve themselves, but the stations were crude and dirty and the food was hardly fit for consumption.

The coach creaked to a stop, and after Maggie descended, the driver lifted her bag down to her.

"Thank you, sir. I hope the last leg of your trip goes smoothly," Maggie said.

"You're welcome, Miz Harper. You'd better get up on the boardwalk yonder before those boots're soaked through," the driver said, pointing to the mud that squished up to her ankles. "Ain't ya got someone meeting ya here?"

"Oh, someone's expecting me, sir, don't worry. I just have to find my way to the newspaper office."

A small town, Gillespie Springs nevertheless had a prosperous look on this sunny April morning. Next to the hotel on her right, Maggie could see signs announcing a millinery and a barbershop. When she turned to look to her left, she saw a bank, a doctor's office, a general store, and across the street from those buildings, the saloon, the jail, a telegraph office and the livery. So where was the newspaper office? Then she noticed the small, new-looking building right across the street.

She narrowed her eyes to read the sign swinging in the breeze beneath the new building's overhanging roof. "The *Gillespie Springs Gazette,* Established 1869," she read aloud. Yes, this was it. The ad in the newspaper seeking an experienced pressman, or printing press operator, had mentioned that the venture was a new one. When she had written offering her services, Garrick Devlin, the editor, had responded with flattering speed.

Of course, Devlin might not have done so had she signed her letter with "Margaret Louise Harper" rather than "M. L. Harper." Pangs of guilt had assailed her all the way from Austin, but she knew she had to find a way to leave there, and if misleading a prospective employer about her sex would secure her a job in another town more quickly, then mislead she would. Surely once she told Mr. Devlin why she was every bit as qualified as a male printer, he'd give her the chance to prove herself.

Garrick Devlin... She'd formed a picture of him in her mind. With a name like that, he must be an older man, probably in his fifties, with a balding head and spectacles perched on his nose. He'd have a plump, comfortable wife and a brood of grown or nearly grown children. Perhaps he'd already be a grandfather, and if so, no doubt he'd be a doting one. He might be skeptical of hiring a woman, but she'd tell him about her experience. Why, she'd started as a printer's devil for her father, a veteran newspaperman, back in Ohio, and progressed to the point that when they got to Austin she'd been John Harper's most-relied-upon reporter.

Devlin *had* to accept her! She just couldn't go back to Austin! She'd rather die than face the knowing looks, the sneers, or the attentions of the officers and officials of the Freedmen's Bureau, who suddenly seemed to find her irresistible—ever since Richard Burke had left her house that night.

Of course he had boasted of his conquest. She'd known it the very next week, when she'd gone with her father to a New Year's Eve ball put on by the army for its staff and the rest of the Northeners who now lived in Texas. She'd seen the ladies whispering behind gloved hands in corners, staring in her direction, only to fall silent when she approached. They were distant and vague when she tried to converse with them, and some even looked right through her and walked away with an angry swish of skirts—as if she were a saloon girl who'd dared to trespass where only ladies were welcome!

Her dance card had been full that night, though, a fact that only seemed to make the officers' wives and daughters hate her more. But she could take no joy in being the belle of the ball, for it was achingly clear that the men who danced with her were only looking to sample the delights Captain Burke had told them about.

Of course her sudden change in popularity—a belle on the dance floor, a pariah among women—could not escape her father's attention, even as absentminded and preoccupied as James Harper could be at the best of times. She'd had to tell him what had happened between herself and

Captain Burke. It was only the second time she'd ever seen her father cry; the first time had been when her mother had died. He hadn't condemned Maggie, though. He'd been so kind and loving that she'd felt worse than ever.

She didn't have to worry about him doing any violence to Burke—though he'd expressed a fervent desire to hurt him—because the captain had suddenly and conveniently been ''called to Washington'' two days after his last meeting with Maggie.

Maggie knew she'd been fortunate beyond measure when her ''monthly visitor'' came as usual two weeks after Burke's departure, for she could imagine no hell worse than having to carry the fruit of her foolish liaison. Now they could put this unfortunate happening behind them, her father had told her, and things could go back to normal.

James Harper had protested when she'd told him she had to leave Austin. Things would blow over, he'd said—but she knew they would not. Her position there was untenable. Even though she was willing to forgo what social life there was for Yankees in Texas, and just live for her work, she could no longer endure her father's pitying kindness in the midst of her disgrace.

Maggie couldn't tell him that, of course. She'd told him she needed a change of scene, to try her wings. He'd been adamantly against her going off alone to take a position, but she had reminded him she was an adult with some limited funds of her own, and in the end he had given her his reluctant blessing.

Now she took a deep breath and began to wade through the ankle-deep mud that separated the newspaper office from the hotel.

Chapter Three

Garrick leaned over the shiny black Washington hand-press that held pride of place in the middle of the office of the *Gazette*, holding on to the sides of the machinery as if it were a raft in the midst of a stormy sea.

Perhaps it was a mistake to have come in today, one day after his solemn-faced brother Sam had brought over the letter from Houston. Full of misspelled words and barely legible writing, the letter had been written by a semiliterate friend of Martha Purdy, the woman who had brought little Johnny to him. She thought he ought to know, she wrote, that Cecilia Prentice had passed away in the third week of March. She had died in her sleep, and her "husband" had barely waited through the brief funeral service before he'd started seeking another wife.

Sam had urged Garrick to stay home today, to take it easy while his mind absorbed the shock of his faithless wife's death. Hiding at home didn't make sense to Garrick. Cecilia had been as good as dead to him ever since she'd left him, he'd told Sam sourly, though deep inside, Garrick had known that wasn't true. Some small voice inside of him had never stopped hoping that a miracle would take place and she'd recover and come home so they could learn to be a family.

And now it would never happen, and there was no point in staying in the new house that hardly felt like home yet, mourning for a woman who'd already been dead for a fortnight. Johnny didn't really understand what Garrick had tried to tell him about his mother, so there was nothing he could do for his son.

Besides, the man he'd hired to be his pressman was a couple of days late in arriving—probably due to the recent spate of rainy weather—and Garrick didn't want the fellow looking high and low for him all over Gillespie Springs when he didn't find him in the *Gazette* office. So Garrick had kissed his son goodbye, told Jovita Mendez he probably wouldn't be back until suppertime, and left his house on South Street. He'd made a brief stop at the general store to purchase a black mourning band to put on his upper arm, but had dodged questions about whom he was wearing it for.

Garrick had been at the office now for three hours and had written several stories about local goings-on. He had no idea, though, if his new employee would arrive before he was forced to discard the longhand copy as old news.

If only he knew how to run the damned press! Garrick stared down at the bewildering, monstrous contraption.

But what if "M. L. Harper" had changed his mind about coming, and was not even on his way?

The damp weather had made Garrick's missing lower leg throb like a toothache. Lord, but he'd swear that he could feel each toe curling with the punishing pain. And the bandaged stump felt red and raw from rubbing against the harness that anchored his wooden limb to his body.

All at once the bell over the door jingled, and he looked up to see a woman letting herself in. He'd never seen her

before, and in the two months he'd been residing in the
small town, he thought he'd met everyone. She wore a traveling costume of coppery brown trimmed with black velvet
at the hem and neckline. Perched on her head was a charming little confection of a hat trimmed with a wide band of
copper ribbon, over which was a narrower one of black
velvet.

It was not her hat that held his attention, however, but
the mass of flaming, auburn-red hair beneath it. He'd never
seen hair that color. When she turned slightly, he could see
it was confined in a demure black snood at the nape of her
neck, but within the netting, curls coiled in fiery profusion,
lit by the sun coming through his window.

He saw green eyes staring at him with wide-eyed astonishment, and wondered what she found so surprising. He
hadn't moved yet, so it could not be that she was shocked
by his awkward gait.

"May I help you, ma'am?" She must be lost, though
how anyone could get lost in a town the size of Gillespie
Springs was a mystery to him. She was probably looking
for the millinery, he decided, taking in her fashionable ap-
pearance. Well, he wished Phoebe Stone joy in her new
customer. Perhaps she was a relative of the mayor, come
for a visit?

"I believe *I'm* here to help *you,* if you're Mr. Devlin,"
she said, smiling a little as she held out her gloved hand.

Her clipped Northern voice raised his hackles immediately. The Yankee who had shot him in the leg had had
just such an accent; Garrick still heard that harsh voice in
his nightmares calling to his comrades, "Well, I was aimin'
for his heart, but I winged him, at least—either way, he
won't be killin' Yankees no more!"

Garrick straightened, and taking his cane from where it
leaned against the press, approached the woman who stood

at his counter. He saw her eyes fasten on the cane and then fly back to his face. He saw the color heighten as she realized he'd caught her staring.

He was used to that reaction from women. "I'm Garrick Devlin," he said, his voice cool. Then he added, with a deliberate lack of courtesy, "Who're you?"

She blinked at his tone, and her smile faded, but her eyes were steady. He saw her straighten her backbone as if preparing to fend off a blow. "I'm M. L. Harper, your new pressman. I'm sorry to have arrived later than I told you to expect me, but the roads between this town and Austin are a river of mud, as I'm sure you can imagine...." Her voice trailed off for a moment, then began again. "But in any case, I'm here now and eager to go to work, if you'll just show me where to put my bag? Ah, I see you have a Washington handpress! It's not the latest in presses, but I have had vast experience using it...."

Her words went on, but he was still focusing on the first thing she'd said. "You aren't M. L. Harper. You're a female."

The smile returned to her face, this time with a teasing quality. "I don't like to argue with a new employer, but I *am* M. L. Harper—that's *Margaret Louise* Harper, sir. And I assure you that while I *am* indeed female, I have had the experience I wrote you about. I was an only child, and my father, frustrated at not having a son to pass on his newspapering knowledge to, trained me in every aspect of journalistic endeavor—pressman, compositor and writer of editorials. I can do much more than the paper folding and coloring in of prints that are all a woman usually is allowed to do on a newspaper. Look, Mr. Devlin," she said, holding up her long, slender fingers. "My hands are small, which makes them more nimble than a man's. I can set more *ems* a minute than any man."

"The hell you say," Garrick retorted bluntly, not having any idea what an *em* was, and for the moment, not caring. He was too furious at the realization that he'd been tricked—and by a female again.

She raised an expressive eyebrow at his rough language, but he was damned if he'd apologize—not when she'd lied to him as she had.

"Indeed I have. Most recently I served as my father's righthand reporter in Austin—"

"You've worked on the *Democratic Statesman*?" he demanded. "I don't believe it."

"No," she said evenly, "for *Freedom's Voice*."

He let his lip curl with all the contempt he felt. "Oh, that carpetbagger paper. I should've known."

"In our circle, the *Statesman* was known as 'that rebel rag,' sir," she retorted sweetly. "Nevertheless, as a journalist I respect newspapers of *any* political persuasion, as our country was founded on freedom of the press, isn't that so? And you *did* send for me to help you with yours."

"I didn't send for a *Yankee, or a woman,*" he growled between clenched teeth. "And you're *both.*" He could feel the throbbing in his leg rise to a pain-filled crescendo. "You lied to me, and I don't like being lied to," he told her. "So you can just take the stage on back to Austin, Miz Harper. I don't like your kind, descending on Texas like a plague of locusts."

"Is it just my geographic origin you object to, or my sex, too? Would you let me work for you if I came in drawling and fluttering like a Southern woman? 'Please, suh, may ah work for y'all?'" the woman mocked in an exaggerated Southern falsetto.

He could feel the rage flooding his system, rage that this lying *female* should dare to mock him! "Miz Harper," he said, allowing his own natural drawl to pour out like acid-tinged honey, "*Southern* ladies stay at home and mind their own business, so I just can't picture that happening. The fact that you're not home tending your knitting tells me that either the Yankees have different standards for ladylike behavior or *you're no lady.* Why else would you have left your cozy place with your father? And yes, there're two things I won't stomach in any employee of mine, *Miz* Harper—bein' a Yankee and bein' a female. So you can just tote that carpetbag on out of here. I lost my leg to your kind, and I won't tolerate you here, *do you understand?*"

He saw her blink back the tears his tirade had caused, and for a moment he felt ashamed. Then he saw her chin rise defiantly.

"In your inexperience, Mr. Devlin, you don't know that most *men* in my line of work have an unfortunate tendency to drink on the job, and get the urge to go on to the next job as soon as you've learned to depend on them. My reasons for leaving my father's newspaper are none of your concern, sir. Suffice it to say that I have reached my majority and am free to look out for my own interests. You said you needed someone to help you operate the Washington there," she said, nodding toward the machine in back of him. "I can do that. You obviously do not know how to do so yourself. Do you want to cling to your hide-bound ideas, sir, or do you want to run a newspaper?"

He had to admire her for standing her ground. She hadn't said anything about his nasty insinuation that she could not possibly be a lady—she'd just coolly reasserted her abilities. Nevertheless, he wasn't going to have a Yankee carpetbagger *woman* running his press!

Just then their duel of words was interrupted by the breathless arrival of Hank Sweeney, the telegraph operator, who'd obviously run clear down the street from the telegraph office past the bathhouse. "Read this, Devlin! This is just in off the wire from Austin!" he said, slamming a piece of paper down on the counter between Garrick and the Yankee woman.

"'Radical Republicans chooses E. J. Davis as candidate for governor.'" Garrick read Sweeney's transcription of the dots and dashes aloud. "'Their ally General Reynolds has ear of President Grant.' Why, this is a disgrace! No respectable man in Texas would vote for this scalawag—yet he's as good as elected since he's got that Yankee general on his side!"

"Wouldn't you like to print that news, Mr. Devlin?" challenged the Yankee woman behind him. "Can't you just picture it as a banner headline of the first edition of the *Gillespie Springs Gazette*? You've got other stories ready, haven't you?" she said, pointing toward the pile of papers filled with his scrawling script. "Say the word, Mr. Devlin, and that edition can be done by *morning*—maybe sooner! I won't sleep until the press has run off the story. Do you want to stand on your pride, and watch me walk away, or do you want to be the editor of a *real* working newspaper today?"

Hellfire, but she had him there, and she knew it, damn her knowing green eyes. If he told her to leave now, it might be weeks before he managed to hire a man knowledgeable in the operation of a printing press. By that time Davis's candidacy would be worse than old news, and how many more exciting stories would remain unreported? The town council had also been eager for him to start operation so they could publicize their community far and wide.

"How many others have you told, Sweeney?" he asked the telegraph operator, turning away from Margaret Harper.

"Why, no one, Mr. Devlin," the man answered, his face earnest.

"See? Your paper's inaugural issue would sell like hotcakes,'' Margaret Harper said in her pushy way. "Why not give me a chance, Mr. Devlin? Let me put out this first edition for you, and you'll see how well I can work. If you don't think I'm as good as I say I am, I'll take the next stage out of Gillespie Springs with no hard feelings, I promise. Please, Mr. Devlin?''

He looked at her, sensing she hated begging, and momentarily savored being in the position of having her plead to him to take her on. And then he saw the pain and the fear deep within those green eyes, and he was ashamed of himself.

"All right, Miss Harper, I'd be willing to employ you for a trial issue, and after that we'll see, is that understood? If I find I can't get along with you, you'll leave?'' He didn't believe for a moment her claim that she would depart without any hard feelings, not with that red hair and those fiery green eyes, or the way she had of raising her chin in the air. There'd be hard feelings, all right, if he told her he couldn't work with her. If she stayed, he knew as sure as he was standing there he'd be apt to spend a good deal of his time clashing with this opinionated, bold woman who was surely no lady. He'd have to make certain she knew who was boss. But he wanted to start up his paper and report this story, and if that meant putting up with this Yankee woman at least temporarily, then that was the sacrifice he'd have to make.

"Sweeney, can I count on you not to blab this story all over town, at least until the paper comes out tomorrow morning?''

"Why sure, Mr. Devlin," the telegrapher said, goggle-eyed. "It's a deal, as long as you'll give me one of the first papers, hot off the press!''

"Does that mean you'll give me a chance, Mr. Devlin?'' Margaret Harper asked in an excited voice. She extended her hand, evidently expecting him to shake it to seal the deal. "You won't be sorry, sir, I promise you."

Garrick was sure he would be sorry, but it was too late now. Bemused, he had just taken her hand in his when the bell over the door tinkled and a familiar voice cried, "Papa, look! We brung your dinner!"

Chapter Four

Maggie whirled around and beheld a little boy dragging a covered basket through the door. Behind him followed a sturdily built Mexican woman with salt-and-pepper hair, her face amused at the child's efforts.

The boy was beautiful, his blue eyes—the same piercing blue as Devlin's, she noted absently—shining as he brought the basket to the man he'd called "Papa." So Garrick Devlin was a father.... Who was the mother of this beautiful child? Surely not the Mexican woman?

"You said you would not be back teel supper, Señor Devlin, and Johnny, he worries that you weel get hungry," the Mexican woman said with a smile. "We pack you a peekneek, yes?"

Maggie saw Devlin's face, set in harshly suspicious and disapproving lines when he looked at her, transform as if by magic as he gazed at his son. He took a couple of awkward steps forward, leaning on the cane, and clumsily knelt down in front of the boy as if he had totally forgotten Maggie's presence.

"Thank you *very* much, Johnny, that was extremely kind of you," she heard him say. "But I'm afraid dinner is going to have to wait awhile. Right now, I need to follow Mr.

Sweeney down to the telegraph office so I can find out some more things about a big story I need to write for the newspaper.''

The boy's face fell. ''But I wanted to eat with you, Papa! Jovita packed a lot of food....''

Devlin looked distressed, but said, ''Johnny, I just can't eat right now. I know you don't understand, but I need to do something else. Perhaps we could have a picnic tomorrow?''

''Mr. Devlin, if I may suggest...'' Maggie began. She saw him frown at her, but rushed right on. ''Why not go down to the telegraph office and wire for the details you need, and we can get your picnic ready for you? Then, while you're waiting for a reply, you can come back and eat with your son. Isn't that a good idea?'' she said with an encouraging smile.

His glare told her in no uncertain terms what he thought of her volunteering her opinion the way she had, but just then Johnny piped up. ''Papa, who's the pretty lady? She talks funny, don't she, Papa?''

''*Doesn't* she,'' Devlin corrected. ''But it's not polite to say so. This is Miss Margaret Harper, Johnny and Jovita. She—'' Maggie saw him struggle to appear calm as he made the announcement ''—is about to begin a probationary period as my printer.''

Maggie saw a flicker of surprise light the onyx depths of the Mexican woman's eyes, to be replaced by a twinkle of amusement. ''Welcome, Señorita Harper. And you are right—Señor Devlin should do as you say about the peekneek. *Andele*, Señor Devlin,'' she said, making shooing motions. ''We will have the dinner all ready by the time you come back. Do not worry, there is plenty for your new employee, too.''

Johnny stared at his father anxiously.

Maggie could tell Garrick Devlin liked nothing less than to be told what to do by a woman, any woman, but for some reason he did not reprove Jovita.

"All right," he said in a deceptively agreeable voice, smiling at his son as the boy crowed with glee. Then Devlin's eyes fixed on Maggie, promising trouble, as he spoke to the telegraph operator. "Sweeney, go on ahead and I'll join you in a moment." He paused, waiting for the man to walk out of earshot before saying, "Miss Harper, come outside with me for a moment, will you? I have some instructions to give you before I go down to the telegraph office."

She nodded and followed him out the door.

He did not pause until he was several yards away from the newspaper office, and did not even look behind him to see if she was following. She could only watch the awkward, stiff-legged gait his artificial limb forced on him until he turned around and faced her.

"Miss Harper, if you're going to work for me, there had better never be a repetition of what you just did," he growled.

"What I just did?" she echoed, trying to think of how best to defend herself, without losing either her job or her self-respect.

"Don't play the fool with me, woman—I don't employ fools. You know exactly what I'm referring to," he snarled. "I'm talking about your meddling back there. I know meddling comes as natural to you Yankees as breathing, but if you wish to remain here you'll keep your Northern nose out of my business, is that clear?"

"*Yes, sir.*" She ground out the words, and watched as he mumbled something and kept walking.

Damn the man! He hadn't even allowed her the courtesy of presenting her side! She had wanted to explain to him, to say, "I'm sorry, but I just couldn't bear to see the boy disappointed, and you would have to wait for a reply in any case, so why not sit down and eat with your child?"

Clenching her gloved fists at her sides in frustration, she turned and stalked back to the newspaper office.

Jovita was just spreading out a tablecloth on the large table at the back of the office when Maggie returned. The boy was capering about, and when Maggie entered, he jumped up and down and crowed, "We're gonna have a picnic! Me an' Papa an' Jovita an' the pretty lady!"

"Yes, you are, *niño,*" Jovita said, smiling at him. "Why don't you watch at the window for your papa and let us know if he comes while Señorita Harper and I spread out the food?"

It was a good way to keep the child from dropping any of the dishes or the jar of lemonade, Maggie thought, as Johnny went obediently to the window to watch down the street in the direction his father had gone.

"Please, call me Maggie," she told the Mexican woman as she went forward to assist her at the table. She saw fried chicken, biscuits, a bowl of black-eyed peas and a peach pie.

"All right, Maggie," Jovita said, her smile warming. "So the *señor* who writes to Meester Devlin is really a *señorita,*" she said. "Eet is a good joke, no?"

"No," Maggie said ruefully. "That is, I didn't mean it as a joke, but I knew he wouldn't consider me if he knew I was a woman. I...I'm afraid he's rather angry—not only because I'm a woman, but also because I'm from the North."

"He weel get over eet," Jovita told her, her black eyes twinkling, "when he sees you do a good job."

"Oh, I intend to," Maggie assured her, buoyed by the woman's vote of confidence. Then she darted a glance at

Johnny, but the boy was staring at a grasshopper making its way over the glass, just out of his reach, and he was paying no attention to them.

Maggie lowered her voice and said, "I'd like to ask while Mr. Devlin is gone—why is he wearing a black armband? And is that why he's so...so cross?"

A shadow passed over the older woman's face, and she, too, checked to see if Johnny was paying any attention to them before she whispered back, "Eet ees for hees wife. She die some days ago, but he just learn of eet yesterday, you see? She was a silly woman, hees wife. She ran away from heem."

Margaret felt her mouth drop open in shock. "She *deserted* him? And their *child?*" Now she understood the undercurrent of rage in his voice when he had spoken to her. His grief was still fresh, and mixed with that grief was an anger he was entitled to feel at his wife's betrayal.

Ah, Maggie, you're so perceptive all of a sudden, a voice within her mocked. *You, who didn't see what kind of man Richard Burke was until it was too late? Maybe Garrick Devlin made his wife's life a hell on earth, as he may very well make yours as his employee.* Somehow, though, her heart was sure that whatever had happened between him and his wife, Garrick had not been at fault, despite his sour temperament.

"Oh, dear," she said aloud. She could hardly have come at a worse time.

"I do not theenk he means to be so cross," Jovita said, laying a consoling hand on Maggie's shoulder. "Eet ees not you. Eet ees hees wife, the war...he lost hees leg in the war, did you know that?"

"Yes, he told me," Maggie said hastily. Actually, he had flung the words at her, hadn't he? As if they were jagged stones.

The Mexican woman shrugged. "Eet ees many things. He has not had the boy a long time. They still get to know each other, you see."

"I see," Maggie murmured, but of course she didn't.

"Hees brother Cal, the sheriff, he tell me much about thees woman who was hees wife," Jovita informed her. "You ask heem sometime, *sí?*"

"Oh, I'm sure it's none of my business," Maggie told the woman uncomfortably, but for some reason Jovita didn't look at all convinced.

"You have never been married, *señorita?*" Jovita inquired.

The change of subject startled Maggie. "No," she said, but she felt the betraying flush creep up her cheeks. Once, she had expected to be Mrs. Richard Burke by this time.

"Ah, but you have a sweetheart, no? He ees back where you came from?" Jovita asked, her face puzzled.

"No," Maggie said, too quickly. "That is…there was someone…but we're no longer, uh, courting."

"Ah…" the woman murmured, and Maggie saw in her eyes that she had guessed much about Maggie's former sweetheart.

She was afraid Jovita was going to probe further, and was wondering how she could politely evade the questions, when Johnny began jumping up and down and shouting that his father was coming down the street. And then Garrick Devlin was silhouetted by the sun in the entranceway.

"Everything ees ready, Señor Devlin," Jovita said, motioning to the food and dishes spread out on the table. "Sit down and eat, you and Señorita Maggie and Johnny. You sent your wire, *sí?*"

"Yes," he murmured, but his eyes were on Maggie, who felt like a jackrabbit must feel when cornered by a cougar. A wounded, irritable cougar.

"Oh, but I wouldn't dream of intruding on your dinner with your son, sir," Maggie assured him, and wasn't surprised to see her remark make his face relax a little. "Perhaps you could tell me if the hotel serves luncheon?"

"Of course you weel not eat at the hotel! There ees more than enough food for all three of you, Señorita Maggie. You weel eat here," Jovita informed her. "*Señor,* I have theengs to buy for your household at the general store," she said. "I weel leave Johnny weeth you while he eats and then come back for heem, *sí?* You can enjoy your son and get to know your new employee," she said with a twinkle in her eye as she started walking to the door.

"You're not staying?" Garrick protested. "But Jovita—" But the bell over the door was already tinkling as the Mexican woman exited.

"Let's eat, Papa! The pretty lady can sit by me!" the boy cried, his eyes moving from his father to Maggie and back again. "Come sit here, pretty lady!"

Maggie bent to speak to the little boy. "Johnny, you may call me Miss Maggie," she said with a smile, then turned to speak to his father. "Mr. Devlin, it's not necessary," she began. "I'll just walk down to the hotel—"

"You'll do no such thing, Miss Harper," Garrick Devlin informed her, his eyes warning her not to protest further in front of his son, who was watching everything that passed between them. "Have a seat next to Johnny, there. I'll need to discuss with you how I intend to run this newspaper in any case, so you might as well sit down and eat dinner with us." He gestured toward the table, his invitation the very antithesis of the famous Southern hospitality.

That hospitality must be reserved for other Southerners, she thought ruefully, for as a Yankee she'd never received it.

Ah, well, he was just her employer. And if he didn't like

her, little Johnny seemed perfectly thrilled that she was going to eat with him and his papa, Maggie thought as the little boy settled himself on the chair between them and grabbed at a drumstick.

"Not yet, Johnny. Haven't I taught you we must give thanks for our food before we eat?"

Before she bowed her own head, Maggie saw the little boy dutifully bow his and squeeze his eyes shut. Then she listened as Devlin briefly drawled grace.

The man had a beautiful voice, even if he was testy in the extreme, Maggie thought. Then she opened her eyes, to find him looking at her.

"Go ahead and help yourself to some chicken now, Johnny, Miss Harper," he said, without looking away from her. "You'll have to forgive my lack of eloquence in prayer, ma'am," he said, irony dripping in the twangy, molasses-coated vowels. "My brother Cal's the preacher in the family."

"But…isn't he the sheriff? At least, I thought that's what Jovita said," Maggie replied, then knew when he raised an eyebrow that she'd managed to say the wrong thing. She ducked her head and pretended to ponder her own selection of chicken.

"Oh, so my housekeeper's already given you my complete family history," he commented. "No doubt you'd have solved all my problems if I'd been gone five minutes more."

"No, Mr. Devlin, I—"

He held up a hand to hush her. "No matter. I'm sure it's just as well that you know my estimable brother Caleb is the sheriff of this little town, after having been a preacher before the war. In fact, you'd probably get along famously with him, as he fought alongside the Yankees rather than

our own Southern boys." There was bitterness in his voice
as he divulged this surprising news.

She felt him watching her again, but she refused to give
him the satisfaction of showing her curiosity.

Johnny's interruption made that easier. "I *like* Uncle
Cal—Aunt Livy, too!" he announced, waving his already-
bare drumstick like a baton. "And I like Grammy and Aunt
Annie, and Uncle Sam and Aunt Mercy—she's gonna have
a baby! And I like my kitty cat!"

"You have a lot of family to like, Johnny," Maggie said,
feeling envious. Since her mother had died, she'd had only
her absentminded father, and she sometimes thought James
Harper forgot her existence except when they worked together at the newspaper.

She turned to Devlin after the boy started attacking a
second drumstick. "So how did you decide you wanted to
run a newspaper, Mr. Devlin?"

"I just got tired of beating all the men and boys of
Brazos County at footraces, Miss Harper," he said with a
sardonic nod toward his wooden leg, which was extended
stiffly out to the side of his chair.

Chapter Five

His sarcasm left Maggie feeling as if she'd just been slapped. For a moment she couldn't get her breath, and then she was angry—so angry that she wished little Johnny wasn't there so she could tell Garrick Devlin off before she quit and went to inquire about the next stage back to Austin. But little Johnny *was* there, and his presence stiffened her resolve. She'd be damned if she was going to let the man bait her into leaving before she'd even started.

"You have a…unique way of informing me it's none of my concern, haven't you, Mr. Devlin?" she replied in a voice that was as unruffled as she could possibly make it, so that the little boy wouldn't notice the tension that thrummed between the adults. "Very well. Perhaps you should tell me what your goals and philosophy are in regards to your newspaper."

He blinked at her composed response. *Point for me,* thought Maggie, *but don't expect me to be so restrained when your child is elsewhere. I haven't got red hair for nothing.*

"My goals and philosophy?" He leaned back in his chair and made a tent of his fingers. "Well, I reckon my goal is to start a newspaper worthy of the name, a paper that will expose the villainy of the carpetbaggers who have polluted our fair Texas soil, and the cancer of the scalawags who would sell Texas itself for the right price.''

She felt herself flushing as she realized he was again attempting to goad her.

"In other words, Texas right or wrong, is that your creed?" she retorted sweetly.

"Precisely, Miss Harper. Johnny, you may not have pie until you have some peas," Devlin commanded his son, who'd taken advantage of his father's inattention to try and cut an enormous slice of peach pie for himself.

Johnny looked sulky. "Does Miss Maggie have to eat 'em, too?"

"Why, yes of course, Johnny," Maggie told him with a smile. "That's one vegetable we don't have where I come from, and I find I quite like them."

The boy appeared intrigued. "You don't have no black-eyed peas?" he asked, looking as if he thought she must come from the moon for that to be true.

"Johnny, finish your dinner and let Miss Harper and your papa talk, please," Devlin said. "Miss Harper, I intend for the motto on the *Gazette*'s masthead to be Forever The Truth For Texas. What do you think of that?"

Didn't he ever give up? "Indeed, I think that the truth is all any newspaper should print, sir. And I'm curious— what did you use for start-up capital, if you don't mind my asking?"

She watched as a guarded look swept over his face, and then a sardonic smile. "Do you mean how did I ever manage to find two bits to rub together after the Yankees moved in and the taxes went through the roof? It wasn't easy, Miss Harper, in the face of that, but like all sneaky rebels, we had some silver buried in the backyard."

She couldn't be sure, but she thought he was being sarcastic again. "All right, but if I may ask, what are you using for operating capital?"

He blinked. "I beg your pardon, Miss Harper?"

"Operating capital," she repeated. "You know, the cost of running your newspaper? The money that buys your ink and paper and pays for any needed repairs to that printing press over there? I see you have enough supplies to start...." She nodded toward the Washington handpress, sitting behind the counter in all its shiny black glory, toward a cabinet full of rows of type cases, cylinders of paper and bottles of ink behind it. Devlin had paid a pretty penny for that press, she imagined, and wondered where the money had come from. None of the former rebels seemed to have any money left after the war, and his clothes, though neat and clean, were far from new or fancy.

"Why, the sale of my paper will supply the operating capital," he said, as if surprised. "I suppose it might occasionally be necessary to sell an ad to the general store, or print a Wanted poster for my brother the sheriff, or a handbill when Mayor Long is up for reelection, but I wish to keep my paper above the influence of those who would purchase space in it, Miss Harper. It's far more important to devote the columns to exposing the evils presently existing in Texas—"

"Lofty ideals, Mr. Devlin, but as an experienced newspaperwoman, I can tell you that your paper will starve for lack of cash nourishment if you think you can run it on nothing more than what the townspeople will pay for it. What did you plan on charging, sir? A nickel? This is a small town, and even if everyone subscribes, you won't make enough to keep it going. No sir, in my opinion, you will have to plan on selling advertisement space regularly. Most papers run each ad for at least six weeks, which is very easy with stereotypes, the woodcut-and-type blocks patent medicine makers furnish. And you will have to do away with job printing during the day if you hope to survive—the paper can always be printed at night.''

He looked momentarily dazed by all the information she had just thrown at him, but then he recovered, and Maggie could see he was restraining himself with some difficulty.

''Opinions are one thing you don't seem to lack, Miss Harper,'' he said at last. ''Very well, I shall sell advertisement space. I imagine the proprietor of the general store will be happy to buy an ad on a regular basis. And then there's the milliner, and the barber—and of course Doc Broughton is always peddling some nostrum or other. Yes, Johnny, you may have a piece of pie now that you've eaten your peas. Here, I'll cut you a slice.''

Maggie decided she wouldn't smash all his optimism in one sitting. She hadn't met the businessmen of Gillespie Springs, of course, but from what she'd seen, a small-town merchant was notoriously reluctant to see the need to advertise when he had the only store of its kind for miles.

She was about to ask another question when Devlin began to speak again.

''Today is Tuesday,'' he said, as if thinking aloud. ''If we succeed in putting out our first edition tomorrow, we'll plan on putting the paper out every Wednesday.''

She nodded, pleased that they were now on a more businesslike footing. ''In your letter, you mentioned that there was a room upstairs that would be my living quarters—does that staircase in the corner of the room lead to it?''

''Yes, but I didn't know you were a female then,'' Devlin reminded her. ''It's out of the question for you to live upstairs now, of course. But you can rent a room at the boardinghouse over on North Street.''

Now it was Maggie's turn to raise an eyebrow. ''Why ever shouldn't I live here? My board was part of the deal you offered, Mr. Devlin, and I doubt I can afford to pay board on the salary we agreed upon," she informed him frankly. "As it is, I will have to buy my meals. And while you are not paying me the fifty cents an hour a *male* pressman could earn at any newspaper back East, I *would* like to be able to save some of my money. All Yankees are *not* born rich, despite what you may think."

"But you can't stay up there, a woman alone!" he sputtered. "It wouldn't be proper!"

"Nonsense, sir. The door can be locked, can't it? Having upstairs quarters will be very handy when we put the paper to bed late at night, as we will probably be doing tonight," she said, then was amused to see him blush at the phrase.

"Miss Harper, perhaps all Yankee women speak as you do, but I'll remind you to keep a civil tongue around my son," he snapped, though Johnny had finished his pie and was once more pursuing a fly on the window glass.

She couldn't help but laugh. "Mr. Devlin, that's a perfectly usual term in the newspaper business," she said, "not a lewd phrase at all. It means finishing that particular edition, and shutting down the press, and—"

"I can guess that," he interrupted. "Just watch how you talk, if you please. Ah, there you are, Sweeney," he said, as the telegrapher rushed in. "Were you able to get an answer from your source in Austin?"

"Yeah, I got lots a' details for ya, Mr. Devlin," said Sweeney, beaming with importance. "It's sure 'nough gonna set the folks in town on the boil, that's fer dang sure!" Then he realized Maggie and the child were sitting there, and he clapped his bony hand over his mouth. "Oh, pardon me, miss."

Maggie could tell her employer longed to inform Sweeney that her language could be much coarser than his "dang," but he restrained himself. "Think nothing of it," she murmured, and then the bell over the door tinkled again, announcing Jovita's return.

"Eet ees time to come weeth me, *niño*," the Mexican woman told Johnny as she entered, holding out her hand to the boy. "After your nap you can help me figure out what to make for supper for your papa, yes?"

"That won't be necessary, Jovita. I won't be home for supper tonight. In fact, I may be very late."

"But you must eat, *señor*, you and the *señorita*."

"You fuss like a mother hen, Jovita, but I promise I won't forget to feed Miss Harper. I'll fetch us sandwiches from the hotel or something. Now go on home with Johnny. I have a paper to get out."

Maggie could see he was fairly fidgeting with impatience to get started. Well, for all his faults, at least Garrick Devlin was an eager newspaperman, and she could forgive a lot in the face of that. She remembered when the stories she'd been writing for her father's newspaper had been all-important to her, too. That had been before Richard, of course. Could she possibly regain her enthusiasm, working for a man who obviously hadn't yet finished fighting the Civil War?

"All right, *señor*," Jovita said. "Well, if Papa must be late tonight, Johnny, what would you theenk of going to visit your *tío* Cal and *tía* Livy?"

"*Sí*, Jovita! See, Papa, she's teachin' me *Mexican!*" Johnny boasted.

"So I hear," Garrick said approvingly. "I'll see you later, son," he added, but his wave was distracted as he snatched the paper, with its dots and dashes and the telegrapher's transcription above it, from Sweeney. "Thanks, Sweeney. Remember to keep this quiet, will you?"

"You bet, Mr. Devlin. Nice meeting you, Miss Harper," said the telegrapher as he backed out the door.

"Nice meeting you, too, Mr. Sweeney. Thank you for your quick work," she added, and saw the man's face light up as he exited.

And then she was alone with Devlin.

"Well, now you have two males in your thrall, my son and Sweeney," commented Devlin sourly behind her. "Stop batting your eyelashes and take your bags on upstairs, if you're still determined to room there. Change into something you won't be afraid to get ink on, Miss Harper."

"I'm sure I don't know *what* you mean, Mr. Devlin," she retorted with some spirit. "But never mind— I promise never to bat my eyelashes in *your* direction. Give me five minutes to change my clothes and I'll be back, ready to work," she said. Picking up her two heavy carpetbags, she headed for the stairs. She hoped five minutes would be long enough to cool both their tempers so that they could get some work done!

The room was small, and sparsely furnished with a bedstead, a chest of drawers, holding a washbasin and pitcher, and a table with a single, rickety-legged chair. A cloudy mirror hung above the chest. There was one window, which looked out over a back street lined with small houses, some of which were little more than rude shacks. Not exactly a scenic view, she thought. She would need to fashion some curtains for privacy at night. And no doubt the room, which was now delightfully airy with the spring breeze blowing through the open window, would be hot as Hades come summer, but at least it was hers alone.

Latching the door behind her, Maggie set her bags down on the bed and pulled out her workday clothes, a skirt and waist of a navy blue so dark it looked black except in bright sunlight. It had been washed and re-dyed many times, but ink stains hardly showed on it. Then, staying away from the window, she stripped off her traveling clothes and hung them on pegs on the back of the door. There would be time later to arrange her garments in the chest of drawers.

Some thoughtful soul—impossible to think it could have been Devlin—had put water into the pitcher, and she poured some onto a towel and used it to wash her face. Feeling refreshed, she combed out her hair and braided the fiery, curly strands.

Garrick Devlin could hardly be more different from the kindly, middle-aged man she had imagined, Maggie thought as she coiled the braid at the nape of her neck with a few hairpins. She had been expecting someone like her father, she realized, someone with James Harper's gentle mien if not his looks.

She estimated Garrick Devlin to be anywhere from his mid-thirties to forty years of age, judging by the lines engraved around his eyes and mouth and the silver mixed into his dark hair. But his cynical, touchy disposition might make him seem older than he truly was. His face was a lean, hawkish one, with high cheekbones, a long, well-shaped nose and narrow eyes of that piercing blue that seemed an echo of the Texas skies. There was an impossibly arrogant set to his mouth that belied the weakness suggested by the cane he kept at his side.

All told, it was a stubborn, disagreeable face, at least when he looked at her—and yet she had seen that face change when he talked to Johnny. She had seen that he could smile, and that his smile transformed the rest of his tense features, relaxing them and making him look years younger and much more approachable—even handsome! she was surprised to realize.

Well, *she* had no further use for handsome, that was certain. All she hoped for was to be able to work with this difficult man to produce a newspaper they could both be proud of. She could teach him much, if he would let her.

If only his stiff-necked pride didn't get in the way! It wouldn't be easy, since he despised what she was and everything she stood for, but she could at least try.

Goodness, she'd better stop pondering over her employer and get back downstairs! It was surely more like ten or fifteen minutes since she'd come up here!

"Took you long enough," groused Devlin, barely glancing up as she reached the bottom of the stairs. He was hunched over the table, a stubby pencil grasped in his right hand, and as she approached, she saw that he'd already covered nearly a full page with his untidy scrawl. She saw him stop and glance at the telegraph transcription, and then his pencil began to race over the paper again.

"I'm sorry, sir, I—"

"Here," he said, thrusting the now-filled sheet of paper at her. "You can start setting the type for this page."

The first thing she was going to have to learn how to do was read his writing, Maggie thought with dismay as she peered at the slanting scrawl. It was nothing like the neat copperplate of his letter to "M. L. Harper." Had he gotten the local schoolmarm to write that letter for him?

"What's wrong?" he demanded, peering at her and letting the pencil fall with a soft clatter to the desk. "Are you disagreeing with my headline story already? I didn't employ you to pass judgment on my opinions, Miss Harper, I pay you to run the press," he growled.

"No, Mr. Devlin," she began, "that is, I don't *know* if I disagree. I—I'm not used to your writing as yet. But just give me a minute or two, and let me study it. I'll ask you if I can't decipher a particular word," she promised, evading the hand that would have snatched the paper back from her.

Sure enough, once read in the light of the window, the individual letters began to sort themselves out and form into words and phrases, though it was particularly tough to tell one vowel from another, for they all appeared to be the same indistinct near-loop shape. Hopefully the arrangement of his flamboyantly slanted consonants would give her the clues she needed.

She turned her attention to the California type cases, the trays of metal letters of various sizes and fonts. At least the standard nine-point type she'd need for the newspaper was arranged alphabetically, she discovered. When she had more time she would arrange it the way compositors traditionally did—capital letters alphabetically in cases on the right, and small-case letters on the left, with the most frequently used ones in the handiest spaces.

She began setting up the rows of type that would become the opening lines of the infant newspaper: the masthead, with the large Gothic capitals proudly proclaiming the name of the paper as the *Gillespie Springs Gazette*; the motto Forever The Truth For Texas right underneath; and then the date April 4, 1869, followed by the words *Premier Edition* and *Garrick Devlin, Editor And Owner*.

That portion completed, she laid out the very first headline: Radical Republicans Choose E. J. Davis As Their Gubernatorial Candidate, Former Union Brigadier General Is Certain Victor With General Reynolds As Ally.

Afternoon drifted into evening as she painstakingly set in rows of metal and wood type the words Garrick Devlin was feverishly scribbling at his desk. Every so often he would hand her another page and ask her how she was coming, and if she thought she was going to be able to finish tonight. Naturally, she could not lay out the pages as fast as he could write, but she kept working, ignoring the ache in her back and the throbbing of her head.

"Well, are you going to tell me we shall have to put off publication for another day?" Garrick Devlin inquired some time much later, coming to stand next to where she was working on the second page.

Maggie looked up in surprise. "Why, no, sir," she said, glancing at the watch she'd pinned to her bodice. Seven o'clock, and she was only half done! "No, I promised you this would be ready by morning, and it will be, even if I have to stay up all night, just as I said."

Was that approval that had flashed so briefly in those cold blue eyes? No, surely she had imagined it!

"Well, Miss Harper, I am all done with the writing, and my stomach is growling."

"Go ahead, go have something to eat," she said without looking up. "I'm not hungry after that big midday dinner," she lied. And then, to her mortification, her own stomach protested, too, loudly enough that Garrick Devlin heard it.

"Why, Miss Harper, I believe you are prevaricating," Devlin mocked, a small smile playing about that arrogant mouth.

"Well, perhaps a little," she admitted, "but I really am eager to get this done, just as I promised. Perhaps I will eat something before we start running off copies." She'd need some nourishment before lifting those heavy trays of type and repeatedly pulling back the devil's tail—the lever that rolled the bed of type under the platen.

"Then I shall have to go over to the hotel and purchase something for both of us to eat, or no doubt I'd return to find you swooned on top of the press," he taunted her in that molasses drawl of his.

"It's not necessary."

"Certainly it is. I promised Jovita I would feed you, and so I shall. *I*, Miss Harper, do not prevaricate. I'll return in a few minutes." With that, he made his way to the door and went out.

Chapter Six

Garrick peered at his pocket watch, willed to him as the eldest Devlin son by his father. It was 3:00 a.m.

"One hundred copies," he murmured as Margaret Harper pulled the last one off of the press. "I believe that will be enough for our first edition, Miss Harper, so I'll bid you good-night."

She stared back at him as if dazed, her green eyes dull with fatigue, her shoulders slumping slightly, and he knew a moment's shame for having worked her so hard on the same day she had arrived on the stage. As soon as he'd finished writing the copy, he'd helped with as much of the work as he could, and had been shocked by how heavy the typeset pages were once the tin letters were locked together. Why, they must weigh a good thirty pounds each, and Miss Harper hadn't even mentioned it, let alone batted her eyelashes at him and praised his manly strength the way Cecilia used to do when she wanted something heavy toted for her.

Then, after some quick instruction by Miss Harper, he'd done the tedious "pulling of the devil's tail" and run off copies of the *Gazette* while she belatedly ate her supper. His right shoulder throbbed as a result, and he marveled that she, of much slighter build, had yet to utter a first complaint.

Perhaps the Yankees were built of sterner stuff than he'd imagined. "You've worked very hard today, Miss Harper. That is to be commended," he said. "If it hadn't been for that story, of course, we needn't have been in such a hurry, but this information can't wait. Naturally I shan't expect such a frantic pace out of you normally."

He saw her chin go up again, the shoulders straighten and the light of battle rekindle those green eyes.

"Nonsense, Mr. Devlin," she said briskly. "Every good newspaperman—or *woman*—thrives on the excitement of getting such a big story to its readers. Don't fear you have to spare me just because I'm a woman. I'm used to working as hard as any man."

He knew a grudging admiration for her stubbornness. Fine—if she wouldn't complain, he'd be damned if he'd let on how much *he* hurt.

"Well and good, Miss Harper, but surely you had better retire for the night. It will be morning before you know it, and we'll need to start planning the next edition."

"Oh…oh, of course," she murmured, as she turned and walked toward the stairs. "Good night, sir."

She hesitated as she passed the remains of their hurried supper lying on the table, the grease-stained brown paper wrapping and a piece of crust from a steak sandwich. "I—I'll just clean this up before I go upstairs, Mr. Devlin."

"Never mind, Miss Harper, I'll dispose of it," he said firmly.

"Very well. Good night, then, Mr. Devlin." He heard her trudge up the stairs, pull the creaky door open—he'd have to oil that hinge, he thought—and shut the door quietly behind her. A moment later an audible click announced that she'd locked the door from the inside.

He turned and surveyed the pristine black-and-white stack of papers. The ink still gleamed wetly on the top copy. Each one was a big sheet of paper folded in half, forming four pages filled top to bottom with his eloquent reporting of the story from Austin and his opinions about it. In just hours the townspeople would eagerly snatch copies from that stack, and his career as the respected editor of the *Gillespie Springs Gazette* would officially begin.

The moment seemed incomplete to Garrick. If his new employee had been a man, as he'd been expecting, he would have invited him to share in a celebratory glass of whiskey. He'd stashed a bottle in his desk for just such an occasion as this, the completion of the very first issue of the town's first newspaper. But of course one did not invite a lady—or even a presumptuous Yankee woman such as Margaret Harper—to share a drink.

The only sort of female who drank liquor was a sporting woman, and he did not associate with those, even when his long-frustrated sexual needs clamored for satisfaction. No, he wouldn't pay for what passed as loving, knowing that if he did find a woman who would provide such services to a cripple, she'd either charge him double or do it out of pity, then laugh about it later with her sisters in the oldest profession.

There was no help for it—he'd have to drink alone, he mused, retrieving the whiskey bottle and a glass from the desk drawer and pouring himself a two-finger measure. The amber liquid burned a fiery path down his throat and hit his stomach like a glowing ember.

The sole of his right foot and his lower calf had begun to throb hours ago, just as they always did when he'd done too much. Now he was exhausted and could no longer ignore the pain to his shoulder throbbing in counterpoint, even with the whiskey warming his stomach. Absentminded with fatigue, he reached down with his fingers to massage his leg, only to recoil when his hand met the hardness of wood instead of the softness of flesh and bone.

Damn it all to hell, when was he going to stop having pain in a limb that hadn't been there for over three years? His eyes darted to the top of the stairs, afraid that Miss Harper had managed to silently creep back out onto the stairway and witness the way the phantom pains had made a fool of him again, but his eyes found only lamplit shadows up there.

Relieved, he gulped the rest of the whiskey, and after placing the glass and bottle back into the desk drawer, he grabbed four *Gazettes* off the top of the stack to take home. He'd give one to Jovita, one to Johnny—he smiled as he pictured his son pretending to ''read'' it—send one to his mother and keep one for posterity. He set another one aside, knowing Cal would come directly here for his copy.

Garrick let himself out into the cool spring night. Suddenly he couldn't wait to reach his rented house, which stood over on South Street behind the bank. In the privacy of his own room, he could pull off the damned wooden leg that daily rubbed the flesh of what was left of his upper leg until the end of stump was irritated raw, sometimes even streaked with dried blood. Tonight would be one of those times, he guessed, for he'd been on his feet far too long today. When he sponged away the dark, dried blood, the stump would burn as if the cloth were made of nettles instead of cotton, and he'd have to set his teeth against the pain so that he wouldn't wake Johnny and Jovita, sleeping in the other rooms.

Sometimes removing his wooden leg and washing the stump was not enough to soothe the pain, and he'd have to reach to the bottom of the brass-bound trunk in which he kept his old uniform and firearms for the bottle of laudanum he kept hidden there. But he hated the sense of weakness he felt after drinking from that bottle. And he knew that once he slept after sipping the liquid tincture of opium, his dreams would be nightmares, full of horrifying sounds and the faces of the dead. He'd be even more afraid to use the drug now that he knew of Cecilia's death. He didn't want to see the ghost of his dead wife floating toward him as he slept, her golden tresses dull with mold.

He remembered seeing what laudanum had done to other men, too, turning them into helpless, sniveling addicts for the rest of their miserable lives. Maybe he was better off not using it, and just putting up with the pain, he decided, even as every step that brought him closer to home became an agony in itself.

"Here's my nickel, Garrick. Sell me a paper," the tall fellow wearing a star on the left side of his vest and a patch over his right eye said with a grin, leaning on the counter in the *Gazette*'s office the next morning.

This must be Garrick's brother Caleb, the sheriff, Maggie thought as she looked up from where she was doing the layout of a rate card for advertising in the *Gazette*. She saw the same lean, high-cheekboned features, though Caleb Devlin's upper lip was graced with a dashing mustache, where Garrick's was austerely bare. Caleb's one good eye was of a paler hue than Garrick's, almost a gray-blue, but both brothers possessed faces that reflected the presence of pain, past or present.

"Cal, I can't take your money," protested Garrick, returning the grin. "You're my brother! I saved you a copy, *gratis*."

"Aw, brother, you're never gonna be a rich newspaperman if you keep refusing money—" the tall lawman began, and then Maggie saw him notice her.

In an instant, he swept off his broad-brimmed hat and smiled at her. "Sweeney told me about your new press-man—um, *lady*," he said, speaking to his brother, a teasing glint in his eye.

"Yes…M. L. Harper was not quite as I expected *him* to be," Garrick replied dryly. "Miss Harper, this is my brother, Cal Devlin."

Maggie stepped forward, encouraged by the sheriff's warm smile, and offered her hand.

"Mr. Devlin, I'm Margaret Harper."

He took her hand and shook it. "Miss Harper," he murmured in that molasses-and-honey drawl that flowed from Southerners so effortlessly. "Call me Cal. Welcome to Gillespie Springs. I see you still have your head, so my big brother must not have bitten it off yet—good! Don't let him. His bark is worse than his bite, anyway. I hear you have lots of newspaper experience, so my brother's lucky you answered his ad. Don't let him forget it."

"Cal, if you're quite finished subverting my authority over my employee," Garrick said with heavy irony, "we have work to do here, and—"

The bell over the door tinkled again, and a dark-haired woman stepped inside, a joyous smile lighting her attractive features.

"Garrick, I just heard the newspaper was out!" she announced, coming forward to stand by Caleb's side. "Congratulations on the start of your business!" She planted a kiss on Garrick Devlin's cheek.

"Why, thank you, Olivia…." Garrick murmured, reddening slightly.

Maggie, still standing near her employer, felt her jaw drop for a second. Wasn't Garrick Devlin wearing a black armband as a sign of mourning for his wife? Who was this woman?

Then Maggie saw Cal Devlin place his arm around the woman's waist and smile down at her momentarily before turning back to Maggie.

"Livy, meet Miss Margaret Harper, Garrick's 'pressman,'" Cal announced. "Miss Harper, this is my wife, Olivia."

"Miss Harper, I'm so pleased you're here to help dear Garrick! And I hope you can come over to supper sometime real soon, so we can officially welcome you to the town," Olivia Devlin said, extending her hand. "Actually, we'd heard about your arrival yesterday—nothing much is unknown in a small town, you know—and I wanted to come meet you then, but Cal said you and Garrick would be real busy, so I restrained myself until this morning. And here you've already helped Garrick print his paper! This is just wonderful, Miss Harper!"

"Why...thank you," Maggie said, startled at Olivia Devlin's flow of words and the unexpected invitation. "I—I'd like that. Please—call me Maggie."

The other woman smiled back at her while her husband gazed fondly down at her. "Maggie, then. And you must call me Livy. I'm so sorry about chattering on like that— I'm afraid Southern girls learn to chatter in the cradle. I'd heard you were a Yankee, but not that you were so pretty! My brother-in-law better be careful, or one of the town bachelors is going to steal you right out from under his nose!" she said, her eyes sparkling.

Maggie felt herself blushing at the woman's compliment, but she was aware that Garrick had tensed beside her.

"You're too kind, Livy," she said, before Garrick could speak, "but Mr. Devlin doesn't have to worry. I'm here to put out his newspaper, nothing more." She stole a glance at her employer out of the corner of her eye, but couldn't tell if her remark had reassured him at all.

"Well, all right, but we'll make sure Garrick doesn't work you like a field hand. All work and no play makes Jane—"

"A hard-working newspaperwoman," Cal finished for his wife. "Livy, we'd better clear out and let these folks get back to work. Here, take this hot-off-the-press newspaper home with you, honey. I'll look forward to reading it tonight after supper. I'll second my wife's invitation, Miss Maggie—you don't mind if I call you that, do you?— we'll expect you for supper real soon. Just as soon as you've had a chance to settle in, we'll set a date."

Smiling, Maggie bid them goodbye, but getting back to work proved impossible at that moment. A dapper man in a bowler hat and frock coat was coming in the door just as the sheriff and his wife left.

"Garrick! Let me see the paper!" he demanded with a beaming smile as he came forward, his arm extended. "This is a landmark day for Gillespie Springs, a landmark day!"

"Certainly, Mayor Long," Garrick said, taking one off the stack with evident pride. "I'll be interested to hear your opinion."

Maggie, who had unobtrusively gone back to her layout on the desk, saw her employer straightening and restraightening the stack of newspapers—a stack already perfectly in order. So he *was* anxious about the mayor's reaction, she thought. She found that fact touchingly human.

Mayor Long held the paper at arm's length in the light of the window and perused it for about five minutes, his shiny black eyes darting over the four pages of type.

"Garrick, this is a fine start, a fine start," he said at last. "An important story, sure enough. But this town has ambitions to grow, you know. I'd like to see more in it about what a salubrious location this is, about the wonderful folks that make up Gillespie Springs, so I can send your paper back East and attract more settlers. You *do* intend to include more of that sort of thing in your next edition, don't you?''

Maggie watched, guessing Garrick was struggling to hold back irritation. ''Well, I suppose so, James, but my primary purpose will be to inform the town of the important issues being decided in Austin, and in dad-blamed Washington, not tell the folks what they already know about their own town and the people they see every day—''

''Nonsense, people love to read about themselves,'' the mayor retorted. ''I'm not saying that what the Radicals are trying to force down our throats isn't important, Garrick, but it *is* less important to your readers, I'm convinced, than what happens around here every day.''

''Well, you're not sending my newspaper up North, are you?'' Garrick replied. ''Seems to me we have enough damn carpetbaggers here already—''

''Now don't get hot under the collar, Devlin, I'm talking about sending it to cities like Atlanta and Richmond and Vicksburg, places where the damn Yankees have ground the folks down even worse than in Texas—'' He stopped abruptly, and Maggie, her eyes on her work, realized she had been spotted.

''Garrick, you didn't tell me there was a lady here, and we've been cursing in her presence. Ma'am, my humblest apologies for our crude speech,'' Mayor Long called out.

As Maggie looked up she saw the dapper little man sweep his hat off his head and do a bow that would have done credit to one of the old Cavaliers of bygone days.

Garrick grudgingly performed introductions yet again. Maggie could feel his irritation at the implied reproof.

''Miss Harper, please accept my apology for my frankness about the Yankees,'' the mayor added. ''I'm afraid feelings still run rather high in the South, but there's no excuse for rudeness in your presence. Actually, I'd already heard about Garrick's new employee and that you were a Northerner, but I didn't realize you were in the room.''

"No apologies needed, sir," Maggie said quickly. "Any Northerner with an open mind can see that there were excesses committed in the name of winning the war, and still are, now that we're trying to create a lasting peace."

"Thank you, Miss Harper. Your graciousness does you credit. Well, I'd better be going, but naturally I'll take this with me, Garrick—" he held the *Gazette* aloft "—and read it word for word at home. Think about what I've suggested, now. Pleasure to make your acquaintance, Miss Harper."

They were alone again, but it didn't last long. There was a steady stream of townsfolk coming into the office of the *Gillespie Springs Gazette*, all eager to buy the first edition of the paper and congratulate Garrick Devlin.

Most of them didn't notice Maggie working quietly in the rear of the office, and so by noon she had the rate card typeset and ready to print.

"I'm going home for dinner, Miss Harper," Garrick announced. He'd hardly spoken to her during the busy morning full of visitors. "I'll be gone for an hour or so. You might as well go over to the hotel and eat while I'm gone," he added, with his hand on the door.

"I'll do that. But first I'll just run off a few of these rate cards. Why don't I take them around to the hotel and the other businesses, to introduce our advertising and printing services?"

His mouth tightened. "Ever the Yankee businesswoman, aren't you? Well, go ahead, introduce yourself and see what you can drum up. But remember, Miss Harper, easy does it. Northern pushiness won't be appreciated here, I promise you."

Maggie bit back a sarcastic retort and watched as Garrick picked up his cane and made his awkward way to the door. It would take a man like Garrick Devlin time to trust her, especially after life had taught him to distrust Yankees and women. Perhaps if she was patient and controlled her temper, she would eventually develop a good working relationship with Garrick and he would even come to value her, though he wished she were neither a woman nor a Yankee. Perhaps, in time, she could make him see that neither of those things mattered. She ignored the tiny voice within that wished he *would* see her as a woman, and a desirable woman at that.

Chapter Seven

Maggie, seated at a small table in the Gillespie Springs Hotel restaurant, ordered a green salad, coffee and a small slice of the hotel's peach pie, thinking not only of her waistline but of her wallet. It would be a long time until she was paid her first month's wages, and until then she'd have to live on the money Papa had paid her for her last few stories.

"Was everything all right, miss?" The sullen voice belonged to the cook, who had also served as her waitress. Was the woman's coolness due to Maggie's accent or the fact that Maggie had declined the heavy "blue plate special"—fried chicken, okra, mashed potatoes and gravy? Or did the woman disapprove of her dining alone?

If it was the latter case, the woman had better get used to it, Maggie thought, for without a stove in her room, she had no other option but to dine out. That's what a man doing her job would do, and the cook would think nothing of *that*.

Maggie couldn't help remembering those days when she and her father had adjourned at noon to that café around the corner from the *Freedom's Voice* office, to eat and talk over the articles they were writing. How she longed for his company now! She couldn't picture Garrick Devlin chatting companionably over a meal with her about the articles they were working on, not if she stayed in Gillespie Springs for fifty years!

"Everything was fine. I—I'm sure I'll be eating a lot of your fine cooking in the future, now that I've come to work at the *Gazette*." She'd hoped the compliment and her conversational tone would thaw the woman out some, but it was not to be.

"Yes, the boss told me about you," the woman said, tight-lipped. "You're that newspaper woman."

Maggie didn't know what to say in the face of the cook's obvious disapproval, and then remembered the rate cards she'd brought with her. "Oh, by the way, might I see your employer for a moment? I'd like to speak to him about advertising in the *Gazette*."

The woman's lip curled. "You can go right through there into the hotel," she said, pointing to a doorway, "and he'll be behind the front desk. But I don't reckon he'll see any need to advertise. Everyone in town knows Bessie does the best cooking in Brazos County. Come suppertime, this place'll be full. You want your supper here, you better come early or be ready to wait for a table," the woman finished, her face smug.

Maggie resisted the urge to look pointedly at the empty tables around her. Except for a pair of old men nursing bowls of soup on the other side of the room, she was the establishment's only customer. "I'm sure everyone in Gillespie Springs knows about your suppers," she began with what she hoped was a winning smile, "but wouldn't it be nice to spread your fame back East? The *Gazette*'s going to be sent to other parts of the country, you know, in an effort to attract new settlers."

The woman considered the idea for a moment, her plump arms akimbo on her ample hips.

"That might not be too bad, if none of the new ones are Yankees," she said, and sailed back to the kitchen.

It was ridiculous to feel snubbed by a cook, Maggie told herself, knowing the woman was watching her now from behind the half door that led to the kitchen. Maggie forced herself to walk unhurriedly through the doorway.

The lobby looked prosperous, with maroon brocade upholstered chairs, freshly painted walls and maroon velvet curtains pulled back with matching silk cords. A varnished cherry-wood banister led up the stairs to the rooms. Behind the counter, his back to her, was a short man with bent over a ledger.

"Pardon me, sir…"

He whirled around, and Maggie recognized the same man who had been introduced to her as the mayor.

"Oh, it's you, Miss Harper! I see that you're surprised that I wear more than one hat, as it were. Did you dine in my restaurant? I hope everything was satisfactory?"

Maggie assured him it was, knowing she'd gain nothing by mentioning his cook's less-than-hospitable attitude. She drew one of the rate cards she'd printed out of her reticule and laid it on the polished wood countertop.

"My employer thought I should offer you the first advertisement in the *Gazette*," she said, hoping God would forgive her for the tiny fib. Of course, she hadn't known the mayor owned the hotel, too, but she was sure Garrick Devlin would approve of approaching James Long first. After all, he had wanted a newspaper started in Gillespie Springs.

Long looked startled, but then he said in a considering fashion, "An advertisement? The hotel? Why, I suppose I could do that, though this *is* the only hotel for miles around.''

"Yes, but you'll want all those prospective settlers back East to know they'll have somewhere nice to stay while they look over the town—so they don't have to leave their wives back home in Atlanta or Vicksburg or wherever,'' she reminded him innocently.

"Hmm, you're right there, you're right there,'' he murmured. "Sure enough then, put me down for a twenty-dollar-size advertisement,'' he told her. "How many issues will that run?''

"For twenty-five dollars the *Gazette* could run it for six months,'' she told him, hoping she wasn't being what Garrick would call "pushy.'' "Think how many people would see it then. And you could also advertise your restaurant's hours and its specialities. If you'll just write down on a piece of paper what you'd like the ad to say, what the rooms rent for and so forth, I'll lay out the advertisement and bring it to you for approval. Then we'll create a stereotype—a layout for the ad as it will appear each time—so it'll be easy to keep placing it in the paper.''

"Is there some way a drawing of the hotel could be included, Miss Harper? I'm real proud of the place—I built it from the ground up, pounded every nail myself. Of course, that was before the war, when I was younger and had my son to help.''

"I'm afraid I'm not talented in doing woodcuts, which is how pictures are made for newspapers, Mr. Long. But perhaps someday the *Gazette* will include them.'' She thought of the fellow who'd done woodcuts for the newspaper back in Ohio. She'd grown up watching the talented man carve pictures out of small blocks of wood. If only they had someone like that to work for the *Gazette*.

Long chuckled. "Well, you're quite a saleswoman, Miss

Harper, and you certainly seem to know the business. You may be a Yankee, but Garrick was smart to hire you."

His approval was like a warm bath after Garrick Devlin's irascibility and the cook's frostiness.

Buoyed by her success, she asked Long whom he thought she should approach next.

"Hmm, you're right next door to Miss Phoebe's millinery, but she's real close with a penny. Couldn't hurt to ask, though. And then there's the general store down the street, and the doctor, and the livery...."

But Maggie did not meet with success in the millinery.

Phoebe Stone, a once-pretty woman with faded blond hair worn in a bun with incongruous ringlets in front of each ear, rushed forward from the back of the store when Maggie entered. She introduced herself and asked Maggie's name, and then, without giving her a chance to state her purpose, began showing her one hat after another.

"I may not be here much longer, you know," she confided. "I've been told my creations would be a sensation in Paris."

"Your hats are charming, Mrs. Stone," Maggie said, when she could wedge the words in edgewise. "It's obvious you have a real talent for what you do, and I'd love to buy half a dozen of these. But I'm afraid I didn't come to buy today, much as I'd like to. I'm here on behalf of the *Gazette,* to speak to you about advertising."

The woman looked as if Maggie had just thrown a bucket of cold water in her face, and smelly swamp water at that. She raised a pale eyebrow at Maggie.

"Well! I really can't see the need, as this *is* the only establishment of its kind in our town, Miss...ah, what did you say your name was?" Without allowing Maggie to answer or to give her promotional speech about the wider audience Devlin hoped to reach, she continued, "I *must* say I'm a little surprised at Mr. Garrick Devlin's sending you over here like this. He knows I'm just a poor widow living on...well, the last few *pennies* my sainted husband left me!" She dabbed at her eyes with a lace-edged handkerchief, though Maggie could discern no moisture there.

"You're not from these parts, so you wouldn't know my husband perished for the Cause in the war," she added. "Of course, you *Yankees* have no idea what deprivations we've suffered here. Why, I don't think I can even spare the money to buy the paper and read it, let alone buy an advertisement," she finished with a dramatic sigh.

Maggie bit back an unladylike snort, for Phoebe Stone's dress, if somber in hue, was of the finest silk, and there was a pearl-bordered cameo pin at her throat.

Phoebe blinked and seemed to reconsider. "But perhaps you should send dear Garrick over to discuss the matter with me *personally*," she said. "He already knows he has a standing invitation to have supper with me some evening, but he's so shy he hasn't taken advantage of it. Now he has the perfect excuse to do so, doesn't he?" she commented with a ridiculously girlish giggle. It seemed as if she had forgotten the offense she had taken at the purpose for Maggie's visit.

Maggie thanked Phoebe for her time and turned to leave.

"I'm just sure that dear man could use some comforting, now that he's *officially* a widower, and since I'm a widow, I think I'd understand his trials better than anyone, don't you?" Phoebe called after her.

"I'll certainly remind him of your invitation, Mrs. Stone," Maggie promised over her shoulder, beating a hasty retreat. Shy? Garrick Devlin was about as shy as a penned-up bear, and just as cranky. Perhaps Phoebe Stone didn't know how fortunate she was.

Surely the town doctor would be a better prospect. As

she'd told Garrick, doctors always wanted to peddle some patent medicine. Going past the hotel and the bank, she waved at Cal Devlin coming out of the jail across the street, and went in the building whose hanging sign read Dr. Broughton, M.D.

Fortunately, the doctor's waiting room was empty, so she knocked on the inner office door and heard a raspy voice bidding her "come on in."

The doctor was more like she'd pictured Garrick Devlin to be—bespectacled, barrel-chested and at least sixty years old. But there was no kindly twinkle behind the smudged lenses of his glasses.

"What can I do for you, madam?" he demanded, looking her over as if trying to uncover her malady. "You don't look sick."

"I'm not, Doctor," Maggie said with a smile. "I'm Margaret Harper, assistant to Mr. Garrick Devlin—" she thought "assistant" sounded better than "pressman" "—whose newspaper began publication this morning, as you probably heard."

She was aware that the old man had stiffened when she'd begun to speak. Oh, no, was it her Northern accent again? Was she going to have to learn a molasses drawl before anyone in town would speak to her?

"No, I didn't," the old man snapped. "Young woman, I've been up since dawn deliverin' babies and seein' an old woman into the next world, so I ain't exactly had time to worry about no newspaper. And now you're interrupting my nap. What is it you want, if you're not sick?"

"Why, the newspaper can be of service to you, sir," she said, in what she hoped was a persuasive tone. When she'd first come in, she'd spied a cabinet labelled Murphy's Patent Medicines—a Remedy For Every Ill," and now she pointed to that. "We'd be happy to advertise the patent medicines you offer for sale, such as those. Surely you have patients that would like to know you have remedies for such ills as—let's see…'' She went over to the cabinet and read, ''Catarrh, dropsy, oedema, leukorrhea—goodness! I've never even heard of such maladies! And of course, you could advertise your various charges—''

''Lady, I've been a doctor for almost forty years, and I never needed nothin' but that shingle hangin' out front to tell folks I'm here!'' he exclaimed, pointing a finger at the door.

Maggie began backing toward it. ''I'm sorry if I've come at a bad time, sir—I'll be happy to call at another—''

''Look, you Yankee carpetbagger, don't you ever bother me again unless you're sick, you hear me?'' he shouted, purple-faced as he advanced on her.

Maggie, finding herself on his front step, was reminded of a maddened bull. Biting back the angry words that rose to her lips, she was just about to turn and leave when she ran smack into a solid wall behind her. A solid, warm, breathing wall.

Garrick Devlin braced himself against the impact of Margaret Harper's body against his, then took hold of an elbow to steady her.

Then, without looking at Margaret, he said quietly, ''Dr. Broughton, I don't believe either of us was brought up to speak to a lady that way.''

The old man raised red-rimmed eyes to him and snorted. ''Devlin, I never have spoken to a *lady* in the wrong way, but this woman you went and hired is nothin' but a Yankee carpetbagger, and after what happened to *you*—'' he glanced meaningfully down at Garrick's wooden leg and cane ''—I'm surprised you'd give a woman like that the time a' day, let alone give her a job a Southern *man* could be doin'."

Garrick felt the woman beside him quivering with suppressed rage. Then he knew an overpowering urge to bloody the old sawbone's nose.

"Whom I hire is my business, Doc," he said, "and if you don't wish to advertise, that's yours. But I won't tolerate your being rude to an employee of mine, especially a lady, no matter where she comes from."

Broughton's mouth hung open for a minute, like an old hound dog's. "You're mighty bold fer someone who brought me his sick boy just last month," he rasped.

"Yes, and I paid you, even though you damn near killed him with your 'treatment,'" Garrick shot back. "He didn't get better till I let my Mexican housekeeper use one of her potions on him. Now, from what I could hear as I came into your waiting room, I believe you owe the *lady* an apology."

"I'll be damned before I apologize," Broughton snarled, and shuffled back into his inner office, slamming the door behind him.

"That old quack," growled Garrick, unclenching his fists as he turned to Margaret.

Her emerald eyes were blazing with unshed tears, her was face flushed, and he was surprised by a sudden desire to hold her in his arms and encourage her to let loose the angry sobs she was trying to contain. But of course, as Margaret Harper's employer, he couldn't do that. It would be improper. It would be taking advantage of her subordinate position. And since she was a woman, she'd see it as a weakness in him and exploit it.

Instead he held out his cane and said, "Would you like to borrow this to use on him?"

His offer had the bracing effect on her that he had hoped.

"To be honest, I would indeed," she admitted with a chuckle, then blinked. "How did you happen to find me just then, Mr. Devlin?"

"Cal saw you go into the office."

"Oh. Well, I certainly wish I hadn't," she said with a sigh. "Perhaps he would have been more receptive if you had approached him. I wasn't being pushy, I swear I wasn't!"

"I believe you. And the newspaper won't rise or fall on whether he buys advertising. Broughton has always been a horse's, um...hind end," he told her. "It isn't just you he's offended."

"But I did succeed in selling Mayor Long an advertisement for the hotel," she said, smiling again. "He'll take it for the entire six weeks."

"Good work," he said, and allowed himself to smile down at her.

"However, I'm afraid Mrs. Stone would like to speak to you personally about the subject," she said, and added with a teasing smile, "over supper."

It took a moment for Garrick to recover from the impact of the Yankee woman's smile before he finally realized what she had said. "That infernal woman," he muttered. "She chased my brother Cal until he made it clear Olivia was the only woman for him. I'm not about to put myself in her clutches."

He'd meant it in all seriousness, but Margaret only laughed. "A fate worse than death, is it?" she teased.

He rolled his eyes. "It would be, with that woman." It would be a fate worse than death to get into any woman's clutches again—he knew it as sure as he was breathing. Lord, he didn't want to get used to Margaret Harper's smiles, but he couldn't help basking in this one for a moment. At least he had made her forget she wanted to cry.

He never could stand up against Cecilia's tears, and she'd used them often.

"Well, I had planned to go into the general store next," she told him. "Shall I do that, or do you have something else for me to do?"

"Why don't you go over and see Cal instead? He said he needed some Wanted posters printed up. I'll go see Tyler about the general store's advertisement," he said.

Margaret nodded in agreement, and he sensed she was relieved she wouldn't have to chance any more rejections right now. He watched the attractive sway of her skirts as she started to walk across the street.

"Well, I'll be horsewhipped," a voice cried out from down the street, "can that be Garrick Devlin?"

Chapter Eight

The voice was familiar, though he hadn't heard it for over three years. Garrick turned and saw a man striding toward him, wearing the threadbare remains of a Confederate soldier's coat.

"Why, Captain Ezekiel Barbee, as I live and breathe," Garrick said, extending a hand. "I haven't seen you since...since the day I was wounded."

The other man shifted his gaze for a moment. "Yeah, I—I sorta lost track of ya, once they took ya behind the lines. I guess I figured ya fer a goner, knowin' that ol' doctor was gonna have t'cut off yore leg. But I see ya made it, after all," the man said, slapping Garrick on the back. "Guess they cain't kill a reb ornery as you, nohow. So, how the hell are ya? Got ya a wooden leg, huh?"

Garrick was aware of Margaret pausing to look over her shoulder at him. The last thing he wanted to do was introduce his Yankee employee to the former captain of his Confederate infantry battalion! Deliberately, he shifted so that his back was more fully turned to her.

"Yes, I get around pretty well now," Garrick said. He hated talking about his artificial leg, but he would if that would distract Barbee.

But Barbee gestured toward Margaret, who was now disappearing into the sheriff's office. "That yore wife? A fine-lookin' woman. But I thought ya said yore wife had yeller hair?"

Garrick forced a look of astonishment onto his face. "How on earth did you remember a thing like that, Cap? No, that's not my wife—I'm sorry to say I'm a widower," he said, gesturing toward the black armband.

Barbee uttered some conventional phrase of sympathy, and to Garrick's relief, did not ask him how Cecilia had died.

"Thank you...but what brings you to town, Captain? Thinking of settling here?" It would be great to have someone he could talk to about old times in the army, besides his younger brother Sam, who'd been in a different regiment.

"Well...I was just passin' through," Barbee said. "I ain't had no regular home since I couldn't pay my taxes, so I been doin' a little a' this, a little a' that. Trailed cattle t'Kansas fer a while...did some horse tradin'.... Don't this town have a saloon? What say we go discuss ol' times over a beer?"

Garrick knew a twinge of guilt as he led the way to the Last Chance Saloon, knowing he should be helping Maggie sell advertising, or writing an article. But it wasn't every day he ran into his old captain! Barbee had been a good leader, fearless in battle, always ready to buck up his men's spirits, or loan them money for a drink or a whore. And judging by what he was wearing and what he'd said, he'd fallen on hard times since the war. Surely the least Garrick could do was spend a little time with him.

It was late afternoon and they had fought most of the war over again, battle by battle, by the time they left the Last Chance. Barbee had bought the first round, then admitted he was nearly broke, so Garrick bought the rest of the drinks. He'd consumed only one glass of beer for every four Barbee downed, yet Barbee seemed little affected except for some slurring of his garrulous speech.

"Well, I better let you get on home to yore lil' boy," he said, clapping Garrick on the back once again. "Thass my horse tied up over there," he said, pointing at a raw-boned dun tied to the hitching post in front of the bathhouse.

"Where are you staying now until you get another job, Captain?"

"Gar, ol' boy, I reckon iss time ya jes' called me Zeke," Barbee said mournfully. "I ain't captain a' nothin' no more. And as fer where I'm stayin'—" he flung his arms wide "—the sky is my roof. It's spring, though, so it's right pleasant campin' under the cottonwoods. Don't you worry none about yore ol' Cap."

"Why don't you come stay with me, Zeke? I've got a small house over on the next street. Actually, my brother and his wife own it," he added quickly, not wanting to flaunt his relative prosperity to the captain. "She inherited a lot of rental houses from her last husband's brother. Most of them are little more than shacks on the street behind the saloon, but this is one of the nicer ones on South Street. There's an extra room."

"Naw, I wouldn't want t'impose," Zeke mumbled, his eyes on the ground.

Garrick felt an aching pity for the man. Zeke Barbee was the man who'd showed him the ropes when he'd been a raw recruit, and he'd saved his life at least twice in the first couple of skirmishes. And now look at him—homeless and forced to drift from job to job.

"There's no point in sleeping out in the open when I got a room to spare," Garrick insisted. "You could stay till you sign on for another trail drive. Why, my brother Sam's leavin' for Abilene with a herd the middle of next month— he's getting a late start because his wife's giving birth to their first child about the first of May. You could sign on with him if you wanted, unless something else came up sooner.''

"I don't know, Gar..."

"At least say you'll come have some supper and stay for the night. We weren't finished talkin' over the Wilderness campaign, were we? And you have to tell me about the part of the war I missed, once the damnyankees got my leg.''

Barbee studied him through bleary, reddened eyes. "Well, all right, Gar, and much 'bliged. Maybe jes' tonight. Hey, is that yore newshpaper over yonder?" he said, pointing at the *Gazette* office. "Ain't ya gonna show me around? Ain't ya proud of it?''

Garrick hesitated, wondering if Margaret was still in the sheriff's office talking to Cal. "Why, sure I'm proud of it, but there's always tomorrow. Aren't you hungry now? Let's go home and have some supper." If he could postpone the visit, he thought, maybe he could ensure that Margaret was elsewhere. Then he knew a twinge of guilt for being ashamed of his Yankee female employee, after all the hard work she'd put in since her arrival. Well, even if his old captain and Miss Harper met, surely the meeting would come off better if Barbee were sober and had the benefit of a bath first. Zeke Barbee was rather a sorry sight at the moment.

"Naw, I wanta see it right now, Gar. No time like the present," Zeke said with drunken persistence, and started across the street toward the *Gazette*.

Maggie was thoughtful as she laid out the type for the notice Garrick's brother wanted printed. There was a band of outlaws preying on Brazos County, stealing horses, cattle and even the occasional chicken. They'd also held folks on remote farms at gunpoint until the people had surrendered what little money and valuables they possessed. Even a stage or two had been held up. One elderly victim had died of fright.

From the descriptions given by some of the victims, it seemed likely there were at least half a dozen men in this outlaw band, maybe more. A farmer had mentioned that one was a black man and another looked like a half-breed Indian, but the rest of the men who'd robbed him were white. The notice warned the citizens of Gillespie Springs to be on the watch for these bandits, and cited a reward of five hundred dollars put up by the stage company for the apprehension of the criminals.

Cal Devlin certainly was a nice man, Maggie mused. He'd asked why Maggie looked a little flustered, and when she had explained about her run-in with Dr. Broughton, he'd told her about his own first days as sheriff of Gillespie Springs.

"Some folks were a little standoffish when they found out I'd been an officer in the Union army," he'd said. "It takes time, but stand your ground, Miss Margaret. They'll warm up after a while."

Intrigued that a Texan—especially a Texan with two brothers serving in the rebel army—had chosen to wear blue instead of gray, she'd asked him about his choice, and he'd told her the difficult decision had been a matter of conscience.

"I lost Olivia for many years because of it," he'd admitted. "But we found our way back to each other, and that's all in the past. You keep showing what you're made of *now,* and the good folks'll give you a chance. The other ones don't matter. Is my grumpy older brother treating you all right?''

Maggie had smiled at Cal's description of Garrick and said yes, Garrick was treating her just fine. Now, while her nimble fingers set the lead-and-tin-alloy letters, her lips curved upward again as she remembered the fierce way in which her curmudgeonly employer had come to her rescue in the doctor's office.

She'd been startled by Garrick's touch—and more surprised still by the tingle it set up within her—when he'd reached out an arm to steady her. She couldn't believe her ears when he'd begun defending her.

He had called her a *lady,* and she remembered the warmth the word had engendered within her because *he* had applied it to her. She knew he didn't really think of her as a lady—no woman who chose to invade a man's world could be a lady in Garrick Devlin's eyes—but he'd been loyal to her as his employee. And then he must've sensed how perilously close to tears she was, and had teased her until she forgot to cry!

The moment had been all too brief, but she'd gotten a glimpse of the nice human being buried under all those crusty, defensive layers. Maybe she and Garrick Devlin would be able to work together, after all.

She wondered about the scruffy, bearded man who had hailed Garrick just as she was about to go into the jail. He'd been dressed in the threadbare, dirty remains of a Confederate uniform, so was some old comrade of Garrick's, no doubt. It had been all too obvious Garrick hadn't wanted to introduce her to him, but that hadn't hurt Maggie's feelings. He didn't look like the sort of man she'd want to meet.

Just then the door opened and she heard Garrick's voice.

She was about to call out from the back of the room when she heard a second set of footsteps.

"Here it is, the *Gillespie Springs Gazette* office," Garrick was saying to the man entering behind him. "As a matter of fact, we put out the first edition today. I—I'd like you to meet—"

"Why, it's that gal I saw ya talkin' to before I hollered out to ya! You didn't tell me you had a pretty *filly* workin' for ya, Gar!" the man said. It was the same fellow whose identity she'd just been wondering about. Now he clenched a fat, stinking cigar between his yellowed teeth.

Maggie bristled inwardly as his dark, avid eyes raked her from head to toe—a look she knew Garrick couldn't see, for the man had stepped forward with his hand outstretched.

"Miss Harper, this is my old captain from the army, Ezekiel Barbee," Garrick was saying. "Zeke, my employee, Miss Harper."

"Well, come closer and shake my hand, Miss Harper!" the man bellowed in the overloud tones of a drunk. "You sure are the prettiest thing I've seen in miles, and thass a fact. And you're working for my old pard Garrick? That just about makes us family, don't it?"

Maggie wasn't about to come any closer. "Nice meeting you, Mr. Barbee, but I, uh, you wouldn't want to shake my hand, really—I'm afraid I'd get ink all over you," she said quickly, holding up the black-stained fingertips that were the bane of any compositor's existence. Printer's ink would probably be an improvement over the encrusted dirt he wore, she thought, but she didn't want to touch him. As it was, the man's eyes made her feel like her dress had fallen off and she was standing there in just her unmentionables.

His mouth dropped open. "Well, I'll be durned. Ya got a *Yankee* working for ya, Gar?"

Already irritated by the man's overbold stare, Maggie

stiffened, more than a little tired of the label constantly being applied to her. She saw Garrick redden, and realized he was embarrassed.

"She's a very experienced newspaperman, Zeke, and the war's been over for a while, you know—"

"Yeah, yore right, Gar," Barbee said hastily. "No offense taken, Miz Harper, I hope?" His tone was apologetic, but his eyes continued to devour her and his hand remained extended.

"None taken," she said with quiet dignity, but made no move to step forward. "Nice meeting you, Mr. Barbee, but I'd better get back to what I was doing."

"Oh, why don't you quit for the day, Miss Harper?" Garrick said. "I imagine you're tired—why not finish whatever you're working on tomorrow? I'll see you in the morning. I'm taking Zeke to my house for supper."

"Yeah, we ol' warhorses is gonna fight the war all over again, only this time the right side is gonna win," Barbee said with a chuckle. "Um, no offense again, Miz Harper."

Maggie didn't bother to respond to his obvious baiting. "See you in the morning then, Mr. Devlin."

She sighed as the door closed behind the two men, and she watched them walk past the window. She had wanted to ask Garrick a question about the layout of the hotel's ad, and the possibility of her writing some of the articles herself, but she hadn't wanted to do anything to prolong the presence of Zeke Barbee.

How could Garrick claim such a disgusting man as a friend? Well, she was in no position to dictate who her employer associated with, Maggie reminded herself. She could only hope Barbee wouldn't be in town for long.

Stretching and rubbing her aching back with her hands, Maggie decided she was more than ready to call it a day, even though the poster was far from completed. She'd had only a few hours' sleep the night before, and now weariness—and emotional exhaustion from the confrontations she'd had today—settled over her like a smothering cloak. Perhaps she'd just get a bowl of soup at the hotel before seeking her bed.

She found that the soup revived her somewhat, at least long enough to write her father a letter. He'd be worried about her and wondering how she was getting along in her new job. He'd be interested in her impressions of her employer and the town. And she found, as she sat down at her table in the room above the *Gazette*, that she was eager to tell her father about Garrick Devlin, to make the testy Texan come alive on paper, so that John Harper could picture him in his mind.

Chapter Nine

Type stick in hand, Margaret Harper was already hard at work in front of the type case the next morning when Garrick entered the *Gazette* office.

"Good morning, Mr. Devlin," she called out as he entered. "I just finished the layout for that notice your brother requested, the one warning the townspeople about that band of outlaws that's been preying on the area. He told you about them, I assume?"

She looked wide awake, her green eyes gleaming. She'd caught her hair back in a single wide braid, but little curling tendrils had escaped around her forehead. As Garrick gazed at her, a shaft of morning sunlight coming in the side window caught the curls and turned them into gold-shot, living fire.

Dammit, but she was beautiful this morning. The thought just added to his moroseness. His leg ached already, as if in sympathy for his head, which throbbed so badly he figured he'd have to be dead three days for it to stop hurting. He was an idiot to have helped Zeke finish the bottle of whiskey he'd brought out of his saddlebags last night.

"You're awful cheerful this morning," he muttered. "Of course I know about the outlaws. As a matter of fact, I came in to write a story about them this morning." He hadn't had any such idea, but he had to do something in the face of her aggravating industriousness.

He saw her lips tighten at his cross tone, and immediately regretted it. It wasn't her fault he had an aching head, or that her beauty attracted him at the same time as it reminded him a woman's beauty couldn't be trusted. "Sorry. Didn't mean to sound so crotchety. Zeke and I stayed up a little too late talkin' over old times." He didn't know why he'd said that last thing—it wasn't as if he owed her any explanation.

She looked away, but not before he saw her try to hide her amusement.

"It was nice for you to run into an old comrade," she said, her voice neutral.

He nodded. "He, uh, thinks you're pretty." Zeke had said it more bluntly than that, of course, but suddenly it was important to him that Margaret like his old friend, though he could not have said why. And it seemed a safe way to express his own secret feeling about her.

Her chin came up and the green eyes kindled.

"That leering saddle bum would think anything in skirts was pretty," she snapped. "I have to admit I hope I won't have to encounter him again."

Her unexpected flash of temper sparked the irritability he had just subdued. "You can't see beyond that gray coat, can you?" he taunted.

She glared right back at him. "Can *you*? Do you think that all men who wore it are automatically good and noble? You didn't..." Her voice trailed off, and she turned away from him. "Never mind. I suppose we'll just have to agree to disagree about your friend Mr. Barbee."

He wondered what she had been about to say, but he'd be damned if he'd ask. "I suppose we shall, Miss Harper," he said, injecting a good dose of frost into his tone. It would be better for both of them if they each remembered she was just an employee, and as such, her opinions about his personal life didn't matter to him.

Garrick advanced toward her until he could see the layout of the poster. "That looks satisfactory," he said, knowing it was churlish to be so sparing in his praise. "Go ahead and print up the poster and take it over to the sheriff's office. Cal can pay us out of his expense fund."

She began to do so as he settled down at his desk to write the story about the outlaw raids. For several minutes there was no sound in the office but the scratch of his pen on paper and the clanking, thumping sound made by the Washington press as she rolled the bed of type under the platen and pulled the devil's tail.

"There," she said, pulling the finished poster out and laying it on the counter. "I'll just let it dry a few minutes before I take it over...oh, there you are, Mr. Jones," she added as the tinkling bell announced a visitor.

Garrick laid down his pen and looked up to see a short, wiry man with skin the color of cherry wood standing just inside the door, his hat in his hand. He clutched a sack in his other hand.

"I'm sorry, I don't have any food here," Garrick said, thinking the man was one of the numerous ex-slaves who'd been set adrift by the Emancipation. He rummaged in his desk drawer for some change. "But here's four bits—if you take it to the back door of the hotel, they'll give you a couple of sandwiches. Tell them Garrick Devlin sent you."

The man smiled, a smile of dignity mixed with gentle amusement. "I'm not here for a handout, Mr. Devlin. I don't want anything I haven't earned."

"I'm afraid I don't have any work for you, either," Garrick said. "I've just begun the paper, and I don't have a lot of...*capital*," he said, with a sideways glance at Margaret Harper as he used her word.

She had rushed forward while he was speaking, an anxious smile on her face. "Mr. Devlin, this is Eureka Jones," she said. "I meant to tell you about him as soon as you arrived, but...I forgot when we started discussing...other matters."

He saw a brief flare of color in those telltale cheeks as she referred to their confrontation over Zeke Barbee.

"Mr. Jones approached me in front of the newspaper office about an hour ago," she continued, nodding toward the Negro as she spoke, "as I returned from getting coffee at the hotel. He showed me samples of his work, and I want you to see them, too. It's my opinion that you should hire him, sir."

"*Hire him?* Samples of his work?" Garrick repeated. Had Margaret Harper lost her mind? Hadn't she just heard him reiterate that he didn't have any work for the man? Wasn't she the one who had pointed out his lack of ready cash, or operating capital, as she called it in her Yankee-merchant way? Or was this just another example of Yankee social meddling? He turned back to Eureka Jones. "I'm afraid Miss Harper misinformed you. I have no work for you, Mr. Jones," he repeated.

Eureka Jones shrugged and turned toward the door.

"Oh, but you *do,* Mr. Devlin!" Margaret exclaimed, extending a forestalling hand to the black man. "That is, it's my *belief* that you'll want to employ Mr. Jones when you see what he can do," she amended, clearly aware that her certainty might have already injured Jones's chances. "Mr. Jones is a talented woodcarver, and he can prove it if you'll allow him to show you what's in that poke."

"A woodcarver? But I don't need—" Garrick began.

"But you do, Mr. Devlin, if you want to do much advertising in your paper, and you've already decided that you do.''

No, *you* decided it, he wanted to argue, but she had already gone on.

''Remember I told you about the *stereotypes,* the blocks of wood that have the words and pictures carved in relief on them, so that you can print the same ad time after time without setting up a new layout each time? Go ahead, Mr. Jones, empty your samples out on the counter.''

The black man shot Garrick a wary look and hesitated until he nodded, then opened the sack and upended its contents onto the counter. A dozen or so wood blocks of sizes varying from small square ones to larger rectangles fell out, clattering as they fell onto the wooden surface.

''You might want to start with this one, sir,'' Eureka Jones said, picking up one of the largest ones and handing it to Garrick.

Leaning on his cane with one hand, Garrick held out the other for the rectangular piece of wood and peered closely at it.

''It's—it's the newspaper office!'' he said, startled at the amount of detail the other man had carved into the wood. ''But what's this below it? The letters are backward....'' At last he deciphered the first line and read it aloud: '' 'The *Gillespie Springs Gazette*...' '' and in a moment, the one carved below it in smaller letters, ''Forever The Truth For Texas.' Why, however did you do this? And so quickly— we just put out the first edition yesterday!''

''I carved it last night,'' the other man confessed, a gleam of pride showing in his chocolate brown eyes.

Garrick quickly began to pick up the others, seeing in one a drawing of the bank building; in another, a row of medicine bottles; in a third, a trio of ladies' hats. Other smaller blocks showed intricate capital letters in various print styles, from elaborate Gothic to plainer forms.

"But this is a wonderful talent you have!" Garrick said. "How did you learn to do such work?"

He saw a shadow cross the man's gleaming dark eyes. "I was a slave in Louisiana once, and my mama worked in the kitchen of the big house. I had my own chores to do, but when they were done, she let me carve things into some yams and potatoes, and then she found me a whittlin' knife the young master had left on the veranda.

"I started carvin' things for the children, toys and such, and then later, blocks with letters on them. The master would pay me a few pennies to carve all the letters in the alphabet on a set of blocks. Then I started experimentin' with makin' the letters backward and stampin' them in ink so's the master's children could play with them. They had so much fun, they taught me how to read so I could have fun with 'em, too."

He looked down. "Mastah didn't like that so much. It was against the law for a slave to read, so he sold me— and my sister—to his brother who was movin' to Texas."

Garrick listened silently, appalled. The Devlins had never had slaves, but he'd known plenty of folks who had. He'd never been comfortable with the casual way slave owners could break up families on a whim. Garrick tried to imagine what it would have been like if *he'd* been denied the right to learn to read.

Eureka Jones cleared his throat. "Well, the war is over and I'm free, so I don't reckon I got to apologize for knowin' how to read now."

"No, of course you don't," Garrick murmured.

"Mr. Devlin," Margaret said, "if you hope to do steady advertising for the businesses in town, you need someone to make these stereotypes for you. Obviously, Mr. Jones can do that. The first design you picked up would be perfect for printing the paper's masthead, wouldn't it?''

Garrick had to admit that it would. "But that doesn't change the fact that I can't afford—"

"But Mr. Jones has told me he'd be willing to work for his food, at least in the beginning, and that he'd be happy to sweep up the shop daily, run errands and help your housekeeper with any of the heavier work that might arise," Margaret said quickly. "Meanwhile, if you're agreeable, I could train him as an apprentice, so that by the time you were able to pay him as an assistant, he would be able to assume whatever duties you would require."

"You've got it all figured out, haven't you, Miss Harper?" Garrick growled, knowing he was going to give in, but unwilling to let his Yankee female assistant think she had won so easily. "But where is Mr. Jones to sleep? I don't suppose you will be giving up your quarters and going to the boardinghouse as I suggested. I certainly can't afford to pay his room as well as his board, no matter how well he carves. And where will you get the wood that'll be needed, Mr. Jones?"

Now it was Eureka Jones's turn to speak up. "There's no problem, Mr. Devlin. I've been bunkin' with my sister over on North Street since I came to town. I've been workin' at this'n'that, but I like carvin' wood best. I just didn't figger she ought t'have t'feed me as well as her own young 'uns. And the wood's no problem, either. She's got a big old pecan tree that fell over in the storm not too long ago— it just missed her little house—and what didn't go for kindlin' is what I been carvin' with.''

Garrick saw Margaret Harper break into a cautious smile as he said, "Well then, I suppose you can consider yourself hired. You can start carving one of those stereotypes for the hotel ad. I think I can count on the owner to be a steady advertiser.''

Now Eureka Jones grinned. "Thank you, Mr. Devlin, sir. I'll make you glad you took me on, I surely will. And you can just call me Eureka.''

"Eureka, then," said Garrick, extending his hand. He saw the other man blink in surprise before he stuck out his own hand and shook Garrick's. "Welcome aboard. Miss Harper can show you what the advertisement for the hotel needs to contain before she goes over to the sheriff's office. And now I'm going to get back to work and see if I can get this article done before dinner. You'll come with me to the house then, Eureka, and I'll introduce you to Señora Mendez, my housekeeper. Miss Harper, I assume you'll be eating at the hotel?''

He saw her try to conceal her smug, satisfied smile at her victory as she said, "Yes, Mr. Devlin." It irritated him that the suggestions she made were, so far, always good ones.

Eureka Jones turned to Margaret and said, "My sister Bessie's the cook over there, Miz Harper. You tell her Mr. Devlin hired me, and I reckon she'll take good care of you, too.''

Chapter Ten

"This is right fine, Garrick," Cal Devlin told his brother the next morning, reading the handwritten copy of the story Garrick had produced about the bandits terrorizing the Gillespie Springs area. Garrick had asked him to check the story before Maggie set it in type.

Maggie watched as the compliment brought a flush of pleasure to her employer's face, but Garrick just said, "I got all the facts down just like you wanted?"

"Yeah, it's all here. I reckon most bandits don't read newspapers, but I'm hoping the word will get around that the good people of Gillespie Springs have been warned and will fight fire with fire. Maybe those outlaws'll move on to greener pastures—not that I'd wish this pack of looting scum on any other county."

"Amen to those cutthroats moving on, at any rate," Garrick agreed. "Well, now that we've got the sheriff's approval, typeset it, Miss Harper."

"Yes, Mr. Devlin."

Cal started to leave, then stopped. "I heard you hired Eureka Jones," he said.

"Word sure gets around quick in a small town, doesn't it?" Garrick observed.

"He's a good man," Cal said. "Good for you for giving him a chance at some steady work. And now I'd better get on back to the jail," he added. "Miss Harper, don't let my crotchety ol' brother work you too hard."

"I won't," Maggie agreed, smiling. Cal Devlin sure was easy to get along with, although she guessed he was nobody's fool. But she decided his older brother was the more handsome man, even if his handsomeness was of the stern, ascetic type. *Now where had that thought come from, and what did it have to do with anything?*

Eureka came in just then, and Cal smiled and nodded to him before reaching for the door again.

But before he could open it, the door swung open and Maggie saw Zeke Barbee standing in the doorway. Cal politely stepped out of the way so he could enter.

Maggie saw Barbee's eyes fasten on the tin star Cal wore on his vest, then jump to his face.

Each man gave the other a long, measuring look before Barbee threw out his hand. "Zeke Barbee's my name, Sheriff. Garrick tol' me about his brother th' lawman. I was Garrick's captain, back in th' war. And his drinkin' and gamblin' pardner."

Maggie noticed Cal hesitate before extending his hand to take the other's. "Cal Devlin. You plannin' on stayin' on in Gillespie Springs?"

His voice was not welcoming, and Maggie saw the other man's eyes narrow in recognition of that fact. "Aw, I'm like the wind, Sheriff. Y'never kin tell which way it'll blow, can ya?" He walked past Cal and into the newspaper office.

Cal raised his hand in farewell and went out the door.

Barbee watched out the window until the sheriff had strode past it toward the jail.

"Your brother don't act like he likes me," Barbee complained to Garrick Devlin. "He looked at me as if he'd like to tell me to get outa town, as if I was an outlaw or some-thin'."

"Aw, I'm sure you're wrong about that," Garrick said. "He doesn't have any reason to think ill of you. Give him a little time—he'll warm up to you. He's just a little jumpy about strangers in town these days, what with those outlaws raisin' hell around here."

Perhaps Cal Devlin had nothing to go on, but was just a good judge of character, Maggie thought. She turned to her typecase to try and escape Barbee's notice. She noted that Eureka had sat down on a seat at the back, as if he didn't want anything to do with Zeke Barbee, either.

"So, what brings you back through town, Zeke? Yester-day morning you said you were headed on to Fort Worth to wait for a cattle drive to come through."

"Naw, I thought better of it. I got a job workin' for a farmer south a' here," Barbee said.

"Oh? Who's that?"

"Aw, you probably don't know him. His name's…uh, Jack Smith. He's an old codger, says he hardly ever goes to town, and when he does he mostly goes down t'Brenham."

What a conveniently common name, Maggie thought. Had Garrick noticed how evasive his old friend was?

"Well, you found work quick," Devlin was saying. "So what brings you into town?"

"The old fellow needed some supplies. I figgered I'd drop in and see ya, long as I was here anyway," Barbee continued quickly. "What say we go over to the Last Chance and have a drink an' some dinner?"

Maggie found the explanation, coupled with Barbee's disinclination to share his employer's name, a little too glib.

Would Devlin think so, too? Would he go off to the saloon to waste the afternoon with his old friend?

To her relief, he declined. "Much as I'd like to, I've got a lot of work to do, Zeke. Maybe another time."

Maggie glanced up to see Barbee blink in surprise. "Nose to the grindstone, huh? That's no fun," he protested.

"I'd better keep my nose to the grindstone, or my boy and I might starve to death, Zeke," Devlin joked. "But if you're going to be in the area, we'll do it again sometime, when I'm not on a deadline."

Maggie looked down to hide how pleased she felt. It was only Friday, and they weren't close to deadline by any means. But she was glad that her employer was taking his responsibilities seriously. And perhaps he had begun to see through his old comrade-in-arms.

She turned back to her work, but felt the moment Barbee's attention settled on her. "Well then, how about you, Miz Harper? A fella don't wanna eat alone, after all. If you'll go with me, I'll even spring for a meal at the hotel—can't ask no *lady* to eat in a saloon, can I?" he said with a laugh that implied he used the word *lady* liberally in her case. His eyes, meanwhile, roamed her body as if the ink-stained dark cloth were sheer as glass.

She wanted to tell him she wouldn't have so much as a glass of water in the same room with him, and would have if Devlin hadn't been standing right there watching her. So she contented herself with saying, "No, thank you, Mr. Barbee, I fear I'm not very hungry at present," and turned back to her work.

"But you gotta eat," he persisted. She could still feel his eyes on her. "Purty little thing like you'd waste away iffen you don't eat reg'lar. Why, I bet a good strong wind would blow you away as it is! A man likes a woman with some meat on her bones, ya see."

She set her type stick down deliberately, wishing she could ram it right into his leering smirk. "It's of no concern to me what a man likes, Mr. Barbee," Maggie said. "I'm here to do a job for Mr. Devlin, nothing more. Good day, sir." She turned away and pretended to go back to work, though the letters she selected added up to pure gibberish. She wondered what her employer was thinking. Would he be angry at her for her curtness?

She heard Barbee give an affronted-sounding sniff. "Skittish little filly, ain't she?" he muttered. "Those cold winters up North make the women like icicles, I reckon."

"Zeke—" Garrick began.

"Well, at least the sportin' women like ol' Zeke Barbee," he said, interrupting him. "Hey, what's that sittin' back there in yore shop, Garrick ol' boy? I heard tell you hired a darky, but I didn't believe it till I seen it just now. Stand up when you're in the presence of a white man, boy!"

Bristling at Barbee's crass words, Maggie whirled around and saw him pointing right at Eureka. As he stood up, she opened her mouth to give Barbee a stinging reproof, despite the warning look Eureka gave her.

But Devlin spoke before she could. "Yes, Eureka Jones is employed by me. Why on earth would that bother you, Zeke? You used to boast about how many black men worked on your plantation before the war." His tone was reasonable, but there was a firm set to Garrick Devlin's mouth and a decided chill in his blue eyes, Maggie noted with surprised approval.

Barbee was a lot more surprised, it seemed. "Back when they was slaves, sure," he protested. "But I'd be damned if I'd have one around now. An' they say this 'un kin *read*. That makes 'em uppity, and an uppity darky is trouble fer shore."

Devlin stepped forward as if putting himself between Barbee's words and Eureka Jones. "Zeke, I think you must've already stopped at the Last Chance, from the loose way you're talking." He glanced meaningfully at Maggie, then at Eureka. "Didn't your mama teach you that if you couldn't say anything nice, you shouldn't say anything at all? I think you'd better leave."

Barbee blinked again and stared at Devlin, a sullen expression on his reddened face, his fists clenched at his sides. "Well, well. I knew yore brother fought for the damn-yankees, but who'd've thought an ex-Confederate could talk like that? You been associatin' with this female carpetbagger too much, I reckon."

Devlin took a step forward, his cane loud against the plank floor. Barbee held his ground.

Maggie held her breath. Would Barbee actually *strike* Devlin, his supposed friend, a man who had a wooden leg? And if he did, would Devlin be able to fight with his wooden leg hampering him? Would he need her help? She had no hesitation about doing so, of course, but Garrick Devlin might not welcome help from a woman. Just in case, she looked around for something heavier than her type stick to use as a weapon.

Out of the corner of her eye, she saw Garrick widen his stance and tighten his hold on his cane as if preparing to use it as a weapon. She decided that if a fight broke out, she would send Eureka out the back door to summon Cal, then join the fray regardless of the consequences.

It didn't come to that. After Devlin and Barbee had stared at one another for several endless seconds, Barbee turned and lumbered out the door.

Garrick, Maggie and Eureka stood frozen for a moment, all staring at the door as if Zeke Barbee were still visible.

Eureka was the first to break the silence. "Mr. Devlin,

I'll understand if you want me to leave. You don't need trouble, any more than I do.''

Garrick lowered his cane to the floor with a thump and sighed heavily. "Of course I don't want you to leave. I need someone to carve these stereotypes and help Miss Harper, and I don't care if the man doing it is black, white or purple. I—I'm sorry about what he said.''

"I reckon I'm used to it, sir," Eureka replied with that innate dignity Maggie admired.

"That doesn't make it right." Garrick turned to Maggie. "And I regret you had to witness his drunken insults, Miss Harper. Hopefully he won't come to the office again, but please inform me if you are ever exposed to his unwelcome attentions on any other occasion, or those of any other man while you are under my employ. My, uh, wooden limb may slow me down, but I will do my best to thrash him within an inch of his life.''

Maggie sensed her prim, businesslike refusal to accept Barbee's invitation had won Garrick Devlin's respect, and now she was warmed by the Southern courtliness in his words.

She found herself smiling wryly at him. "Oh, believe me, there are worse lechers than that among the Union army and their associates," she said. "Ever since I began working at my father's side, some men have thought I was fair game. I've always been able to persuade them otherwise." *Except for once, when I let down my guard,* she thought, remembering her ill-fated "love" affair with Captain Burke.

Garrick didn't smile back. "Nevertheless, I feel as if I owe you some sort of an apology. Would you consent to come home to dinner with Eureka and me, rather than going to the hotel to eat today?''

"Oh, Mr. Devlin, no apology is owed me, at least by

you," she said quickly. "Fending off unwelcome advances is the lot of an unmarried woman who works in a man's world."

"Not in a business run by *me*, it isn't. And I don't know if Barbee has indeed left town," he argued. "I don't like to think of you eating alone over in the hotel, under the circumstances. Besides," he said with a little smile, "Johnny has been asking to see you."

It was the last sentence that persuaded her, of course—it had nothing to do with that *smile*. She had seen him smile at his child, but hadn't known that stern, austere man could smile so persuasively at a woman.

"Oh, well, if *Johnny* wants to see me, then of course I must accept," she said lightly. "If you're sure your house-keeper has enough, of course. I'm quite charmed by your little boy, Mr. Devlin."

He seemed relieved at her acquiescence, but tried to cover it in a smile of parental pride. "Yes, Johnny doesn't know a stranger," he said. Then he made himself busy consulting the pocket watch hanging from a gold fob at his waist. "Very well, then, perhaps we should go now. It's nearly noon. And of course there will be plenty. Jovita cooks enough for a platoon." He stepped forward and held the door open. "After you, Miss Harper. Eureka, you're coming? Jovita said that since it's warm for April, she'd like you to help her beat the rugs outside after dinner."

"I'd beat rugs all afternoon for one of Señora Mendez's meals, Mr. Devlin. Why don't I just run on ahead and tell her to set another place?"

Garrick had been counting on Eureka's buffering presence during the short walk to his house. He started to say that it wasn't necessary for him to run ahead, that Jovita would cope very well with the unexpected addition of Margaret. Then he realized that letting Eureka go on ahead solved a problem for the woodcarver, too. As a black man in the South, he might attract unwelcome notice if he walked abreast of Garrick and Miss Harper. Some folks might think of that as confirmation that he was "uppity." Yet he had his pride, and he shouldn't have to walk subserviently behind them, as if he were still a slave. Garrick mentally cursed the need for men like Eureka Jones to have to tiptoe so gingerly around white men's prickly sensibilities. And he resolved to have nothing more to do with men like Zeke Barbee, who still thought of a human being like Eureka as a *thing*.

"That'll be fine," he said, and watched as Eureka took off, envying him his easy, loose-limbed lope. Garrick looked back to see that Miss Harper's eyes were on him, and though he could discern no pity there, he sensed that she had guessed the tenor of his thoughts.

His mind was still whirling about the confrontation between Zeke and Miss Harper, too. Despite his bedrock belief that a woman's place was in the home, he was embarrassed that the Yankee woman had been offered disrespect in his place of business—and by a man he had thought of as his friend. Even a meddlesome female Yankee didn't deserve that.

But there was more to his feelings than shame that Miss Harper had been treated with disrespect. Garrick had been surprised by the rush of undiluted rage that had swept through him when he'd seen the way Zeke Barbee was looking at her—as if she were even less respectable than a soiled dove.

Margaret Harper had been perfectly adept in the way she had refused Barbee's invitation. It was obvious that she had practice in doing so, as she had claimed. So why had Garrick been so angry?

He thought about it and was astonished to realize that

the first emotion he had felt, when Barbee first began to speak to Miss Harper about going to eat with him, had been *fear*. He had been afraid that despite the negative remarks she had made about Zeke Barbee earlier, she would somehow find his invitation appealing and accept. Barbee might be just a hired hand for some farmer at present, but he was not a bad-looking fellow, and more importantly, he was a *whole* man. He didn't get around with a wooden leg and a cane. Margaret Harper wouldn't have to shorten her stride to walk with him, as Garrick noticed she was doing now in order to keep in step with him as they made their way down the side street that led to his home.

By refusing Barbee's invitation with such obvious disdain, she'd set Garrick's fear at rest, but that still left him to puzzle over the anger he'd felt at Barbee. Why had it been so out of proportion to the event?

He retraced the confrontation in his mind and realized he had felt the worst of his fury when he'd followed Barbee's gaze and seen his hot, greedy eyes trained on Margaret Harper's *breasts*.

Garrick had felt a surge of possessiveness then, as if something that belonged to him had been threatened. He'd felt like a stallion whose mare was being approached by a rival stud.

He almost laughed aloud at the damn foolishness of the idea. *You don't even like her, remember? She's bossy and meddling, and she's a Yankee.* And even if she weren't all those things, his stallion days were over. How ridiculous of him to feel like he could possess anything as splendid as Margaret Harper, with her fiery red hair, challenging green eyes and trim figure. She wouldn't need to settle for anything less than a whole man, so any possessive feelings he might have were a waste of time. He had awakened in a sweat during the night, not because he was dreaming of his lost leg, or having a nightmare about Cecilia again, but because he had been dreaming of doing intimate things with the woman who walked beside him now, chattering about the weather. *Useless.*

And even if she *would* look twice at him, why open himself up to hurt again? Just because she had turned Barbee down was no guarantee she wouldn't leave Garrick as soon as a prosperous man with sound limbs came along.

He realized with a start that she'd been speaking. "I'm sorry, Miss Harper. You were saying?"

She gave him a sidelong look. "I *said,* Mr. Devlin, Texas springs are so beautiful! The sunshine is so bright! It's never gray and blustery here, as it can be back in Ohio in April."

Jarred out of his thoughts, he retorted, "You'll get more than enough sun in Texas, Miss Harper. By the end of one of our summers you'll be positively longing for snow and gray, gloomy days."

Miss Harper disagreed. "My father and I arrived in the middle of the summer, Mr. Devlin. I think I'm hardy enough to survive."

"You won't miss the snow? We hardly ever see any here. I think I've only seen it once or twice—except for during the war, of course, when I was farther north." He remembered winter days spent huddled around a campfire, cursing the white stuff, but it had looked so pretty as it fell....

Miss Harper appeared thoughtful. "Perhaps just on Christmas Day. It seemed odd this year to look out the window and not see it lined with snow and hung with icicles." Her face was sad just then—was her sadness due to the lack of snow on Christmas or was there something more?

He wanted to see her smile again. "You ought to get out

into the countryside in May, Miss Harper. There are carpets of wildflowers—bluebonnets and pink primroses and so many kinds of yellow flowers that it looks like the streets of heaven paved with gold...." Against his will, he had a sudden vision of taking the carriage out into the country with her and having a picnic among the flowers.

"Why, Mr. Devlin," she said lightly, "I had no idea you could be such a poet. Perhaps you should write verse—or novels."

He looked quickly to see if she was amused at him, but those green eyes held no mocking light, just interest.

"I'm no poet—I'm a newspaperman," he said gruffly, "and high-flown language like that has no place in a newspaper. I just...like lookin' at the countryside when it's all in bloom, that's all. And here we are," he said, relieved that they had reached his house and he would no longer be alone with Margaret Harper, who aroused such opposing emotions within him.

Chapter Eleven

"Papa, bring Miss Maggie home for dinner *every* day," Johnny urged that night when Garrick was putting his son to bed. "She's so pretty. Don't you think she's pretty, Papa?"

Garrick had been thinking how he had enjoyed being able to look at Margaret Harper while she interacted with his son, and the question caught him off guard. "Pretty? I don't know, son...I suppose so," he managed to say. *She's not just pretty, she's beautiful, so beautiful that Cecilia's golden loveliness was like a pale shadow in comparison.*

"Papa, she likes me—I can tell," the little boy said. "She's very nice to me. Can she be my new mama?"

If he'd been startled by Johnny's earlier question, he was thunderstruck now. Where had the child gotten such a notion? But Garrick didn't want to make Johnny feel guilty for asking the question. He'd have to choose his words carefully.

"You're right, son, Miss Harper likes you, and I've seen her be very nice to you. But your mama just died. I'm still sad about that. A man doesn't generally marry again for a long time after his wife dies. Sometimes he never does." That was saying enough for now. As Johnny grew older,

Garrick could explain that he would never marry again, though Johnny would be nearly grown before he really understood the role Garrick's lost leg played in his decision.

Garrick watched as Johnny considered what he'd said, his childish brow furrowing with concentration.

"You miss your mama, don't you, son?"

Johnny nodded, his face solemn. "Mama was sick for a long time. Then she went to heaven." How awful it must have been for the boy to see his mother suffering and wasting away in her sickbed, while the only tenderness he'd been given had been what Martha Purdy could spare when she'd come to nurse Cecilia.

"*You* won't get hurted and go to heaven, will you, Papa?" the boy asked after a long moment, his lower lip quivering, his blue eyes suspiciously moist.

Garrick's heart ached at the realization that his son feared losing him, too. He reached down and smoothed the boy's hair away from his forehead, saying, "Johnny, I'm not going to heaven for a long, long time. You'll be a papa with children of your own by that time."

The child seemed only partially satisfied.

"You like Señora Jovita, don't you?" Garrick asked.

"Sure, Papa," Johnny replied in his childish treble. "But she's like a grandma, not a mama. Mamas are young and pretty like my mama—or Miss Maggie. You like Miss Maggie, Papa?"

"I like her fine, Johnny, but Miss Maggie didn't come here with the notion of marrying me. She came here to work on the newspaper."

"She could do both," the boy persisted. "I'll ask her."

"No, Johnny!" Garrick said quickly. "That's something grown-up folks ask one another."

He realized he'd made a mistake as soon as the boy's blue eyes lit up.

"Then ask her, Papa, *please?* As soon as it's a long time? Tomorrow's a long time, ain't it?"

If only things were as easy as they seemed to a child.

"*Isn't* it," Garrick corrected gently. "And no, it isn't a long time till tomorrow, especially as late as it's gotten while we've been talking. I'd better start on that story I promised to tell you before you get too sleepy—the one about when your uncle Cal, uncle Sam and aunt Annie were children and our papa bought us a pony."

"I'm not sleepy at all, Papa," Johnny insisted, but the droop of lids over his eyes belied his words. Johnny was asleep before Garrick got to the part where Sam got bucked off and broke his arm the very first day they'd ridden Midnight.

"Ees Johnny upstairs, Señor Garrick?" Jovita asked the next morning, when Garrick descended the stairs.

"No, I haven't seen him," he said, reaching the bottom. "Didn't I hear him going out into the backyard to play?"

"*Sí,*" said Jovita, her brow furrowed. She turned and looked out the back window. "But now I do not see heem."

Garrick shrugged. "He's probably gone back into the barn, chasing his kitten—or going to see Toby. If the sugar bowl's empty, that's probably where he is." His son loved to stand on a box and offer lumps of sugar to Garrick's brown gelding.

"No, I check, *señor*. He ees not in the barn."

Uneasiness stirred in the pit of Garrick's stomach. "He must have wandered out of the yard, then." Dear God, where could he have gone? There were so many ways a child that small could get hurt.... There was an open field in back of the house, and beyond that, a creek. It wasn't deep, but it didn't take much water to drown an adventuresome three-year-old.

Damning the handicap that slowed his steps, Garrick sent Jovita ahead of him into the field. But they found no Johnny picking wildflowers there, nor, thank God, was there any sign that he had reached the creek.

Maybe he had wandered down South Street to the west, attracted by the big empty Gillespie mansion. There was an iron fence around the place, but could a tiny boy wriggle through the bars? Devlin shuddered to think of Johnny getting into the abandoned slave cabins, cutting himself on broken glass or rusty nails....

They reached the front of the house again. Jovita was winded, but trying not to show it. Garrick had just confided his fear about Johnny getting into the Gillespie mansion grounds.

"I weel run down there, *señor*. You go up to Main Street, yes? Maybe Johnny goes there?" Then she stopped stock-still, pointing, and cried, "*Señor*, there he ees!"

Garrick looked up. Coming down the side street was Margaret Harper, and she was holding Johnny's hand.

They met at the intersection.

"Johnny, where have you been?" Garrick cried, relief flooding his heart as he knelt awkwardly in the dusty street to hug his child. "Papa's been very worried about you!"

The boy looked guilty, his lip trembling, his face pale. "S-sorry, Papa."

"I know Johnny didn't mean to worry you," Margaret Harper said, an amused smile on her face. "Your son came to see me to propose marriage."

Had Johnny gone and asked Margaret Harper to marry his papa, in spite of what Garrick had said? Embarrassment mingled with the relief and anger he felt. "I'm sorry if my son's been matchmaking, Miss Harper. I assure you, it wasn't anything I—''

She gave a silvery laugh. ''Oh, I know that's the last thing *you'd* be thinking of, Mr. Devlin! And he wasn't proposing a match between you and me—he asked me to marry *him,* you see. Of course, I explained to him that while I was very flattered and honored, I was a bit too old for him....''

Johnny favored her with an adoring look that perversely irritated Garrick as much as Margaret's amused, tender smile did. ''While you were being flattered and honored, Miss Harper, I was looking for his body in the creek. Johnny, let go of Miss Harper's hand and go into the house. You're in big trouble, young man.''

He saw the smile fade from Margaret's lovely face. ''I'm so sorry you were worried, Mr. Devlin. I assure you, I brought him back as soon as I could—''

''Just another adoring male for your collection, eh, Miss Harper?'' he snapped. He felt instantly ashamed of his churlish response, knowing he was taking his leftover fear and anger out on her, but he wasn't about to apologize, not in front of Jovita and his child. ''I'll join you at the office in a while,'' he said, taking Johnny's hand and turning back toward his house.

The workday provided no opportunity for Garrick to apologize, either. Maggie was hard at work when he arrived, not revealing by so much as a reproachful glance that she was hurt by his overreaction, but her normal enthusiasm seemed muted.

Go on, tell her you're sorry you snapped at her like you did, his conscience urged him, and he would rise to go and beg her pardon, only to have Eureka come in, or Maggie leave on some errand. And so the day passed without the apology that burned within his soul, and Garrick had gone home. He was determined to set things right first thing in the morning, before any other event could intervene.

Johnny fell asleep early that night, just as the sun set. No doubt he was worn out from making his first proposal of marriage, Garrick thought tenderly, smoothing the brown hair away from the child's eyes before kissing his brow and leaving the room. *Son, someday another pretty girl will say yes. Hopefully you'll choose better than I did.*

It was too early for Garrick to sleep. He knew if he went to bed now he'd just toss and turn. The balmy April breeze that stirred the curtains hanging over the open window in his room beckoned him outside.

Maybe a walk around town would help him get drowsy enough to sleep, he thought, going downstairs and out the front door, being careful to close it softly behind him. Jovita had already retired to her room, but she would hear if Johnny awoke.

He fully intended to turn left when he reached Main Street, so that his walk would take him past the bank, the saloon, the livery stable and the church, but he found himself taking out his key and unlocking the front door to the *Gazette* instead.

He'd just go in and make his peace with Miss Harper, he resolved, and then he'd go home. Surely he'd sleep better, not having to anticipate the necessary apology all night.

"Miss Harper?" he called softly, as he let himself in the shadowy office. There was no answer.

He lit the lamp that sat on the counter, and took it with him to the stairs. "Miss Harper?" he called, more loudly this time.

Still no answer. Could she be asleep already? He wouldn't want to wake her, even to make an apology.

But then the lamp revealed the open door at the top of

the stairs. Surely she wouldn't leave it open if she was there, but just to be certain, he climbed to the top of the stairs and looked within. The room was empty.

Where could she be at this hour?

A thousand suspicions assailed him then. Visions of Maggie Harper dressed in her best and out for a stroll in Gillespie Springs Park with some bachelor in town—Garrick couldn't think of any man living here right off that wasn't married, but maybe some drummer staying at the hotel had struck up a conversation with her and was even now making time with her in the shadows of a cottonwood tree. Or maybe she was sipping whiskey at the saloon, surrounded by a herd of admiring cowboys.

Damn! That's what came of trusting a woman! They were sweetness and light to a man's face, but as soon as he turned his back—!

He clumped ungracefully down the stairs, telling himself he was just going to continue on his walk as he'd originally planned. He'd pass by the saloon on the opposite side of the street, and he would *not* look in to see if Margaret Harper was there.

He'd made it as far as the street, and was just passing the side street that separated the *Gazette* from the bathhouse, when a movement at the corner of his eye caught his attention. A shadowy figure was making its way toward the back of the *Gazette* building, as if intending to go in the rear entrance.

Margaret Harper! What twilight tryst was she just sneaking back from?

"Miss Harper, is that you?" he barked, in a voice he'd once used to wake up sleepy sentries.

The figure gave a small cry, dropping something she'd been carrying in her arms. It tipped over, and something light-colored spilled out in the dirt at her feet.

She didn't seem to notice that, however, for her eyes were trained on his face. "Oh! Mr. Devlin! You—you startled me," she said as he approached.

I'll just bet I did, he thought grimly.

"Were you looking for me? Did you...need me for something? Is some story brewing? I was just over at the bathhouse," she said.

As he drew abreast of her, he could see that what she was saying was true.

Her hair was down, hanging in loose strands over her back. Damp tendrils of curly hair ringed her forehead, which was still pearled with moisture. He could smell the scent of soap rising from her skin.

A new vision replaced the ones his suspicious mind had conjured, one in which he saw her bathing in a tub in the bathhouse, running a lathered cloth luxuriously over her soft skin, between her breasts.... He felt his groin tighten at the thought.

"I—I wanted to wash my hair before going to church tomorrow," she explained unnecessarily, then seemed to remember the basket his bark had startled her into dropping. "Oh dear," she murmured, stooping quickly to pick it up.

Garrick's eyes followed her movement, and he had a quick glimpse of some still-wet, lace-trimmed undergarments that were now spotted with dirt from the street, before they were wadded up and stuffed once more under a concealing towel. Then she straightened again, and even in the fitful light afforded by the lanterns hung at the entrance of the cribs behind the bathhouse, he could see that she was blushing furiously.

"I had some washing to do, too," she said, looking everywhere but at him.

Now he imagined seeing her dressed only in the lacy

white camisole and drawers she'd been washing. Still wet, they would cling to her charms, outlining them.... If she only knew how irresistible she looked, fresh from her bath and blushing like a bride. Her lips looked dewy as rose petals at dawn.

"*Did* you need me for something?" she asked finally, when the silence lengthened between them in the quiet spring night.

Yes, I need you, he thought. Aloud, he said, "Need you? Why, no, Miss Harper. I was just out for an evening stroll...."

But now she was looking him in the eye again, and he couldn't lie to her then. "Well, um...that's not altogether true. I...I did need to see you. I wanted...that is, I wanted to say I was sorry for speaking so gruffly to you this morning. I—I'd been frightened when I couldn't find Johnny, but that doesn't excuse the way I snarled at you."

With a relieved expression, she set her basket down again.

"That's all right, Mr. Devlin. I'm not a parent, but I think I can understand. Are we friends again?" she asked, holding out her hand.

Garrick took it, feeling as if he didn't deserve her easy forgiveness. Her hand was smooth beneath his, and soft— how could she have such soft white hands when she did such hard work, and was always having to remove printer's ink from them?

"Friends?" he said. He'd never had a female *friend* before, one who was not a relative by marriage. "Certainly we are." The feelings he had at the moment were a great deal warmer than friendship, but the shadows would hide that from her. "It's very good of you to be so understanding, Miss Harper."

"Not at all. Good night, then," she said, still looking up at him.

He was caught, trapped by the lamplit emerald clarity of her gaze. She seemed in no hurry to pull her hand from his, and he couldn't have moved at that moment if the whole state of Texas depended on him to do so!

"Good night, Miss Harper," he said, but couldn't seem to make himself drop her hand so she could move to unlock the back door. His gaze dropped to her lips, which were slightly parted and still glistening as if bedecked with dew. Slowly, as if in a dream, he lowered his head and touched his lips to hers.

He heard her quick, surprised intake of breath and raised his head, but not before his brain had registered her lips' overwhelming softness.

"I can't imagine why I did that, Miss Harper," he said quickly, letting go of her hand and expecting to be slapped for his impertinence.

She blinked, as if even more startled that he'd said that than by the kiss itself.

"Then don't even *try*, Mr. Devlin. Good night." With that, she picked up her basket again, walked over to the back door and unlocked it, disappearing within before he could think what to say.

Chapter Twelve

Two weeks later, Maggie lay a sheet of paper half-filled with her neat copperplate script onto the desk where Devlin pored over the latest news off the telegraph. The paper had just come out yesterday, but they were already hard at work on the next edition. "Here's my story on the sewing circle's weekly meeting."

He glanced at it and grumbled, "Rather short, Miss Harper. How am I supposed to fill up the ladies' section with this? Can't you come up with some *details*?"

"Such as? The fact that Miss Amanda Harris dyed her dress so she could pass it off as new, or the news that Phoebe Stone was wearing yet another of her famous hats?" Maggie retorted. "And I didn't think you wanted me to report gossip, but I could always cover the rumor that Edna Arnold is *enceinte* with her ninth child...." Maggie took a breath and said, "Nothing of any lasting importance *happens* at these meetings! Perhaps it would be easier to come up with details, Mr. Devlin, if you would let me cover a story with some *substance*."

"Miss Harper, I hired you as my printer, not as a reporter—" he began.

"I know that," she interrupted, "but I've finished typesetting everything you've written and every print job we've been able to obtain. I used to write front-page stories for my father's paper. It's frustrating, not being able to write anything more challenging than this!'' She stabbed a finger at the story lying on his desk.

"Are you finished?" He drawled the words in that effortless way Southerners had, and the effect was like a bucket of cold water being thrown in her face.

"I'm sorry. I didn't mean to speak to you like that. You were perfectly honest with me about what the job entailed. It's I who have been trying to make it something more," she said, turning away so he could not see her blinking back tears. She was sure she had just reinforced Garrick Devlin's cherished belief that Yankee women were pushy, unfeminine shrews.

But it was better that he think that of her than she tell him the other reason for her reluctance to attend these feminine gatherings. When she went to them, she was all too conscious that she was seen as nothing but the Northern interloper in their midst, a woman who had dubious claims to being a lady because of the job she had taken. Olivia Devlin and her friend Mrs. Long, the mayor's wife, did their best to make up for the other ladies' chilly civility, but their efforts only seemed to accentuate Maggie's feeling of isolation from the others.

As the silence stretched out between them, Maggie was glad that Eureka Jones had gone to chop some wood at Garrick's place and wouldn't witness the stern reprimand that was undoubtedly coming. Surely she must have dreamed that time when Garrick had kissed her by the back door, for he'd given no indication since then that he ever remembered having any softer feelings for her.

Maggie turned around, determined to face it head-on, her chin up.

"Miss Harper—" Garrick began, then stopped as down the street, the church bell began to ring. "What in blazes—?" It was Thursday, and the middle of the day, not Sunday morning. Then they saw a couple of the men of the town run past them in the direction of the tolling bell.

"Something must've happened," Devlin muttered, rising and reaching for a leather-covered notebook, and the cane that was never far from his hand. "Come on, Miss Harper."

As they stepped out into the street, they could see a crowd gathering, not at the church, but in front of the jail. The church bell had merely been the means Cal had used to summon the inhabitants of the town from their homes.

If she'd been by herself, Maggie would have picked up her skirts and run. Youths and grown men, even girls dashed past them, calling apologies over their shoulders as they kept running. But as much as she wanted to, Maggie wouldn't, for she was all too aware that the man at her side was frustrated at his inability to go faster than the awkward gait forced on him by his artificial limb.

"What's going on, Davy?" he shouted at one of the young men.

"Sheriff's forming a posse!" the youth cried.

"Why?" Devlin called after him, but the boy's reply was swallowed up by the breeze.

They were the last to reach the jail, and arrived just as Cal Devlin began to speak.

"Y'all have heard about the outlaws raiding around the area, thanks to the stories in the *Gazette*," he said, nodding in his brother's direction, "and from word of mouth. Up to now they've been content to take money and steal a few head of cattle here, a chicken or two there, and my deputy and I haven't had any luck catchin' up to 'em. But I've just gotten word they hit the Blevins farm this afternoon, and killed Hal Blevins and wounded his son so bad he may not live. They stole every bit of stock they had. I'm hereby formin' a posse, and I'd like every able-bodied man to saddle up and meet me in front of the livery stable in an hour, armed and ready to ride—ride hard. I'll trail those sidewinders all the way to Mexico if that's what it takes."

"I'm comin'! Count on me, Sheriff!" someone called out, and then another and another called out similar promises. Some of the men began to head in the direction of their homes to get ready.

"Did the Blevins boy get a look at any of 'em?" one of the remaining men in the crowd asked. "Did he say what they looked like?"

"No, he wasn't able to talk," Cal said, his scarred face grim. "He was shot up pretty bad. That's all I know right now. Those of you who can join the posse, go get ready." He turned and disappeared into the jail office.

Maggie, glancing at Devlin out of the corner of her eye, saw the longing in his expression as he gazed after the departing men.

"You'd like to go, wouldn't you?" she asked softly. "An eyewitness account *would* make a fine feature story, right enough. But there are other stories in this event, Mr. Devlin," she told him. "For example, I think—"

"Like to go?" he interrupted, his blue eyes kindling. "Of course I'd *like* to go. What's more, I *am* going. What kind of man stays safely in town like a coward? I want to be right there when they catch those bas—those outlaws," he said. "I wouldn't mind putting a bullet in one of 'em myself!"

"B-but…Mr. Devlin…" she stammered, forcing herself not to drop her gaze from his chill blue gaze, "what about…what about your—your leg? Can you…can you ride? Hard, like your brother said?"

He gave her a withering stare, his jaw clenched tightly. "*Yes, I can ride.* I don't ride often, because it's more comfortable to take the buckboard, but I'll keep up. Now, what I need *you* to do is run ahead to the house and tell Eureka I need him to start saddling Toby. Tell Jovita to pack me something to eat, too—anything! If they can do that while I'm gathering up my gear, I can get to the livery before the posse leaves."

"But I was thinking we might get an even better story if we go out to the Blevins farm and interview Mrs. Blevins," Maggie countered, hoping he'd see reason. "We could take the buckboard that way, and you wouldn't have to—"

"But I *want* to, Miss Harper, don't you see that? You aren't my mother, woman, and even she knows better than to coddle me because of my leg, dammit!" he replied with a contempt that precluded further argument. "*Now go!*" he said, making shooing motions.

Of all the pigheaded notions... But she ran nonetheless, knowing there would be no making him see reason.

Half an hour later, standing with Eureka, Jovita and Johnny outside the small barn in back of the house, Maggie watched as Garrick tied his bedroll and saddle bags in back of Toby's saddle and stiffly mounted the chestnut gelding. Toby looked startled and sidled uneasily for a moment, but as Garrick spoke soothingly to him and settled himself in the saddle, he offered no further resistance.

Maggie had to admit Garrick Devlin looked like a different person on a horse—confident and commanding. She could imagine him leading a charge, his saber held high to rally his comrades as shells exploded around them. He looked years younger than he did in the *Gazette* office.

She waited until he had waved and cantered down the street in the direction of the livery stable, and Jovita had ushered a very excited Johnny Devlin back inside for his nap.

"Do you think he'll be all right?" she whispered to Eureka as they watched Devlin disappear around the corner.

"I don't know, Miss Maggie," Eureka murmured, his brown face creased with worry. "That horse is a good one, but he hasn't been ridden in three months o' Sundays, or my name isn't Eureka Jones. The saddle was all dusty and covered with old feed sacks. Miz Jovita says she hasn't seen him ride the whole time she's worked for him—he always takes the buckboard."

Maggie sighed. There had been no stopping the man, that was for sure. All she could do was pray that he would meet with no harm. And he might even come back with a wonderful firsthand account, as he hoped.

"Eureka, does Mr. Devlin have another horse?"

The ex-slave looked startled. "No, ma'am. He doesn't have need of another horse. Why? You're not fixing to ride after the posse, are ya? Mr. Devlin'd be fit to be tied if you did that."

"No, Eureka, don't worry, I was just thinking about riding out to the Blevins farm. I could hire a horse, I suppose, if there are any left at the livery...." Maggie chewed her lip in indecision. The money she'd brought from Austin was just enough to last her until the end of the month; if she hired a horse she might have to skip a couple of meals, but perhaps if she returned with a good story Devlin would reimburse her the hiring fee.

"Miss Maggie, there isn't likely to be anything left fit for a lady to ride," Eureka said. "But my sister'd loan you her mule. He isn't fast, but he's gentle, and the Blevinses don't live too far, anyway."

And so it was that half an hour later, Maggie was riding west out of town at a teeth-rattling, bone-shaking trot. Eureka's sister didn't own a sidesaddle, so Maggie rode astride on the worn, hard Mexican saddle. Thank God no one was outside to see her clattering past! She was already a pariah as a Yankee, but since riding astride caused much of her petticoat and several inches of stocking-clad lower leg to show, being seen would further shred her reputation! She'd be in less of a hurry on the return trip and could always hook her leg decorously around the saddlehorn once she reached town.

"And then…then he pulled a pistol…an' shot my Hal," the new widow, her face pillowed against Margaret Harper's breast, said with a gulping sob. "All because he came upon 'em drivin' off all our cattle! I heard the shots from the house and came runnin'. I knew it was somethin' bad…. And my poor boy…" She waved a bony, trembling finger across the farmhouse kitchen at her son, whose still, white arm dangled limply from the table upon which he lay. A frock-coated Dr. Broughton, his back to them, was examining the boy's wounded thigh. "He was just tryin' to protect me from them devils…." A fresh wail broke from the woman.

Margaret held her trembling form, stroking her back comfortingly as she listened. For the dozenth time she wished Devlin had come with her rather than gone with the posse, so he could be taking notes in the small, leather-bound notebook she'd seen him pull out of his breast pocket. She hoped she could remember the account just the way Clara Blevins had told it.

"Mrs. Blevins, what did they look like, these outlaws?" Maggie asked in a low voice.

"I done tol' Tom Baker standin' yonder," she said, indicating a solemn, long-faced farmer standing by the door.

"He's my neighbor, the one that rode t'town to get the sheriff...."

"I know you did, and I know it's difficult to talk about this, but just in case the posse doesn't find these outlaws today, your description will be of invaluable help...."

Concentrating on her answer, Clara Blevins forgot to cry. "They was five of 'em. They all wore bandannas over their faces, so I couldn't rightly tell much a' what they looked like, but one was a stocky fella with yeller hair, another was tall and had dark hair an' eyes, another looked like mebbe he was a half-breed renegade. There was a black man, too.... But what I remember most was that the last feller, the one that shot my Hal—he had on a gray, raggedy coat, like those our soldiers came home in! Oh, Lord, how could someone who fought on our side do such a thing?"

He had on a gray, raggedy coat... Maggie closed her eyes, thinking of the worn-out, threadbare jacket Zeke Barbee had been wearing. Was it possible—? She'd have to tell Garrick about this. He wouldn't like it, but perhaps this was a helpful clue that would lead to the gang's arrest!

"Missus Blevins," the doctor called from the kitchen table, glowering when he noticed that it was Maggie who was holding her. "There's not a whole lot else I can do for this wound—the bullet's passed on through. He'll probably get better, if he don't get a fever."

"But we can't just leave her out here by herself, a woman alone with a wounded boy!" Maggie argued. "What if the outlaws come back?"

Her neighbor spoke up now. "I'll take 'em to my place—it ain't too far down the road. My missus can take care of her. Reckon me and my sons'd better take turns standin' guard till they catch these sons a'—beggin' yore pardon, Miz Blevins, and you too, ma'am," he added, including Maggie in his apology.

Reassured, Maggie turned back to Mrs. Blevins. "Ma'am, we'll publish your description of the outlaws in the *Gazette,* don't you worry," she promised. "Maybe these fellows'll have the sense to leave Brazos County. I'll be going now—thank you for talkin' to me."

Clara Blevins wiped red-rimmed eyes and nodded, and Maggie made her way out to where she had tethered the mule beneath a shady live oak. She ached in every joint south of her waist and wasn't the least eager to clamber back aboard the rawboned mule, but she was eager to write down her story while it was still fresh in her mind.

She had finished her story and was just crossing to the hotel to eat her dinner when Mr. Tyler, proprietor of the combination general store and post office, hailed her from down the street.

"Hey, Miz Harper! I got a letter inside for you, from Austin!"

"Oh, thanks, Mr. Tyler! I'll be right there!" Maggie said, hastening forward as he obligingly unlocked the store to fetch the letter. It would be wonderful to have a letter from her father to take her mind off of how Garrick and the posse were faring, at least for a little while.

She read the two-page missive while she waited for Bessie to bring out the fried chicken dinner that was the special tonight. She smiled at some parts, laughed aloud over others. But the last paragraph, right before her father's flourishing signature, made her thoughtful:

I read with interest your description of your new editor-employer, Mr. Garrick Devlin. Daughter, he sounds as if he is a bundle of contradictions. Difficult, yet an interesting man. And reading between the lines, I believe you find him fascinating, do you not? Be

careful, Maggie—I wouldn't want you to be hurt
again.

Your loving father,
John Harper

Well! She'd have to write her father and set his mind at
ease. She'd tell him that he had no reason to worry, that it
was highly unlikely she would ever be willing to trust a
man again, and if she *did,* it wouldn't be Garrick Devlin.

Yet when she sat down at her table with pen in hand that
night, another Garrick emerged on paper in front of her:

"Father, Garrick Devlin is a man who has experienced
much tragedy in his personal life—I told you about
the loss of his leg in the war, and his wife's betrayal—
but while it has made him wary and bitter, it has not
changed his basic honorable *goodness.* Undoubtedly I
am not the right woman for him, but I pray he will
find the lady who *is,* for he will make the risk of loving
him well worth her risk. He is one who certainly deserves the love of a good woman...."

Chapter Thirteen

The posse didn't return by the time Maggie lay down to sleep that night, but she really hadn't expected them to. After all, it had been the middle of the day by the time they had ridden out of town. Maggie, familiar with military bivouacs through her father's association with the army, assumed nightfall had probably forced them to stop and make camp. She pictured them around a fire near a stream somewhere, swapping wild stories over coffee and tin plates full of beans. Half of them would doubtless be smoking the smelly cigars their wives didn't allow them to light up around the house. It was probably the best time some of those men had had in years.

Or perhaps they had even caught the fugitives and had set up shifts of paired men to guard them through the night. Maggie could imagine seeing the five outlaws marched through the streets tomorrow, their hands tied behind them. A trial would begin, and probably soon afterward, a hanging.

The posse didn't return the next morning, either, or the next afternoon. Maggie went ahead and typeset her interview with Clara Blevins, her fingers busy while her mind wondered how her employer was doing. As the afternoon went on, she became more and more anxious. Had Devlin, handicapped by his artificial leg, fallen off his horse and been injured? Had the posse been ambushed by the raiders? Was he wounded? Killed?

It was five o'clock, and having printed up a notice for the Baptist church regarding the funeral service planned for Hal Blevins—hardly the most cheerful subject matter— Maggie felt anything but hungry. Yet what was she to do with the rest of her evening? She'd already picked up a letter from her father at the post office and written a long answer to it. Now she had nothing to read, no mending to do....

Perhaps Olivia Devlin would like some company? She would be alone while she waited for her sheriff husband, and might appreciate it if Maggie paid a call. It was better for Maggie than trying to force supper down when she wasn't hungry, or pacing in front of the plate glass window that looked out onto the street.

She had just stepped off the plank walkway into the street and turned left, intending to walk down to Cal and Livy's house, when she heard thudding hoofbeats coming from the opposite direction.

The posse had returned. Down the street she could see the riders, led by Cal Devlin, some stopping at the livery to drop off hired mounts, others trotting on in pairs or loose groups of three or four. The men were grim faced and weary, and there was no sign of any captured outlaws—or Garrick.

She felt as if an icy hand had gripped her throat. Her heart thudded so hard it threatened to escape from her chest. Seeing Cal dismounting at the jail, Maggie picked up her dark skirts and started running.

"Where is he? Where's your brother, Cal? He isn't..." She couldn't put the horrible thought into words.

Cal Devlin looked up from where he was untying his rifle from the saddle. "Evenin', Miss Maggie. No, he isn't hurt. Just tired. He'll be along directly," he added, jerking his head in the direction the others had come from.

"You didn't…you didn't catch them?"

Cal shook his head. "No, though we found their trail easy enough, following the Brazos south. But they apparently swam the river a ways and then split up the next day. We lost them," he confessed, his voice thick with disgust.

And then the cloud of dust cleared somewhat and she saw Garrick, bringing up the rear on his brown gelding. She froze, ignoring the urging of her heart to run to him, knowing he wouldn't appreciate her doing so.

Paralyzed, she watched him ride toward them. He nodded to Cal, then rode right on past as if he didn't even see her. Her eyes darted back to the sheriff.

"Miss Maggie, he's just really, really worn out," Cal said, his face full of concern as he stared at his brother's retreating figure. "I'd give him a wide berth if I were you. He gets all snarly when he's bitten off more'n he can chew like this."

"But why did you—" she began, not wanting to sound accusatory, but afraid that she would.

"Why did I let him go with the posse?" he finished for her, a rueful smile forming on the mouth that was so like Garrick's, but more relaxed. "Miss Maggie, we're both grown men, but Garrick's my older brother. And he's bull-headed—maybe you noticed that. The more you tell him he shouldn't do something, the more that's what he's determined to do."

Maggie nodded, understanding exactly what Cal was telling her about Garrick Devlin's personality. But she also knew she couldn't just leave him alone until he'd gotten over whatever had made his face so masklike and unyielding. She turned and walked quickly in the wake of his ambling mount, though she dared not call out to him.

She caught up to him just as he pulled up at the hitching post in front of the *Gazette* office, and she breathed a sigh of relief, for she had been afraid he meant to turn down the side street and go straight to his house.

As Maggie climbed up onto the plank walkway in front of the hitching post, Garrick dismounted, moving slowly and stiffly, as if he was sixty years old.

"You're back!" she said, greeting him brightly, not knowing what else to say.

He went on tying the reins to the post, then turned toward her. His face had a pale, taut quality, as if he were holding something in. There were deep lines etched around his tightly held lips. But it was his eyes that finally drew her attention, eyes that looked like those of a soul tormented in hell.

She moved forward now, throwing caution to the wind, her gaze scanning him hurriedly, sure that Cal must have been wrong, that Garrick Devlin must be wounded. What was wrong with the rest of the men—with his brother Cal—that they couldn't see from his face that he was wounded?

"Gar—Mr. Devlin, what's wrong?" she cried. "Where are you hurt? Are you shot?"

"*Whoa,* Toby," he said, as the gelding started at her sudden flurry of skirts. "I'm not shot, you silly Yankee female!"

"But…you look…"

"Played out," he snapped. "Before I go on home I'm going to come in and have some of that whiskey I keep in my desk drawer, as you no doubt know, Miss Harper. If you're going to act shocked and disapproving, you can go on up to your room and shut the door." He started making his way to the entrance, moving as if he were barefoot and every step carried him over hot coals and broken glass.

She said nothing about his insinuation that she had inspected the contents of his desk. "Of course I'm not shocked by a man drinking whiskey, Mr. Devlin," she said matter-of-factly. "In the evenings, before he retired for the night, my father often had a glass of it." She started to say she'd even taken a sip or two herself on occasion, but Garrick interrupted her.

"I'm not even gonna use a glass, Miss Harper," he growled as he went through the door she held open for him. "What do you think of that?"

She ignored his disagreeable question and followed him inside. "While you drink, you can tell me about your expedition."

"Nothin' to tell." He sagged into his chair, shoving his wooden leg under the desk as he yanked open a drawer and drew out a half-full bottle of whiskey. He pulled out the cork and raised it to his lips, and she watched the dust-streaked muscles of his throat work as he swallowed. "You can see we didn't bring any shackled outlaws with us, and I'm sure my brother's already told you we lost their trail."

Hovering near the desk, Maggie nodded. "Very well, then, I'll tell you what I did yesterday afternoon after you left. Or perhaps I should just show you the article I wrote. It's subject to your approval, naturally," she added, walking to the rear of the office, where she'd left her draft of the interview with Clara Blevins. She wouldn't tell him it was already typeset and ready to be printed.

"Bet you'd like to say 'I told you so,' wouldn't you?" he jeered as she handed him the copy. "You got an interview with the widow, while all I did was go on a wild-goose chase."

He seemed determined to pick a fight. "No, I wasn't

thinking of it that way," she said in a neutral voice. "Your account of the posse's pursuit would still make very interesting reading, even if you didn't capture the raiders. I thought we might run the articles together."

"Ever the managing female, full of ideas, aren't you, Miss Harper?" he muttered.

His quarrelsomeness was beginning to prick the edges of her own temper. "You are, of course, free to do as you wish," she said, keeping her eyes fixed on some point above his head.

Devlin glared at her again before lowering his eyes to the paper. He began to read, pausing to take another swig from the bottle once or twice. Maggie saw that the whiskey had produced a little faint color in his cheeks to replace the gray.

She could tell when he had finished the final sentence, for he dropped the paper as if it were on fire.

"'As has been mentioned, one of the murderous renegades was wearing the threadbare remnants of a Confederate uniform jacket. The *Gazette* joins Mrs. Blevins in deploring the fact that one who may have served at the side of some of our town's Confederate veterans could have so shamefully turned against his fellow Southerners in such a heinous fashion.' I suppose you just *had* to include that bit of Yankee editorializing, Miss Harper."

Her temper, which had been smoldering up till now, finally ignited. "Well, *shouldn't* the *Gazette* deplore it? And it's not as if I didn't describe the others—the other two white men, the black and the half-breed Indian...and since you brought it up, have you thought of whom you've seen recently wearing just such a garment?"

He didn't try to pretend he didn't understand. "Zeke Barbee wouldn't do such a thing, and you have no right to accuse him just on the basis of a ragged gray jacket. The

South is full of men wearing parts of old uniforms because they can't afford anything newer, thanks to the carpetbaggers stealing us blind!'' He lurched upright, clenching his teeth—in anger, she thought. ''I'm going home, Miss Harper, and when I see you tomorrow—'' He staggered suddenly, leaning heavily on his cane. His face was suddenly white and beaded with sweat.

Maggie stayed where she was, thinking he'd just had too much whiskey on an empty stomach. But a groan escaped him, startling her. Then, by the light of the setting sun coming in the side window, she saw the dried blood on his right trouser leg.

''You *are* wounded,'' she breathed, rushing forward. ''Why did you tell me you weren't? Sit down, Mr. Devlin!'' she ordered, pushing the chair in back of him. ''I'll run and get the doctor—''

''*No*,'' he said, sinking into the chair, his eyes shut. ''That old quack sawbones isn't coming near me. And anyway, there's nothing he can do. I'm not wounded, dammit.''

''I don't believe you,'' Maggie said, trembling, but keeping her voice steady. ''Why would you be bleeding if you're not wounded? Maybe no one shot you, but perhaps you scraped against a tree or something?''

''I've just done too damn much. Give me a minute and I'll ride on home.''

''No, you're going to let me have a look.''

Devlin opened one startled eye. ''Miss Harper—''

''I did some nursing during the war,'' she informed him briskly. ''Stay right there—I'm going up to get some water and a cloth—and a blanket to cover you so you can take those trousers off. You can't go home like that—you'll frighten your little son to death.''

He opened both eyes at her last remark, blinked and

closed them again, letting his head fall back with another groan.

Maggie hurried up the stairs to her room and grabbed her pitcher of water, a big bowl, a clean towel and the blanket off her bed, half convinced she'd find Devlin gone when she went back downstairs. But he was still there, slouched in the chair, so still and pale that she thought for a moment he was dead.

She took a second to step to the door and flip the sign to Closed, then pulled the shade down over the front window that looked out on the street.

"Mr. Devlin, I'll hold the blanket up while you pull off your trousers," she commanded. "Then sit back down and I'll clean your...your leg."

Maggie still thought there was a very good chance he'd refuse to move, but he just mumbled, "Shut your eyes." She complied, and a moment later, felt him pull the blanket out of her grasp. She waited until she heard him settle himself on the chair again, then opened her eyes to find him watching her, her blanket covering his lap and his good leg.

She swallowed, remembering how her aunt had forbidden her, an unmarried girl, to do any of the actual physical care of the wounded soldiers, and how she had often disobeyed her aunt's orders and assisted the nurse in charge with bathing the most critically ill of soldiers when her aunt was occupied in one of the other wards. It wasn't as if any of them were well enough to take liberties with her. One of them had actually breathed his last while she was sponging his fevered brow. If she'd been able to do that, she could do this, too....

Maggie forced herself to lower her eyes from his and look at the lifeless, wooden imitation of a limb that joined a swathing of cotton cloth above the hinged wooden "knee." The cotton was streaked with dry brown stains, interspersed with the newer, brighter crimson streaks of fresh bleeding.

She put her hand to her mouth to stifle her gasp, then knelt beside him, pulling the bowl over and pouring water from the ewer into it.

"Can you show me how to…unstrap it?" she said, hoping her fingers wouldn't shake when she touched him.

"I'll do it," Devlin said. She watched as his fingers, obviously well used to the task, nimbly worked the belts and straps that attached the manmade limb. A minute later, the limb fell to the floor with a thud.

Now there remained only the stained cloth covering what was left of his own right leg. Taking a deep breath, she found the pin that fastened the wrapping, then began to unwind the cloth.

She heard him stifle a groan after she unwrapped the first foot or so and began to tug gently at the fabric stuck to his skin with dried blood.

"Soak it off," he said through gritted teeth.

"Here, drink some more of this," she said, handing him the whiskey bottle before picking up the pitcher and pouring some of the remaining water onto the blood-encrusted bandage. She waited until he took several swallows, hoping the water would loosen the cloth from his flesh. It did.

The rounded, scarred end of his upper leg was fiery red where it had rested in the socket of his wooden leg.

"Dear God," she breathed. It had to have been agonizing, just walking into the office from his horse!

"I haven't ridden more'n once or twice since the war, and then just long enough to prove I could stay on," he muttered above her head. "I was a damn fool to think I could suddenly gallop all over creation like Sir Galahad or something." His voice was full of self-contempt; his eyes were tightly shut, as if he could not bear to look at her while she gazed at the truncated remnant of his leg.

He flinched as she touched the water-soaked towel to his leg and began to sponge away the dried blood. Glancing up, she saw him stick his forefinger between his teeth and bite down. *"Go ahead. Do it,"* came the muffled order. His forehead was once again pearled with sweat.

Not another sound escaped the clenched teeth as she bathed Devlin's leg, then gently rinsed it. He barely breathed. His eyes were tightly shut, and if it weren't for his rigid posture, Maggie would have thought he had passed out.

"I'll be right back," she said, rising and climbing the stairs again to her room, returning with a bottle of rosewater lotion, which she rubbed gently over the irritated flesh.

"You're gonna have me smellin' like a damn flower," he growled, taking another swig of the whiskey.

What to use for a fresh wrapping? She certainly couldn't replace the bloodstained cloth around his leg, now that it was clean.

Spying one of Eureka's carving knives left on a table at the back of the office, she got an idea. Rising, she went and got it, and keeping her back to Devlin, raised her skirt and began to tear her serviceable, workday petticoat into strips. Moments later, the limb was once again wrapped in clean bandages.

"Th-thank you," he said, his voice thick. He had opened his eyes, but hadn't raised them from the floor. Devlin reached for the straps attached to his artificial leg to pull it toward him.

"But you can't put that right back on," she protested. "It's too inflamed. You'll make it bleed again." Besides, he had drunk too much whiskey—she could tell from the slurring of his words and the fumbling way he had grabbed at the leather strap. But she knew better than to mention his intoxication as a reason to stay put—drink made most men even more bullheaded.

"Can't...shtay here...."

"No, but I'll get help to get you home," she insisted, and started for the door, thinking of finding Eureka Jones. With a backward glance, she discovered Devlin still trying to reach for the wooden leg, so she went back, picked up the leg and took it upstairs with her. He wouldn't be able to reach it there.

"*Stay there,*" she ordered firmly. "I'll be right back."

"Contrary, meddling Yankee female!" he shouted, and with that cry ringing in her ears, she shut the door firmly behind her.

Chapter Fourteen

Garrick entered the *Gazette* office the next morning just in time to see Margaret Harper descend the stairs, not in the usual dark dress she wore while working around the press, but in a dress of some stiff black material—and a hat. It was the latter article that sent alarm bells ringing inside his head. He stopped just inside the door.

"Good morning," she said as she reached the last step. He couldn't gain any clue about her mood from her expressionless face or voice.

"You're not—you're not leaving, are you?" *Did I—was it my fault…?* Garrick couldn't say it, couldn't voice his fear that she had been so repulsed by the ugly sight of his amputated leg yesterday that she was now dressed and going to wait for the stage that stopped here at noon.

She blinked in obvious surprise. "Leaving? No, I'm not leaving—I'm going to the funeral. I—I wasn't sure if you were going…I thought one of us from the *Gazette* should attend…."

Funeral? Then he remembered. Of course—it had been two days since Hal Blevins had been gunned down by the outlaws. They would be laying him to rest in the cemetery next to the Baptist church today.

"Did you...did you bring those flowers for Mr. Blevins's grave?" she prompted, nodding toward the bouquet he'd totally forgotten he was holding.

He shook his head, dizzy with relief that she wasn't leaving—at least until after the funeral. Maybe if he said all the right things, she'd agree to stay on.

"No, they're for you."

Garrick saw the gold-shot lashes that shadowed her cheeks fly up, and went on before she could misinterpret his gesture. "It seems I'm always apologizing to you.... These are to say I'm sorry for—for yesterday," he said, nodding toward the bright yellow-and-red blossoms. "I was—I was just awful to you, Miss Harper, talking to you the way I did—and then for you to have to see...to tend my leg as you did...well, that was way beyond what any woman—what any *lady* should have to do, especially for a man you aren't even related to. I just want to say I regret it, and to let you know that I'll understand if you want to resign your position here—"

Margaret Harper held up a black-gloved hand to stop him. "But, Mr. Devlin, I don't want to leave—unless you want me to, that is." Her green eyes looked enormous against the ivory of her face.

Awash in relief, he took a step forward, drowning in those green pools. "No, I don't want you to leave, Miss Harper. Of course I don't. I want you to know there will be no repetition of...of anything that happened yesterday. I will never take a drink in front of you again, and I am appalled that you had to see—"

"That's not necessary, Mr. Devlin. You were exhausted and in pain when you got back yesterday. I knew that. And as for your...leg, I only did what any Christian would do. How is it...I mean, how are you?" she asked, and he saw her cheeks bloom with pink.

"Better," Garrick said quickly. He didn't want to talk about his leg, about the flesh that was still reddened and raw, but definitely improved after her ministrations. He could still smell roses on his skin when he'd inspected the leg this morning.

"Here, take these," he said, holding out the bouquet. "Maybe you have something upstairs you could put some water in for them? I...I owe you a new petticoat, too," he added, thinking of the embroidery-trimmed strips of cotton she had wrapped around his leg, "but I don't suppose it would be proper for me to buy you one, so I'll put something extra in your pay envelope to compensate you for sacrificing it for a grouchy old rebel."

He savored the amused way she smiled at his self-deprecation. She dipped her face close to the yellow-and-red blooms. "Mmm, these are so pretty, so colorful. Thank you."

"Indian blanket, that's what they're called." He was sorry they weren't roses or lilies, or some other delicate blossoms suitable for giving a lady. He hadn't planted any flowers in his yard, and these had been growing wild in the field behind his house. But the vivid wildflowers suited her, somehow.

"I'll just put them in my pitcher for now," she said, turning toward the stairs, "and then I'll be right down. If I'm going to the funeral service, I'd better get going."

"You can ride with me. I brought the buckboard, so I could give the leg a rest today," he called after her. It was proper that he attend the funeral, representing the newspaper, and if she attended, too, it would give him an excuse to enjoy her company a little longer before they went back to their formal roles of employer and employee.

The entire town attended the funeral of Hal Blevins, even folks who normally didn't darken the door of the Gillespie

Springs Baptist Church. Hal Blevins's widow sat in the front pew, her face pale as bleached bones against the stark black of her mourning. She was flanked by the mayor and his wife, and the Blevinses' neighbors, her wounded son still being too weak to rise from his sickbed.

The rest of the pews were packed; Devlin and Margaret had gotten two of the last spaces, and had been forced to sit so close together that she was aware of his slightest movement. Maggie said a small secret prayer of thanks for the feeling of peace that now lay between them. She had expected Devlin to be embarrassed after she had bathed and dressed his leg, but she'd never dreamed he'd think she might quit in disgust. Goodness, had he thought she was that much of a shrinking violet? Had his late wife been such a woman, for him to expect all other women to be shrinking violets like herself?

The preacher was suitably eloquent in his eulogy, praising Blevins as a good Christian husband and father. Cal, pale and solemn, got up to speak, too, pledging as sheriff his unending efforts to bring the murderous raiders to justice so that no more innocent people would die so needlessly.

Now the coffin had been lowered into the ground and the clods of earth had been dropped on top of it. The townsfolk of Gillespie Springs were filing out of the churchyard and into the street.

Garrick and Margaret walked to the buckboard, accompanied by Olivia Devlin, whom Garrick had offered to drive home, since Cal was meeting with his deputy and the mayor to plan their strategy to capture the outlaws. Garrick was just about to hand Margaret into the buckboard when a female voice called out, "Mr. Devlin! Wait up a moment!"

All three turned to see Phoebe Stone bustling toward them. "Oh Lord," groaned Devlin and Olivia simultaneously under their breath.

Black certainly didn't do anything for the milliner's faded looks; if anything, it made her look more pinchmouthed and washed out. But the gleam that lit Phoebe's eye as she sailed toward Garrick was anything but faded.

"Oh, *there* you are, Mr. Devlin," she trilled. "I was hoping I'd catch you before you left— I'm sure you're so dedicated, you're going right back to that dusty old newspaper office!"

The *Gazette* office was one of the newest buildings in Gillespie Springs and had hardly had time to get dusty, but Devlin restrained himself from pointing that out. Instead, his face set, a polite half smile on his lips, he inclined his head and murmured, "And what may I do for you, Mrs. Stone? Did you want to arrange an advertisement in the *Gazette*? Miss Harper—" he nodded toward Maggie "—handles that aspect of the business, if so."

Phoebe made the smallest pretense of nodding toward Maggie in turn. "Oh, I'm afraid there's nothing your *employee* can do for me, Mr. Devlin. I was hoping you might be able to come to my house this evening—I know it's short notice, but you won't mind that, will you?" She rushed right on, not giving Devlin a chance to say he minded even if he did. "This really needs a *man's*—er, that is to say, your *editorial* touch. I've been thinking about starting a mail-order millinery business, rather on the order of *Godey's Lady's Book,* only it will be *bigger,* naturally! I'd like you to proofread the text I've written to run beneath my own fine pen-and-ink drawings of my creations, and catch those pesky little errors that are bound to creep in when one works at the fever pitch of inspiration...." She ended with an elaborate flourish of bony fingers just as she ran out of breath.

"Mrs. Stone," Devlin began, "I'm flattered that you think me capable of assisting you with such...such a creative endeavor, but I'm afraid I'm already engaged for the evening. My sister-in-law here has invited Miss Harper and me to supper."

Maggie suppressed a surprised outcry and held her breath. She saw Olivia eye Devlin in surprise, but merely nod in confirmation, murmuring smoothly, "Yes, we've been meaning to have Maggie over for supper to welcome her to Gillespie Springs for *ages*...but she and my dear brother-in-law are always so busy...working on the newspaper," she said, her tone and arched eyebrow imbuing her words with hidden depths of meaning.

Maggie saw Phoebe Stone's complexion lose what little color had enlivened it and become even more sallow than before. With one eyebrow raised, she eyed first Devlin and then Maggie until Maggie felt herself flushing under the woman's piercing scrutiny.

"So that's how it is...." she said, her voice an insinuating hiss. She pursed her lips. "*Well*...I perfectly *understand* why you don't have time to help a poor widow. Good day," she said, wrenching her eyes away from them and, head held high, gliding back toward the groups of people conversing in the churchyard.

Silence blanketed the wagon until she was safely out of earshot.

Devlin cleared his throat, his eyes on the ground. "I— I'm sorry, Miss Harper. I regret using your name in a lie to evade that woman's clutches. And Olivia, I hope you will forgive me as well—the first thing that popped into my head was the invitation you extended to Miss Harper just after her arrival.''

While Maggie was still trying to think of the right thing to say, Olivia Devlin gave a nervous chuckle. "No apologies are needed to *me,* dear brother-in-law—I still remember how that woman chased after my Cal! But I must add my regrets to yours and apologize to Maggie, now that I embellished the tale so shamefully. All I could think about was how she'd be after you, Garrick, the next time she saw you if I didn't do something to discourage her, and I said the first thing that occurred to me, too. Now you and Maggie will be the talk of the town gossips—and Phoebe is the worst of them. I'm so sorry, Maggie!"

Olivia Devlin's smile was so sweet it would have melted a stone statue, Maggie thought. And while she wasn't angry, she was still wondering how this incident would affect the peace that had been achieved just an hour ago between Garrick Devlin and herself.

"I understand, *really* I do," she began. "I could see Mrs. Stone could be a very insistent lady—"

"That's putting it mildly," muttered Devlin.

"Oh, but why don't we make it the truth?" Olivia suggested. "I mean, the two of you having supper with Cal and me tonight? You never know, Phoebe Stone might just have her spies watching our house this evening to see if it's true! And I *have* been meaning to have you to supper ever since you arrived in town, Maggie, I've just not felt very well lately, but I'm all right now. Garrick, of course you must bring Johnny, too? I just adore that precious little boy!"

Maggie was amused. Olivia Devlin's words, despite her soft Southern drawl, were like a spring flood. "Well, I—"

Devlin cleared his throat again and interrupted. "Thanks,

but it's not necessary to include Johnny and me. Jovita will have already planned supper—''

Olivia interrupted him in return. ''Now, Garrick Devlin, I know full well Jovita visits her family on Saturday night. She used to be my housekeeper, remember? I'll expect all three of you promptly at six—that is, if *you're* agreeable, Maggie?''

Before Maggie could even glance at him for some clue as to his feelings, Devlin said, ''You might as well give in and say yes, Miss Harper. When Olivia wants something, she gets it, as my brother Cal has learned all too well!''

Chapter Fifteen

"Garrick, have another piece of pie," Olivia Devlin said, not even waiting for an answer as she cut a piece and placed it on his plate. "Maggie, Johnny, how about y'all?"

"Thank you, but I couldn't eat another bite," Maggie said. It was wonderful to have a break from hotel food; Bessie was a good cook, but she couldn't compete with Olivia Devlin. "Everything was delicious, especially the glazed ham."

"Aunt Livy, I'm full up!" said a solemn-faced Johnny Devlin, holding out his plate. The little boy had been on his best company behavior throughout the meal, but he was starting to fidget now that he was done and the grown-ups gave no indication of leaving the table.

"You sure cleaned your plate, Johnny," Olivia said approvingly. "Would you like to see some puppies? There's a little black dog that seems to have adopted us just in time to have a litter. They're out in the barn, if you'd like to see them. Don't worry, Garrick, she's very gentle. She won't mind if Johnny touches them."

Johnny Devlin's blue eyes, so like his father's, became round as the dinner plate he'd just eaten every bite from, and he cried, "*Puppies?* Wanna see 'em! May I be 'scused?'' Without waiting for an answer, he ran from the table.

"He's a great little boy, Garrick. You've a right to be proud,'' Cal said, leaning back in his chair and watching Johnny out the window that looked over the backyard.

Maggie noted the quiet pride that shone in Garrick's eyes as he, too, stared out the window at his child. "I am,'' he said. "I realize my marriage to Cecilia wasn't a total tragedy when I look at my son.''

"Yes sir, I hope we have one just like him,'' Cal murmured, smiling at his wife. Olivia smiled back at him, a smile radiating such happiness that for a moment Maggie couldn't help but feel a pang of envy. Cal and Livy had made her feel very welcome, but she missed what they so obviously had together—what she had so erroneously thought she had with Richard Burke.

Almost unwillingly, she glanced at Garrick. Her feelings for him had grown from a grudging admiration of what he had become in spite of all he had endured—from his war wound to his shabby treatment at the hands of his faithless late wife—to an attraction she felt was hopeless. They were forging a good business relationship, but he would never trust a woman again, not after the way Cecilia had treated him. And he would never see Maggie as anything more than that unladylike, pushy Yankee woman.

If only she could be more like Olivia Devlin, the kind of woman Garrick obviously admired, the epitome of Southern womanhood! Yet Maggie had to be honest with herself and admit that she couldn't be like Olivia, content to make her home and husband her world. Maggie couldn't imagine giving up her work on the newspaper. And she was no better at trusting than Garrick. She had once trusted a man, and look where that had led!

She saw Garrick glance from Olivia to his brother and

then gaze more closely at Olivia before looking back to Cal. "Brother," he said slowly, "are you trying to tell us something?"

A big grin spread across Cal's scarred but handsome face.

"Yep, I reckon I am," he said, taking Olivia's hand in his. "Olivia is...that is to say, we're going to become parents come September."

"We wanted you both to be the first to know," added Olivia, the brightness of her smile warming Maggie's heart. She felt touched that she had been included in this very special family moment.

"Well, that's just grand!" Garrick said, the biggest smile Maggie had ever seen him smile lighting his face. "First Sam and Mercy and now you two! Mercy's due any day now, isn't she?"

"That's a fact," Cal agreed. "The Devlin family is really growing."

"Congratulations," Maggie said. "So that's what you meant when you said earlier you hadn't felt well lately."

A lovely flush of pink suffused Olivia's cheeks. "Yes," she said. "I thought I'd given away the secret right then. But that...that sickness didn't last, and now I feel better than ever. I just know everything will be all right this time," she said, and a swift secret look passed between her and Cal.

Was Olivia referring to an earlier miscarriage? Maggie wasn't sure how long Cal and Olivia had been married, but she didn't think it had been all that long. Ah well, it must be wonderful to be this close to a man, to communicate with him almost without words, she thought.

"So I'm gonna be a double uncle in the space of...lets see—" Garrick counted on his fingers "—six months." He grinned. "Well, that's wonderful. Olivia, you just let me know if there's anything I can do to help, especially if this brother of mine gets a notion to take off after those raiders again.''

Maggie saw a cloud pass swiftly over Olivia's features.

Garrick had evidently seen it, too. ''Aw, durn my awkward tongue, Olivia. I didn't mean to bring up—''

But Olivia Devlin's eyes were once again serene. ''Garrick, I know my husband has a dangerous job as sheriff, but I wouldn't for a moment want him to shirk it because of me.''

Johnny came pounding in the back door at that point, clutching one of the tiny puppies. Outside they could hear the anxious yipping of the mama dog, which had followed them from the barn.

''I want dis puppy! Can I keep him, Aunt Livy?'' he said, holding up the fat, wriggling, yellow-black-and-white animal.

Olivia knelt down, her skirts billowing around her as she examined the puppy. ''Oh, Johnny, that's a girl puppy, not a boy puppy. And those puppies are just a month old, not yet old enough to leave their mama.''

Maggie watched as the little boy's brows furrowed at this information.

''Can I keep him—her—when she's old 'nuff?''

''That's something you must ask your papa.''

Solemnly, Johnny turned and asked the same question of his father.

Garrick hesitated. ''Johnny, you already have a kitty....''

''Oh, *please*, Papa?''

''I seem to recall *you* had quite a menagerie, Garrick,'' Cal interjected with a grin. ''We all did. Puppies, kittens, frogs— Ma drew the line at mice and snakes, though.''

Garrick sighed. ''All right. We'll soon be drowning in pets, especially if this one's female, but if you'll help take care of her...you can have her when Aunt Livy says she's old enough to leave her mama. But you'll have to be very gentle with her, and always hold her with both hands—''

Johnny jumped and let out a shriek of delight worthy of a Comanche brave, causing the puppy to squeak plaintively. ''Yippee! I'm gonna name her Maggie!'' he cried, beaming at the puppy's human namesake sitting next to his papa.

Maggie covered her mouth in surprise. ''That's a big honor, Johnny, thank you,'' she told the child.

''And now I think you'd better take 'Maggie' very gently and carefully back to her brothers and sisters, Johnny,'' Garrick directed his son. ''It's time to take you home to bed.''

''Good night, y'all,'' Cal said minutes later, his arm draped about his wife's waist as they stood on the porch. Garrick settled himself on the wagon seat with Johnny between him and Maggie. Johnny was still chattering about his soon-to-be pet, but it was obvious from his slowing words and droopy lids that he was sleepy. And in fact he fell asleep, leaning against his father, before they reached the *Gazette* office.

''You don't have to see me inside,'' she said, when Devlin automatically started to lay his son down on the seat so he could do just that. ''You'll wake Johnny up, and anyway, I have my key.''

He looked uncertain, but finally said, ''All right, but I won't pull away till I see your lamplight in the window. Good night, Miss Harper. I enjoyed the evening. And I...''

She waited, wondering what he was going to say, watching his austerely handsome features by the light of the rising moon. Finally she had to fill the silence. ''I enjoyed it, too. Your brother and his wife are wonderful people. They'll be good parents.''

Garrick nodded. "Yes, at least Johnny will have cousins...."

Since he won't have sisters or brothers, Maggie knew he meant. It was a shame, she thought. Garrick was a good man, and certainly young enough that he should not have closed the door so finally on that part of his life.

"Good night," she said at last, when she saw he was not going to say anything more. "Thank you for giving me a ride."

"My pleasure, Miss Harper."

Was it your pleasure, Garrick? she wondered. *Do you do anything that really gives you pleasure?* Opening the door to the *Gazette* office, she lit the lamp she'd left there and waved out the window to Garrick. She watched as he turned the wagon, then kept watching until he was out of sight.

When Maggie went for breakfast at the hotel Monday morning before starting work, Bessie told her the news. There had been yet another raid on a Gillespie Springs area farm. No one had been killed or wounded this time, but the farm buildings had been burned to the ground and all the stock driven off. The survivors were taking refuge with relatives who lived in town, and once again a posse was about to be formed.

Maggie hurried back to the *Gazette,* to find Garrick already there, watching from the window as the riders assembled down the street.

"Are you going?" Maggie asked, trying to keep her voice calm. *Lord, don't let him go again, out of some misguided sense of male duty, and come back in agony once more!*

Devlin shot a look at her. "No," he muttered. "Don't fret, I learned my lesson the last time. Here," he said, crossing to the counter, where a piece of paper lay, "read the editorial I wrote while I was waiting for you."

She took the paper and perused his handwritten words.

The piece gave a quick summary of the raiders' depredations, then went into Garrick's solution: "'The occupying federal troops, who have hamstrung Texans attempting to govern themselves by imposing impossible, so-called ironclad oaths and similar repressive, dictatorial measures,'" she read aloud, "'could better occupy themselves by assisting the occupants of the state to capture and try such vicious criminals as the gang operating in the Gillespie Springs area. Surely that would be a more worthy task for them than growing fat, blue-clad bellies on the fruits of Texas labor....'"

It was hard to stifle a chuckle at the image he'd evoked, but his words worried her, too. "Should you *really* be writing such inflammatory prose? Aren't you concerned that these same 'repressive dictatorial measures' won't be enacted against you?"

The glint of battle lit his eyes. "Freedom of the press is a constitutional right, isn't it? Or is that only for the Northern states?"

"Well, certainly, but prudence might dictate—"

"Prudence be damned, Miss Harper!" he snapped. "I will *not* be muzzled like a biting dog! I only wrote the truth!"

Maggie had learned to love these political debates with her employer. "Then you may instead find yourself penned up like a dangerous bull, Mr. Devlin! And while I agree with you that the federal troops should be helping catch these outlaws—"

"Bull? I remind you of a dangerous *bull*, Miss Harper?" he retorted. "Better to be a dangerous bull, I think, than a tame mouse!"

"Are you saying *I'm* a tame mouse, Mr. Devlin?" she said, warming to the debate. "And no, I wasn't saying you were like a bull, only bullheaded, so bullheaded that you'd chance daring the federal troops shutting down your precious newspaper—"

"Bullheaded, is it? Well, let me tell you, Miss Harper, it'll be a cold day in Hades before I'll let a passel of Yankees tell me what to write!"

Maggie was trying to formulate an answer when Olivia Devlin came hurrying in. "Oh, Garrick, I was hoping I'd find you here! In the middle of all that—" she pointed down the street, indicating the rapidly forming posse "—Cal just got the most wonderful news from the telegraph office!" She waved a piece of paper. "It's from Sam! It says, 'Come see new baby, stop!' I'll bet the proud new papa sent a telegram because he can't bear to tear himself away! And he's such a tease—why, he doesn't even tell us if it's a daughter or a son! We were hoping that all of us could go see the new baby as soon as it was born. But now, of course, Cal can't go...." Her voice trailed off and her face looked wistful.

Then the bell over the door tinkled again and Maggie saw Cal striding through the door.

"Well, if isn't Uncle Cal." Garrick greeted him with a grin.

"Well, I'll be switched—it's Uncle Garrick," Cal retorted, grinning back. "Look, I've got to leave—you know about the posse. Kristof, my deputy, is gonna stay and keep an eye on the town. But there's no reason y'all can't go see our new nephew or niece," he reminded them. "I'd rather not leave Livy in the house alone, on the edge of town an' all."

Garrick hesitated. "What direction did the raiders go? Is it safe to be on the road?"

"They galloped off to the south again, and since you're going west on the main road, you should be all right. Just take your rifle and pistol, and keep a sharp eye. I know you'd do that anyhow."

Garrick nodded. "Well, it sure looks like I'm getting the easy job...but all right, I'll do it."

"Wonderful!" Olivia said, clapping her hands together. "You go home and get Johnny, and I'll go pack us a picnic!"

"Tell Ma I'll be there to admire her new grandchild as soon as I can," added Cal, his hand already on the doorknob.

Olivia stepped over to kiss her husband goodbye, murmuring, "Now you be careful, darlin'."

Olivia looked momentarily sad as she watched her husband stride out the door, but then joy replaced the sadness. "Oh, I just can't wait to hold Sam and Mercy's little bundle, and imagine how we'll have one of our own in the fall...and just wait till you meet them, Maggie! Sam is the youngest Devlin brother, and he's just as handsome as the devil, and Mercy is as sweet as she can be—"

"Me?" Maggie said, mystified. "Well, I suppose I'll meet them *sometime* but—"

"Sometime?" Olivia said with a musical laugh. "Maggie Harper, you're coming with us, so you'll meet them *today!* They live with Mother Devlin on the farm outside Bryan, only an hour's ride or so, and there's no reason why you shouldn't come too, is there, Garrick?" She went on without waiting for an answer. "Oh, it's going to be such fun, riding over there together!"

"But I have the new editorial to typeset," Maggie said, holding up the paper she'd never put down, and carefully not looking at Garrick. He hadn't spoken, so she was sure taking her with them was the last thing he wanted to do.

"And anyway, I wouldn't dream of intruding on a family event like that—"

"What if *I* want you to come?" Garrick said suddenly, shyly meeting her startled eyes. "That editorial can wait until we get back, and we both know it."

"You'd be perfectly welcome, Maggie," added Olivia. "Like Johnny, Mother Devlin doesn't know a stranger. Neither do Sam or Mercy."

Maggie barely heard her. It seemed she couldn't take her eyes from Garrick's piercing blue ones. Her heart beat very fast as she pondered his surprising words: *What if I want you to come?*

"Very well, then," she said, feeling a rising sense of excitement. "Yes, I'll go—just give me a few moments to change my clothes!"

Chapter Sixteen

Garrick enjoyed the wagon ride to the Devlin farm more than anything he'd done in years. Olivia had begun singing, and Johnny joined in. He didn't know the words, but he didn't let that dim his enthusiasm. Then Maggie began to sing along, and her voice mingled with Olivia's in sweet harmony. Finally, Garrick had added his baritone, realizing he hadn't sung since the early days of the war.

They reached the farm shortly after noon. Everyone came out to greet them, including the Reverend Jeremiah and Charity Fairweather, Mercy's father and sister, who had arrived from Abilene, Kansas, in time for the birth.

Olivia helped Johnny off the wagon first, then, while Sarah Devlin was hugging her grandson, Garrick descended and helped Maggie down.

He knew his family was startled at the presence of an unfamiliar woman by his side, but their expressions were cautiously welcoming—even his widowed, sometimes vinegary sister Annie's.

"Mother, Reverend, Annie, Charity, Sam, this is Miss Margaret Harper, my assistant at the *Gazette*," he said. "Uh...Olivia thought—that is, Olivia and *I* thought—it would be nice for her to see the farm, and meet y'all."

"Please, call me Maggie," he heard her murmur as she stepped over to greet them.

"Maggie, you're certainly welcome. We're glad that Garrick brought you," Sarah Devlin said, taking one of Maggie's hands between both of hers, and Annie, still goggling somewhat at Maggie's Northern accent, echoed the sentiment.

His brother Sam, however, was characteristically less restrained. "I'd heard you were a Yankee, but Garrick didn't tell us how pretty you are! You're sure a clever fella, Garrick, gettin' a pretty lady to help you on your paper! Makes workin' purely a joy, doesn't it?" His eyes sparkled with good-natured humor.

"Forgive my brother Sam, who's never learned proper restraint," Garrick said repressively. "And where's Mercy, Sam? Do I have a niece or a nephew?"

Sam's grin rivaled the sun for radiance. "I'll let Mercy show you—she's in the bedroom," he said. "Right this way," he added, beckoning.

They followed Sam into the sprawling fieldstone farmhouse and down the hallway to the bedroom that Garrick, Cal and Sam had shared as boys. There they found Mercy sitting up in bed, her nightgown covered by a shawl. She was holding not one, but *two* sleeping infants.

"Twins?" breathed Garrick, stunned.

Mercy smiled proudly. "Surprise! Their names are Mercedes and Wyatt—for the two people back in Abilene who had the most to do with introducing us."

"Babies, Papa," whispered Johnny in awed tones. *"Two* of them!"

Garrick picked his son up so the boy could see better. "Hard to believe you were once that tiny, isn't it?" he murmured, and his throat felt tight at the thought. He'd never got to see Johnny when he was that size, had never even known he existed. His eyes burning, he introduced Maggie to Mercy.

"Hello, Maggie. I'm so happy to meet you," Mercy Fairweather Devlin said in her sunny way. "I'm sorry our son and daughter aren't awake to greet you and their uncle Garrick."

"But wait around, and they will be. They've got big howls for such little tykes," Sam said with a rueful grin. "Aren't they the prettiest little babies you ever did see?"

Garrick agreed. "In a few years, they're going to be a real handful—double trouble. You'll have to keep your shotgun loaded because of the boys that will be hanging around your daughter," he predicted, and was amused to see his brother's dismayed face.

"They couldn't be any worse than the three of us boys were," Sam said with a groan.

Everyone laughed.

"May I hold one?" Olivia breathed. "I need the practice, you see." Her joyous face explained her meaning, and further celebration ensued.

Garrick realized, as they all sat on the porch after supper, enjoying the spring evening, that he'd gone all day without thinking about his leg.

"You're certainly good at that," Charity Fairweather, who was holding baby Wyatt, remarked to Maggie. The latter was sitting in the old cane-bottomed rocker next to Garrick, rocking baby Mercedes. "Did you come from a large family?"

Maggie raised her head, which had been lowered to the baby's while she nuzzled the infant's soft cheeks.

"No, I was an only child. I've always loved babies, though," she said. "I just haven't had the chance to be around too many of them."

How natural she looks. Garrick found himself imagining her with her red curls dangling over *his* baby's face, and was more disturbed than he cared to admit at having such a thought.

He stood up. "Well, I expect we'd better be heading back," he said. "It'll be dark soon."

"Not yet, Papa!" Johnny pleaded from his position on his grandmother's lap.

"Yes, you're not taking my grandson away already, are you?" Sarah Devlin objected. "He and I are just getting to know one another again. Why don't you leave him here for a few days?"

"Yeah, why don't you do that? I promised Johnny I'd take him fishin' tomorrow, isn't that right?" Sam said, ruffling Johnny's hair.

"Yeah!" Johnny cried. "Wanna go fishin', Papa!"

"But I didn't bring any of his things," Garrick protested.

"Garrick, he'll be fine," his mother assured him. "It's warm enough for him to sleep in his underclothes."

"I reckon it'd be all right, then...."

"'Ray! I get to stay wit' Grandma! I get to go fishin'!" Johnny cheered.

Garrick, feeling a mixture of chagrin and pride at his son's self-sufficiency, murmured, "And here I was worrying about him missing me."

"Cal and I will bring him back once Cal comes to fetch me home," Olivia told him.

Then suddenly Garrick realized Johnny's staying meant it would be just himself and Maggie in the wagon going back to Gillespie Springs.

His face must have registered alarm, for Sam said, "He'll be fine, Garrick, don't you worry. There's no problem Ma can't handle, and you won't be that far away, anyway. You and Maggie go ahead and enjoy that big ol' moon risin' over yonder," he added, pointing to where the moon had indeed appeared above a tall live oak by the entrance gate.

All Garrick needed was a full moon to illuminate Maggie Harper's lovely features! The thought sent panic and excitement simultaneously zinging through his veins. "We're not...I mean, Miss Harper's just..." His voice trailed off. What could he say that wouldn't sound ridiculous? He'd be lying if he said he didn't have feelings for the Yankee woman sitting next to him, but he wasn't about to impose them on her. Maggie Harper was beautiful enough to have any man she wanted, and wouldn't have to settle for a damaged fellow like himself.

"Good night, son," Sarah Devlin said, as if she sensed his uncertainty and didn't want to give him time to say the wrong thing. "And Maggie, you come back here anytime. You don't need to wait for Garrick to invite you."

He heard Maggie responding in a pleased fashion, and was warmed by the way his family had accepted her. He shouldn't be surprised.... The Devlins weren't the sort to let geographical origin influence their feelings about a person, especially since Cal had served with the Union army and Sam had married a Kansas girl.

Johnny was more than willing to let his father go home without him, but he insisted on having Garrick himself tuck him into bed, so it was fully dark by the time Garrick and Maggie pulled away from the farmhouse in the wagon.

"Miss Harper, I hope Sam didn't embarrass you," he began, once they had rounded the bend in the road and the Devlin farm was no longer visible behind them. "I mean, jabbering about the moon and all," he said, feeling her gaze upon him. He didn't dare look at her.

"Embarrass me? No, of course not. And don't you think,

now that we've spent the whole day together, you could call me *Maggie?*"

He looked at her, and knew it had been a mistake to do so. Just as he had feared, the moonlight did magical things to Maggie Harper's already lovely face, turning the green eyes into dark, mysterious pools, glistening on her cheekbones and soft, inviting lips.

He took a deep breath and found for some reason it was hard to fill his lungs. "All right, I suppose I could—Maggie. I just didn't think it would be proper, since you're my employee...." All he could think of was how much he'd like to kiss those lips.

"Good. And I shall call you Garrick. It's such a forthright, unusual name," she said. "We can always go back to 'Miss Harper' and 'Mr. Devlin' when we are in the *Gazette* office, if you think it best."

He liked the way his name sounded when she said it, with her clipped Yankee consonants, so different from the drawling, slow-as-molasses accents of those around him. She always said just what she meant. "My mother named me for the English Shakespearean actor, David Garrick," he told her, since continuing to talk gave him an excuse to keep gazing at her. "Papa didn't like it, because he was Irish, and he said it was too fanciful a name for a Texas boy, but she could always sweet-talk him into seeing things her way."

"I liked your mother a lot. I like your whole family, in fact," she said.

"And I could tell they felt the same about you." *Now* what was there to say? This was the sort of conversation sweethearts should be having, not the two of them!

"Maggie..." he began.

"Garrick?"

There was silence again.

"Oh, nothing..." he managed to say at last, after he had tightened his grip on the reins so he wouldn't take her into his arms. "I was only going to say that I have come to value you very much as a friend as well as an indispensable employee."

She seemed disappointed in his praise, so much so that she momentarily turned away. Then she looked back at him, and her eyes were once again untroubled and gleaming with...what?

"As long as we're making moonlight confessions, Garrick, I will tell you that I've come to feel similar sentiments toward you, and..."

"And?" he prompted.

"And I hoped you might kiss me in the moonlight."

One second he was gazing at her in blank astonishment, the next he was fulfilling her wish, with his arms around her, pulling her close. And she was kissing him back, her lips soft and moist and utterly willing. One distant corner of his brain registered the fact that he had dropped the reins, but the gelding wasn't inclined to take advantage; he merely dropped his head and started cropping the grass that grew in lush springtime profusion at the edge of the road.

Garrick was just about to pull away when he felt her mouth open under his, and instantly, he was lost. His tongue entered her mouth and his grip on her deepened until he could feel her breasts like twin points of heat pressing against his chest. Seemingly of its own accord, his hand rose up to cup a breast as his long-denied manhood swelled to life.

"Garrick..." she said with a sigh, when they remembered to breathe again. And as she sagged against his chest, her hand happened to fall just above the point where his wooden leg joined what was left of his real one.

Maggie wasn't aware of it, but to him the effect was like a bucket of cold water splashed in his face.

"I—I'm sorry," he said quickly, and pulled away, before she could voice outrage that he had so forgotten himself. A darted glance at her showed no anger or even uneasiness on her face, though, just desire, the same desire that was clamoring within him and demanding to know why he had stopped.

"Sorry? But I was enjoying—"

"So was I," he snapped, before she could tempt him to lose his head again. "Way too much. And it's loco, that's what it is."

"Loco to show my feelings for a man I've come to care for?" she asked in a quiet voice. "To—to l—"

He cut her off with savage haste. "You don't. You don't care for a cripple, for a man who isn't whole. I won't let you throw yourself away like that."

She blinked at the vehemence of his words.

"You've seen me. You've seen my leg," he continued, before she could deny his self-description. "I'll be blunt, Maggie, can you really bear to think of *that* in your bed? Because that's what it would mean, sooner or later, if we go on kissing and touching. I'm not a boy to be fobbed off with a few kisses and caresses in the moonlight, Maggie— I'm a man. And I'll be damned if I'll open my heart to another woman who's going to run screaming from my bed."

"You think because your wife—"

He cut her off even more quickly than before. "Don't even soil your mouth speaking of that slut."

"Garrick, you're speaking of Johnny's *mother!*" she cried, her lovely face aghast. But there was more there than just horror at his merciless assessment of Cecilia, though he couldn't guess what troubled Maggie further. "And I—I'm far from perfect myself, Garrick, but I—"

He interrupted her ruthlessly once again. "Cecilia was too squeamish to stay in my bed, but not too squeamish to bigamously wed the first man who'd keep a roof over her head. I sincerely doubt you've committed any sins comparable to that."

Maggie looked down at her hands, and he saw they were trembling.

"Then I don't understand why you stopped."

He started to tell her again how he would not allow her to throw herself away on a cripple, but this time she interrupted him. "You are not your *leg,* Garrick. That is a part of you, yes, but when one loves, one loves the *whole* person. And there is much in you to love."

She had as good as said she loved him. He stared at her for a long time, and she faced him as unflinchingly as a veteran soldier under grapeshot.

He wanted to say he believed he loved her, too, that he was willing to try to trust her, but the words wouldn't come.

"I just don't know...." he muttered at last. "I have to think of Johnny. If it didn't work out...he's already lost his mama. I can't take a chance on that happening again."

He thought she would protest that she was already coming to care very much for little Johnny. He knew it was true from the way her eyes lit up whenever Johnny spoke to her. But she didn't; she merely hung her head in mute acceptance.

After a moment he awkwardly leaned over and picked up the trailing reins, clucked to Toby, and they were once more on their way back to Gillespie Springs.

Chapter Seventeen

Pride warred with Maggie's love for Garrick all the way to town. Half a dozen times, she opened her mouth to tell him that he couldn't discourage her so easily, that she'd show him her love was steadfast and he could trust her not only with his own heart, but Johnny's, too.

In the end, however, neither pride nor love won, for she kept silent out of shame. The way Garrick referred to his late wife "—that hussy—" had given Maggie a hint of how he would feel if he ever learned the truth about her.

How could she have allowed herself to forget what she was? Thanks to Richard Burke and her own foolishness, *she* was damaged goods just as much as Garrick's late wife Cecilia had been! The fact that Maggie had been unmarried and thus free to give herself to a man, even the wrong man, did not mitigate the matter.

She imagined telling him that she was not a virgin. He would feel betrayed and cheated all over again. And he would turn from her in scorn.

No, she was not worthy of a man like Garrick Devlin.

"I don't mind tellin' you, brother, I'm about as discouraged as I've ever been," Cal said to Garrick the next afternoon in the *Gazette* office. "If only we could discover the raiders' hideout! But every time they ride off after a raid, it's as if they vanish into thin air."

It was Tuesday, and Garrick, Maggie and Eureka had been hard at work preparing yet another edition of the *Gazette* for printing when Cal and the rest of the posse had returned, dirty and exhausted, to Gillespie Springs. He'd stopped at the *Gazette* just to let Garrick know he was back and intended to clean up before going to the Devlin farm to pick up his wife and Johnny.

"They must be moving around a lot, or you'd have found the hideout," Garrick consoled him. "But you'll catch them eventually. They're bound to get greedy sometime and slip up. And maybe that editorial I wrote about the army's obligation to help you will reach the right ears. Maggie always sends a couple of copies to her father in Austin, and this time she asked him to be sure and show it to all those bluebellies hanging around the capital."

"Maybe." Cal's lips lifted in a ghost of a grin. "I never thought I'd hear *you* wanting the federal army to step in, Garrick."

"They might as well do something to earn their keep!"

"I won't argue with that. Reckon I'd better be goin' now so you can get back to work. We probably won't start home till the morning, though."

Garrick nodded in agreement. "There's no need to rush back tonight. I doubt Ma would let you, anyway, Cal. She'll want to fuss over you. And tell Sam goodbye for me—now that the babies are here safely, he'll be gone soon on that trail drive, won't he?"

Maggie joined Garrick and Eureka in saying goodbye to Cal, but her mind was elsewhere. It was not lost on her that Garrick had not returned to the more formal way of addressing her, but still referred to her as "Maggie."

Maybe it meant nothing, but she was determined to take it as a sign that however much Garrick was determined to deny himself in regard to her, something had changed on the road to Gillespie Springs a few days ago.

"That's it, Eureka," Maggie said hours later, as she handed the still-damp page to the black man. The smell of wet ink filled her nostrils. "The last copy. We'll be all ready to sell them tomorrow. Thanks for staying so late. I don't know how we ever did that first edition without your help."

"That's all right, Miss Maggie," Eureka said. Garrick had left an hour ago to cover a special meeting of the town council. "Now you get on over to the hotel and get your supper. Bessie told me she was fixin' chicken fricassee tonight, and she's gonna save you a special piece of her pecan pie. I'll stay and tidy up."

"Mmm, chicken fricassee and pecan pie sounds wonderful, Eureka," Maggie said as she took off her work apron. "But why not leave the tidying till morning? You're bound to be as tired as I am, and it can certainly wait till then. You're always up with the roosters, anyway."

Eureka grinned and stretched. "I reckon you're right, Miss Maggie. I'll skedaddle on home, then." A couple of minutes later, he let himself out the back door.

Maggie looked with satisfaction at the neat stack of newspapers on the counter, ready for sale in the morning. Several owners of outlying farms had already approached Garrick about purchasing subscriptions to the paper. Yessir, Garrick, Eureka and she could really be proud of what they had achieved in a short time, she thought as she lit the lamp she always left burning to assist her upstairs when she returned from supper. Wrapping her twilled shawl around her shoulders, she moved toward the back door, intending to lock it.

An evening breeze coming in tickled her ear and brought the faint sounds of laughter from the row of rooms called cribs across the side street. The cribs were the combined working and living rooms occupied by the town's trio of soiled doves.

The door was ajar; Eureka must not have shut it firmly enough, and the breeze had blown it open.

Then a bulky form blocked the shadowy opening.

She froze. *"Who's there?"*

The figure started forward, even as she quickly retreated and picked up the lamp.

"It's me, Miz Harper, Ezekiel Barbee," he said, just as the lamp she extended illuminated his smirking features. He wasn't wearing the tattered gray jacket. In fact, Zeke Barbee, dressed in a frock coat and string tie, could have almost passed for a gentleman, if one could ignore the leering eyes, cat-with-a-mouse smile and the stubble of beard shadowing his chin.

Maggie couldn't. There was something about Zeke Barbee that made her feel like she had touched something slimy. She wondered where he had gotten the new clothes.

"The *Gazette* office is closed right now. Mr. Devlin..." She stopped, knowing instinctively she shouldn't tell him her employer was occupied elsewhere. "You'll have to come back tomorrow."

"Oh, I ain't interested in *newspaper* business," he drawled. "And I didn't come to see ol' Pegleg Garrick. I knew he went off to some meeting."

Simultaneously, anger at the crass reference to Garrick's artificial leg mingled with apprehension within Maggie. The hairs at her nape prickled. "I'm going to have to ask you to leave," she said in a firm voice. "I was just about to lock up."

"I know you was. I seen that darky leavin'," he informed her smugly, his eyes not on her face but her bodice. "I came to take you to supper."

"Indeed, Mr. Barbee? I cannot imagine what made you think I would go anywhere with you," she said with chilly, clipped precision, then backed up in the direction of the front door. She was miserably aware that the street outside was deserted. Eureka was gone, and the other townsfolk were either home having supper, at the meeting Garrick was covering or down the street in the Last Chance.

"Now, is that any way to talk to a nice gent like me?" he wheedled.

She began to retreat still farther.

"Not so fast, Miz Harper," he snapped, snaking out a hand to catch her upper arm. "I just thought that since I've hit a spot a' luck and got me some fancy duds, you oughta *reconsider* my invite."

Her jaw fell open in astonishment, and fury swamped her fear. "You are obviously under the mistaken notion that it was only your clothes that kept me from accepting your, ah, invitation before. Let me set you straight, Mr. Barbee. I will not now or ever willingly breathe the same air as you, sir, not even if you appear before me clad in velvet and a top hat. Do you understand?"

His eyes narrowed as she spoke. "Mighty uppity fer a woman who's been spendin' the last coupla hours since ol' Garrick left fraternizin' with that *darky*," Zeke Barbee sneered. "So I figger you doan need t'be givin' yourself such airs, woman. I doan unnerstand why my ol' pard Garrick wants such a female around, but—"

His nasty, insinuating tone reached through Maggie's apprehension and ignited her temper. "Not that it's any of your *business,* Mr. Barbee, but Mr. Jones and I were *working* together. And you have your nerve even showing your face in this town! Where's your raggedy old gray jacket? Did you leave it at the scene of one of your murderous sprees?"

Now the piglike eyes narrowed to slits. Barbee's skin paled beneath his windburned tan. He lowered his voice and, putting fisted hands on his hips, demanded, "'Murderous sprees?' What're you jawin' about, woman?"

She allowed herself a thin smile. "I think you know, Mr. Barbee. It's very coincidental that both eyewitness accounts of the raiders menacing this area have included a man of your description wearing a tattered rebel jacket. You're going to get caught, and very soon. And then you'll hang. If I were you I'd ride out of Texas as fast as a horse could carry me and never come back."

Alarm sprang once more to the fore as she felt his hot, stale breath on her face. *What had possessed her to be so defiant when there was no one here but Barbee and herself?* She could feel her heart thudding in her ears, and her mouth had grown dry as a Texas creekbed in August.

Zeke Barbee lowered his head until it was inches from hers, and snarled, "Well, you *ain't* me, and I reckon you oughta be nicer t'me. I'm gonna teach you how, Miss Uppity Yankee...." Clapping a hand over her mouth even as she opened it to scream, he yanked her against him.

"No, you're not," came a voice from the shadows. A most welcome voice.

Barbee whirled, and in his astonishment he let go of Maggie. "Git out of here, darky!" he snarled. "This ain't none o'your concern!"

Quickly, Maggie dashed out of his reach behind Eureka, who cocked both barrels of the shotgun he held. "I'm saying it is. Now vamoose, you trash, and make it quick, or I'll blow your sorry carcass to hell."

Barbee just stood there, glaring at both of them. His fists clenched and unclenched.

"But I have a message for Miz Maggie, from someone she used t'know," he said, reaching a hand up to his breast pocket.

"Freeze! Hands in the air!" ordered Eureka. "I'm no fool to believe such a story and let you go for your gun!"

Rage blazed anew in Barbee's eyes as he raised both arms. "You cain't kill me, darky," he snarled. "You'd hang for killin' a white man, and you know it."

Eureka didn't waver. "You'd be just as dead, wouldn't you, you polecat?"

Barbee's gaze turned to Maggie. "But I really do have a letter for ya, Miz Maggie," he said. "Tell him to at least let me give it to you."

She was not about to take a chance, either. "I don't believe you. We certainly wouldn't have any friends in common."

He shrugged, as much as a man can shrug when his arms are pointing toward the ceiling. "It's your loss, Miz Maggie. I guess your friend will just have to contact you some other way. I'm gonna leave now, okay?" Cautiously he began to back toward the rear entrance.

Maggie and Eureka watched him until he disappeared out the back door, and a moment later they heard the sound of a horse's hooves breaking into a trot and then a gallop.

Carefully Eureka stuck his head out the back door. "He's leavin'," he said, then pulled the door closed and locked it.

Now Maggie shook like the last leaf on a tree in a windstorm. "Th-thank you, Eureka," she managed to say. "Why did you happen to come back?"

The black man smiled, revealing gleaming white teeth in the lamplight. "I remembered I left the blocks I was carving for Johnny here, and I wanted to work on them tonight after supper. And as I turned back, I saw that no-account white man sneakin' in the back door. So, quicklike, I ran home—it isn't but a couple of shacks down the street, you know—and got the old shotgun. I figured he was up to no good."

"You don't really think he *did* have some letter for me from someone?" Maggie asked. "I can't imagine who." The thought caused a prickle at the back of her neck.

Eureka shook his head. "Naw, he was jest tryin' a ruse to go for his gun." He rubbed his forehead. "Miss Maggie, we got to let Mr. Devlin know this happened."

Maggie remembered Garrick telling her to inform him if Barbee ever bothered her again, but she nevertheless rejected the idea. "No we don't," she said, thinking how Garrick would receive such news. Though he'd had a confrontation with Zeke over his hiring of herself and Eureka, he'd nevertheless defended his former comrade when she'd accused Barbee of being one of the raiders. Pride forbade her to complain about Barbee again.

Besides, Barbee wouldn't be back, now that he'd been so firmly repulsed.

"You're not to tell Mr. Devlin, Eureka," she repeated. "Promise me. It would just worry him, and he has enough to worry about. Barbee won't come back."

Eureka scratched his head. "I don't know about that, Miz Maggie. Folks like him don't take to being crossed."

"I'll lock my door every night. And I'll sleep with the derringer I brought from Austin under my pillow." It was a small fib—she didn't own any sort of firearm—but she could turn it into the truth with a visit tomorrow to the general store.

"You have a derringer? Show me you know how to load and fire it," he challenged.

She was taken aback. "Are you accusing me of *lying*, Eureka?" she asked indignantly, but she saw he was not about to budge. She sighed. "All right, I don't own a gun," she confessed. "But I could buy one tomorrow...."

Eureka studied her. "Okay, Miz Maggie. But I'm gonna walk you over to the hotel and back. And I'm gonna sleep downstairs here tonight in case that trash tries to sneak back during the night. Mr. Devlin won't ever know—I'll be up sweepin' by the time he comes in."

"But you can't sleep on the floor!"

"Miss Maggie, I've slept on worse many a night when I was a slave. It won't hurt anything."

Maggie sighed and bowed her head in acquiescence. "All right." Truth be told, she would feel uneasy being alone here tonight. There had been something about the way Barbee looked at her....

Chapter Eighteen

Maggie had no time the next morning to wonder if her sleepless night—one she'd spent worrying about Barbee's advances—showed on her face. A near-constant stream of customer traffic had the tin bell over the *Gazette* office door jingling merrily as the townspeople of Gillespie Springs bought the latest edition of the newspaper. It seemed "newspaper day" was becoming an eagerly awaited event. Often the purchasers would linger to scan the pages before they left, discussing them with their neighbors. They appeared to be interested in the articles on the state and federal governments' actions, but as Mayor Long had predicted, loved most to read about themselves. Garrick had given them plenty of both kinds of articles.

Maggie, watching the saloon keeper slap Garrick on the back and compliment him on his editorial, was glad for her boss. Garrick had really found his niche in the community.

He was happy to give credit where credit was due, too. "My assistant wrote that," he said, when Mrs. Long praised an article Maggie had written about the founding of the town.

Maggie, coming forward to thank the mayor's wife, felt a rush of pleasure at the title "my assistant." It was an acknowledgment that he had really accepted that she was capable of doing more than operating the press.

Phoebe Stone, who had come in with the mayor's wife, just sniffed and murmured that *she* hadn't been interviewed for the article, and after all, she and her husband had been among Gillespie Springs' first families. Then she darted a malicious look at Maggie before turning to Garrick.

"Oh, are you going to our Celebration Day at the park, Garrick?" Phoebe inquired in that voice that always reminded Maggie of a pigeon cooing.

Garrick looked blank.

"Hasn't anyone told you? Haven't you seen the signs that must've been printed right here?" Phoebe chided. "It's tomorrow! Why, there's horseracing and a shooting contest for you men, as well as pie, embroidery and quilt judging for the ladies. I frequently win all three," she admitted with a modesty so patently insincere it was all Maggie could do not to roll her eyes. "The preacher judges the pie contest, and he *is* partial to my peach pie, bless him."

"I must admit I'd forgotten about it," Garrick said politely. "But you may be sure the *Gazette* will cover all the events."

Phoebe's answering smile was malevolent. "Oh, but your lady love can't compete in the pie contest, can she? I mean, she lives in that little bitty room up there—" she lifted her eyes meaningfully toward Maggie's room upstairs "—and takes all her meals at the hotel, doesn't she? I can't imagine not having a stove to cook up my confections!" She shuddered elaborately.

Your witch's brew is more like it, Maggie thought, struggling not to clench her fists in irritation. Garrick looked decidedly uncomfortable at the woman's calling Maggie his "lady love." Beside Phoebe, Mayor Long's wife looked as if she'd like to put her hand over the milliner's mouth but didn't quite dare.

Phoebe, preening, turned to Maggie. "But perhaps you *are* able to do stitchery up there of an evening? Have you something you could enter in one of the needlework contests?"

Furious at the other woman's patronizing, Maggie decided to rescue Garrick.

"You're mistaken that I'm Mr. Devlin's lady love, Mrs. Stone," she said smoothly. "And it's quite true that unlike most women, I've had a type stick in my hand more often than a rolling pin or a needle. But working at the side of such a professional newspaperman as Mr. Devlin has always given me an excellent outlet for *my* sort of creativity."

Phoebe Stone looked as if her corset was suddenly too tight.

"A most *unladylike* sort of creativity, I vow," she said with another sniff, and sailed out of the office like a ship under full canvas, her skirts swishing behind her.

Martha Long stayed where she was and gave them both a rueful look.

"I swan, she gets worse and worse, since her husband was killed in the war. I'm so sorry you had to be on the receiving end of that poison tongue of hers, my dear," she said to Maggie. "She's lonely, that's what, but what man would get near enough to let her sink her claws into him?"

She shifted her gaze to include Garrick. "But I had no idea you two were courting," she said in delighted tones. "I think that's won—"

Maggie cut her off, not wanting Garrick to have to say it. "But it's not true, Mrs. Long. Mr. Devlin and I are professional colleagues, nothing more."

The mayor's wife was clearly not convinced. "I understand the need for discretion perfectly, my dear. Never fear that *I* will give away your delicious secret before you are ready. And now I'd better run. The mayor does like his dinner promptly at noon, and I haven't prepared a thing.''

There was a temporary lull at eleven o'clock. Cal had just left with his copy, followed out by Eureka, who took a stack of the papers to peddle on North and South Streets.

They were alone.

"Maggie," Garrick said in the sudden silence, "I'm real sorry about that old biddy's babbling—Phoebe's, I mean, not Mrs. Long's. Mrs. Long means well, and she won't gossip.''

"Phoebe Stone doesn't bother me, Garrick," Maggie said with as much dignity as she could muster. "I'm used to spiteful women. There were a plethora of army wives just like her where I used to live.''

And she'd been gossiped about by all of them, she thought, remembering the painful aftermath of her seduction by Richard Burke. "I'm just sorry your name is getting dragged into the mud along with mine," she added, looking at him.

He made a dismissive gesture, then said something that astonished her. "But I think it'd be real nice if we attended Celebration Day together, Maggie—you, me and Johnny. What do you think?''

She stared at him, dumbfounded. A day spent at Garrick's side, eating picnic food and watching Johnny play, sounded like heaven. But his words were a complete contradiction of what he'd said on the way back from the Devlins' farm. And Phoebe Stone's hurtful words, and the memory they engendered of similar barbs uttered by the army wives, still stung.

"You're very chivalrous, Garrick," she said, dropping her eyes. "But I can't take advantage of that. I'm sure it's wisest that we stick to our decision of the other night.'' She made herself suddenly busy gathering up the score of newspapers that were mailed to subscribers outside of town. ''You wanted these sent—I think I'll just walk over to the post office and take care of that.'' Pulling open the desk drawer where he kept the petty cash supply, she dipped her hand in and came out with enough coins to cover the cost, and then headed for the door.

''But Maggie—'' he began.

She pretended not to hear him as she hurried out. She had to leave or she'd cry right in front of him.

The ''post office'' took up the back corner of the general store. Cyrus Tyler greeted her from behind the counter and took the newspapers from her.

''Here's a letter for you, too, another from your father in Austin, looks like. That'll be two bits for mailing the *Gazettes*. Mighty fine day, isn't it, Miss Harper? Oh, and I really like the look o'the advertisement the paper did for the barbershop, with that pitcher of the barber pole an' all. Reckon that Eureka Jones could make me a pitcher like that for the general store?''

''I'm sure of it, Mr. Tyler,'' Maggie said, pleased that Tyler was finally agreeing to advertise. She had explained to him about the stereotype process before, but all that mattered to the storekeeper was that the carved blocks made a ''pitcher.'' ''I'll tell him you're interested,'' she added, ''and I'm sure he'll start on it right away. Of course, he'll submit a copy for your approval before we go ahead.''

Not ready to go back to the *Gazette* office and face Garrick again, she decided to go find Eureka. What street was he likely to be on by now? North Street, where the poorer folk rented humbler dwellings, or had he made it to South Street, where the mayor and the more prosperous lived?

He was probably still on North, she guessed—Eureka did

love to talk. She reversed her direction to go down the side street that led to North Street.

"*Hssst!*" a female voice called softly from somewhere to her right. "Miz Harper! Over here!"

Whirling around, Maggie saw a face peering out from the narrow alleyway between the general store and the doctor's office. A female face, one whose sallow, rice-powdered cheeks bloomed with rouge like two pink flowers.

"Who are you?" Maggie said, inching closer and peering into the alley. The overhang of the general store prevented much light from illuminating the passageway.

"Name's Ruby Timmons. We're neighbors— I work in the cribs over behind the bathhouse. I been followin' you since you left the *Gazette*."

"Why not come on out if you want to talk?" Maggie said warily. She couldn't see anyone lurking behind the woman, but there was something about going into that tight space that made her uneasy.

"'Cause I don't want that nosy sheriff to see me, that's why," the woman said, nodding in the direction of the jail across the street. "He told me not to set foot on Main Street till the decent folks were in bed."

Knowing Cal Devlin as she did, Maggie very much doubted the fair man had issued such an edict, but she let it pass. "What was it that you wanted to say to me?" she said, standing in front of the alley while the woman withdrew into the shadows.

"I got a tip for ya," she said, then added, when Maggie hesitated, "I know everyone's all afire to find those outlaws that've been causin' such a uproar. Well, one of 'em paid for my services the other night and he told me where they camp."

Maggie digested that bit of information. "One of the

raiders, um, spent time with you? Why would he tell you such a thing and chance your telling the law?'' she asked skeptically.

"He figgered we was both on the wrong side o'the law, I reckon. And he told me 'cuz he had such a fine time he wanted me to bring the other girls out to their camp and have a party with them—if you know what I mean,'' she said with a sly wink. Then her voice took on an indignant note. ''As if we'd trust them out there not to slit our throats rather than pay us! Do they think we were born yesterday? No thanks!''

"So why tell me? Why not tell the sheriff?'' Maggie retorted.

Ruby Timmons spat in the dust at her feet. ''Like I said, Sheriff Devlin an' I don't see eye-to-eye. I don't think he would believe me. Now you—I know you write some of the articles in the paper—bet you didn't think the likes of me could read, did ya? Well, I'd like to benefit a fellow workin' woman— I thought an adventurous gal like yourself could use a leg up, so to speak. You could go investigate the hideout, and write a big ol' story about it.''

"But why would you betray a...a customer?'' Maggie persisted.

Ruby Timmon's beady brown eyes snapped in the dim light. '''Cuz he likes t'play rough,'' she said matter-of-factly. ''He left me with bruises and bite marks—in places *you* can't see, of course. I don't need that.''

Maggie was convinced. Ruby Timmons was just another unfortunate female, at the mercy of a cruel man. *There but for the grace of God...* ''So where is this place? And why hasn't the posse found it?''

The woman guffawed. ''Not so fast, Miz Reporter Lady. I have to work for my living. They haven't found it 'cause them outlaws never stay in the same place fer too long. But I have d'rections to where their camp is right now.''

Maggie frowned, jolted out of her idealistic thoughts. "I didn't come prepared to pay," she stalled, though she had five dollars in the reticule she carried.

"No money, no information," the woman said. "And I want *you* to be the one doing the investigatin'—not that Devlin you work for, understand?''

Maggie started to tell her that once she paid for the information, she'd use it as she saw fit, but decided not to argue. The sporting woman might change her mind about telling her, and it was important that the raiders be stopped before they did any more damage or cost any more lives. And the more she thought about it, the more she thought it would have to be she who did the investigating, anyway. Garrick and Cal were both highly likely to discredit information from such a dubious source. If Maggie was stealthy enough when she rode out to the hideout, she could check the veracity of the woman's story before ever telling Garrick. She felt a thrill of excitement at the thought of doing some real eyewitness reporting, something more than the reports from the women's sewing circle meetings.

"All right, here's a half eagle," she said, reaching into the reticule and handing her the gold coin. "It's all I have."

"It'll do," the woman said, grabbing the coin with greedy rapidity. "Now, here's how you get there," she said, lowering her voice still further. "You take the road that runs east outa town, and go on that for three miles or so, till you come to the live oak that's got struck by lightnin' down its trunk. Then you turn an' follow the lil' path that leads away from it till you come to a creek. Turn west, and follow that creek till you see three stones together, and cross the creek there. Then turn east and go till you cross a cottonwood down across the path, and turn right, and keep going straight till you come to a cave stickin' outa the rock. That's their camp, and I reckon you'll see them there, less'n they're out raisin' Cain somewheres else then!'' She guffawed again as if she found the idea hugely funny.

Maggie repeated the directions back to her, hoping desperately she could remember them until she could write them down on some paper, and that she'd be able to tell east from west out in the countryside.

''That's it. You're a right quick learner, Yankee lady,'' the woman said. ''Good luck. Maybe you'd like to write about the cribs next.''

Obviously, she wasn't expecting a straight answer to that, for she gave a hoot of laughter while Maggie was still struggling to frame a polite reply. Then she turned, and, without another word, backed down the alley away from Maggie.

Chapter Nineteen

"Miss Maggie, why are you talkin' to that no-account woman?" a voice behind her said.

Maggie jumped, then relaxed somewhat as she recognized Eureka. "Oh! Where did *you* come from?"

"Across the street." He indicated his empty arms. "I sold all the papers I took with me."

"Eureka, that's great—but you startled me! I was going to look for you. Mr. Tyler has finally realized the need for a weekly advertisement, you see, and—"

"Never mind about that," he said, his eyes narrowed as he stared down the now-vacant passageway between the two buildings. "What was that—that trashy woman talkin' to you about? She's got her nerve, talkin' to a lady like you—"

"Easy, Eureka, she didn't do any harm," Maggie said reassuringly. Apparently he hadn't been close enough to overhear her conversation with Ruby Timmons, and she was glad. One glance at his suspicious brown face and she realized she couldn't tell him the truth any more than she could tell Garrick. Which also meant she didn't dare ask him for the loan of his mule again, as she had on the day she had interviewed the newly widowed Mrs. Blevins. Maggie would have to rent a horse from the livery, drat it.

"She was, um, just making the suggestion that we might like to do an article about the, um, the place she works...." Maggie felt her cheeks redden. "I was...well, I was trying to find a tactful way of saying that I didn't think my employer would agree to that."

Eureka snorted. "You got that right. Mr. Devlin isn't that hard up for things to write about."

"Yes, well...I've got to be going. I have something to do in my room. You'll get started on Mr. Tyler's stereotype, won't you?"

"Sure enough, Miss Maggie. Say, you have those trousers and jacket of mine done?"

She had offered to mend a pair of Eureka's old pants that had caught on something at the *Gazette* office and ripped, after he had admitted his sister was "no great shakes" with a needle. Once she had agreed to mend the trousers, he had shyly produced a jacket with a rent, too.

The mention of his clothing gave her an idea. She'd mended the articles, but she found herself saying, "No, I'm afraid I haven't got to them. But I'll do them this evening and you can have them back in the morning, all right?"

"That'll be fine, Miss Maggie. Thanks."

She could feel his eyes on her as she walked back toward the *Gazette* office. Had he guessed there'd been more to the conversation than what she'd reported?

Maggie still dreaded encountering Garrick when she entered the office, but to her surprise he wasn't there. She started upstairs to write down the directions, but then a scrap of paper tacked to the printing press stopped her.

Dear Maggie, have gone out to try some target practice west of town. Thought I'd see if I was still any good—

I used to be the best sharpshooter in my regiment—
before humiliating myself at Celebration Day. Why
not take the rest of the day off yourself? You've been
working very hard lately. Perhaps you will see things
differently (about coming to the picnic with us) after
a good night's rest. Garrick.

Maggie smiled at the first part of the message. Apparently
Phoebe's needling had resulted in one more contestant, anyway. And how convenient that he was already occupied in
the opposite direction from where she was going, so he
wouldn't see her riding out of town!

But as for seeing things differently, Maggie knew she
couldn't weaken the stand she had taken by agreeing to go
to the picnic with Garrick and his son, no matter how much
she wanted to. Both she and Garrick were all-or-nothing
people, and Richard Burke had stolen a very important part
of what made up her "all."

Pushing the thought ruthlessly to the back of her mind,
Maggie hurried up the stairs and sat down at her table,
where she kept a pile of scratch paper and a pencil in case
inspiration struck. She scrawled down the directions to the
hideout, hoping she was remembering them correctly. Had
it been west or east she was supposed to turn at the creek?
West...

Then she turned to the matter of her attire. She wouldn't
be able to ride close to the hideout without being de-
tected—a horse made too much noise. She would have to
be on foot to sneak up on the raiders. Therefore, she would
need to wear men's clothing for stealth and ease of movement.

How fortunate that she hadn't given Eureka's mended
trousers and jacket back yet! Eureka wasn't nearly as tall
as Garrick, so his trousers should suit her well enough. The

only shirtwaist she had was white, but if she buttoned up the jacket, the whiteness shouldn't be too visible.

Stripping off her dress and petticoats, she found that while Eureka was short, he was still taller than she. She had to roll up the cuffs to walk without tripping. And he was bigger around the abdomen than she was, so the pants sagged comically around her hips. She made a belt out of a length of twine she found downstairs, then went back upstairs to arrange her hair.

Undoing the neat coil at her nape, she combed out the thick curls, then braided her hair and pinned it higher on her head, so that the floppy-brimmed hat Eureka had left on a peg by the back door would cover it. She didn't want the bandits to catch sight of her because of her vibrant hair color.

Now she was ready to go. She made a ridiculous picture with her obviously feminine high-buttoned boots peeking out from the rolled-up cuffs of Eureka's trousers, but with any luck she would encounter no one she knew. She would get to the livery stable from the back, by cutting over to North Street, and if she walked with her head down, no one would take much notice of her—providing she could get past Eureka and Bessie's house without being seen! Sticking the folded directions into a pocket, she descended the stairs and went out the back door.

Fooling the liveryman wasn't possible, of course, since he visually inspected everyone who rented his horses. She knew by the way he goggled at her as she held out the fifty cent rental fee that he recognized her.

Maggie ignored the look and requested a horse that was both biddable and capable of a gallop if required. She planned on spying on the outlaw camp, then leaving the vicinity unseen, but one never knew. "And fifty cents will allow me to keep the horse the rest of the day, if necessary?''

The liveryman nodded and grudgingly began saddling a roan gelding that looked as if he had seen better days.

Maggie raised an eyebrow. "Are you sure that one has galloped anytime in this decade?''

The liveryman raised a bleary eye from the cinch he was fastening under the horse's belly. "Aw, Downy used t'be a cavalry horse. He kin run from sunup to sundown in about half an hour, providin' you give a rebel yell when you need him to giddap.''

"A rebel yell...?''

The liveryman gave a disdainful snort. "I clean fergot you were a Yankee," he said with a straight face. "Like this.'' And he let out a cry that not only yanked the roan's head out of his manger, but should have awakened the dead in the cemetery across the street, too.

"Mmm, I see—or rather, I hear," Maggie murmured, her ears ringing. She fervently hoped she could utter such a noise if the need arose, even while she prayed it wouldn't.

Garrick could not have said what made him suddenly uneasy as he sighted down the barrel of his trusty old rifle—and just as he had the tin cans all set up in the vacant field west of town, too! It was a perfect day for target practice, warm and sunny and glorious, as only a spring day in Texas could be. A mockingbird trilled from a nearby cottonwood.

This was nonsense. He'd never been one for believing in intuition, or "the sight" as his Irish-born father had called it. But there would be no target practice for him today, not until he did something to quiet the unspringlike icicles of apprehension about Maggie that now stabbed his spine. And that meant proving to himself that she was all right.

Maggie had seemed to have a burr under her saddle all morning, especially before the steady stream of customers had made him too busy to keep watching her. She'd been jumpy as a mule on jimsonweed. He had no logical reason to think that she could be in danger, but nothing about his feelings for the Yankee woman had ever been logical, had they?

Toby looked at him with mild protest as he began resaddling him, for Garrick had just hobbled the brown gelding and set him to grazing the lush spring grass. He submitted with resigned docility, however, even allowing the curb bit into his mouth with only a token show of resistance.

"I know, old boy, it doesn't make any sense," Garrick muttered, wincing from the red-hot needles of phantom pain traveling up his right leg as he swung into the saddle. "I'll probably find her up in her room, and she'll look at me like I'm loco as a lizard with sunstroke. That'll suit me just fine, mind you, so then we'll ride back out here and you can get back at that grass, okay?"

Finding the storm-damaged live oak had been easy enough for Maggie; the lightning that had struck the gnarled old tree had split the trunk in two. The black-scarred halves of the bisected trunk leaned away from one another at crazy angles.

Following the rest of the directions was more tricky. She found the path leading away from the blasted tree and into the woods without difficulty, and reached the creek, but she was disoriented out here so far from town. Was west right or left? The thick leafy cottonwoods that shaded the creek made it difficult to check the sun's position, but by backing up a few yards she was able to see it clearly. By now it

was afternoon—the sun would be descending toward the
west. Therefore she should turn left, she reasoned.

She was to follow the meandering creek until she found
three stones together. But was that *in* the creek, or by it?
Peering about until her eyes swam with the effort, she kept
the roan moving forward, wondering if she'd missed the
landmark and why she'd let the sporting woman talk her
into this expedition. It hadn't been the way she'd talked to
Maggie as one "working woman" to another, Maggie
thought. No, it had been the appeal to her vanity as a newspaperwoman. She'd been imagining the admiration she
would see on Garrick's face—and the praise of the townspeople, especially Cal—for her daring investigation! *In-
trepid,* they would call her. *Fearless.*

Fool, she called herself now. She had no good reason to
trust the whore, and even if the woman's motives had been
just what she said they were, no reason to think she could
find the camp *and* get back to town safely. Lord, if only
she had a pistol with her!

There—there was the downed cottonwood, just ahead.
"You stay right here, Downy old boy," she said, dismounting and tying the roan's reins to the trunk of the tree.
Before she went on, though, she unfolded and consulted
the paper she'd put in her pocket.

"Turn right at the downed cottonwood," it said. And
sure enough, now that she was looking for clues, she could
see a faint hoofprint in the earth, crushed grass and bent
stems of plants that indicated recent passage that way. Re-
folding the paper and sticking it back in the breast pocket
of Eureka's coat, she said a silent prayer and moved forward at a crouch, taking care to avoid stepping on twigs
that would snap underneath her feet.

It was supposedly a straight path to the outlaws' hideout
from here, but how far? Her joints ached from the strain of

her crouched posture, and her nerves screamed. Overhead in the trees, a catbird's cry startled her so badly she almost cried out.

Then the wind changed, and a breeze brought her the odor of smoke. And a snatch of a voice—a male voice, deep throated and coarse. An answering voice, and a bark of laughter. The scrape of metal on metal, like the sound a fork might make against a tin plate. Oh, yes, she was very near the camp. Just ahead lay a small grove of magnolia saplings, each about three feet high, clustered around the fallen magnolia that had given them birth, and then, by its death, allowed them to grow.

Maggie dropped to her hands and knees and began crawling forward, an inch at a time. It had rained during the night, and the shaded, grassy earth was cool beneath her fingers.

She peered between the broad shiny leaves of one of the young magnolias. At first, all she could see was a row of horses tethered to a picket line strung between two loblolly pines, their heads toward her. She peered to the right, then jumped. She had expected to see the outlaws, but still the sight startled her.

There were four men, two of them sitting near the campfire with tin plates in their laps. One of them, a stocky man with scruffy yellow hair, had just taken a drink from a tin cup and was setting it down. The other, a black man, was forking beans into his mouth.

Of the two men who were not sitting, one, whose coppery complexion and lank, overlong black hair proclaimed his Indian heritage, was cleaning a pistol. So far, these three matched the descriptions given by Mrs. Blevins.

The fourth man had his back to her, preventing her from seeing his face as he leaned over to retrieve something from the saddlebags lying atop his upended saddle. But he wore a tattered gray jacket, and when he straightened and came back to the campfire, she was not surprised to recognize Zeke Barbee.

She watched him stick a wad of tobacco in his mouth and start chewing. *Garrick,* Maggie thought, *you didn't want to believe my suspicions, but now I can prove it.* She had no sense of triumph at being right, however, only a sour taste in her mouth.

But Mrs. Blevins had said *five* men had raided her farm—where was the fifth? Had he left the band? Had he been a casualty of some later raid far from Gillespie Springs?

And then she saw him, standing between two of the horses while he curried one of them. He was a tall man with dark hair and a mustache—"A tall man with dark hair and eyes," Mrs. Blevins had said. The man was too far away for Maggie to see his eye color, but there was something familiar about him—something about the mustache, the way he moved....

He looked like Richard Burke.

Even as Maggie formed the thought, she discarded it. Richard Burke had gone to Washington—he couldn't be there and back in Texas at the same time. And this man was wearing ordinary clothes—denims and a striped shirt, not a blue uniform. Ambitious to advance in the army, Richard wouldn't have left it—and certainly not to join a band of outlaws.

There were lots of dark-haired men with mustaches such as her seducer had worn. He was a familiar type, that was all.

Well, she'd seen them, all five of them, and now it was time to steal away from the camp and report her findings to the Devlin brothers. She wondered how Garrick would take the proof that his old comrade was one of the killers.

Just as she was about to start backing up, Zeke looked at the yellow-haired man and said, "So, you think we oughta hit that ranch along Thompson Creek, the one with all the fancy horseflesh?"

"Hell, yeah, I think so. Jest think o'the kinda money we could make on them if we was to sell 'em in N'Awlins. I don't know why we ain't doin' it today."

"'Cuz I said we ain't, thass' why. I felt like restin' up after that bit o'fun we had yesterday over by Navasota. And I told you, them whores in town are gonna come out and treat us real nice."

"You white men are led around by what's between your legs," observed the half-breed, his voice contemptuous. "I say we go get those horses, and don't stop till we're across the border in Mexico. We can have women anytime."

"Shee-it, you can't make much money on hosses in Mexico," the black man commented.

Go ahead and debate where to sell the horses, Maggie thought with a grim smile. *You aren't going to need to decide, because before you can stage this raid you're all going to be captured.*

She knew she should go, but still she lingered, watching the man currying the horse, wishing he would offer an opinion so she could hear what his voice sounded like. But he just continued his grooming and kept silent.

That settled it—he couldn't be Richard, she decided. Richard wouldn't have held back; he had the habit of command and would have been telling the rest of them when the raid was going to take place and how they were going to do it.

She didn't dare stay any longer. She began to back up, still crawling, keeping her eyes fastened on the lounging outlaws.

She had just reached sufficient cover to rise to a crouch,

but as she began to push herself up, something cool and smooth passed over her right hand.

She smothered her shriek as the snake disappeared into the grass, but not quickly enough.

The half-breed's head jerked up. "What was that? I heard something."

"What?"

"A sound—over there."

Just then one of the horses in the tethered line nickered, and a second later, Maggie heard her own horse, about a hundred yards away, utter an answering whinny.

"Someone's there!"

Maggie was up and running before she even heard the shout. She'd gone about a dozen yards when a shot rang out and half a second later, a bullet splintered the wood of a post oak beside her.

Without thought, she ran at a right angle from the damaged tree.

"Damn! You missed him!" someone shouted behind her. Now the sound of thudding feet came to her ears, and she began to run even faster, instinctively zigzagging as more shots rang out in her direction. She could see the roan gelding just ahead, plunging in agitation against the restraint of his tied reins. God, even if she reached Downy unharmed, how could she untie him and jump on in time to escape her pursuers?

"Don't let him get away!" shouted another voice.

"Shuddup, he ain't gonna—"

And then she felt her hat catch on a low branch. Wrenching her head away, she left the hat behind, and felt her pinned-up braid come loose and flop onto her shoulders.

"Hell, it's a *woman!*" The shout rang out behind her.

"We still can't let her get away!"

She was close enough to the roan to see the whites of his eyes as he reared.

"Easy, boy, easy!" she called, praying she could free him without having him plunge away from her before she could mount—and before she got struck by a bullet.

Another shot rang out, and she dived for the ground, sure they wouldn't miss her this time. But it hadn't been her the gunman was aiming at. She heard a scream, an unhuman one, and saw the roan, his back creased by a bullet, wrench away from the downed tree, the old, brittle leather of his reins no longer able to withstand his terrified efforts to free himself. A moment later he was galloping down the path in the direction they had come.

She ran, following the creek westward, even though she had fully absorbed the realization that with her horse gone, she had lost all hope of escaping. Inevitably, the outlaw running behind her would catch up with her.

All she could do, as despair weighted her thoughts, was keep running. She had to *try*. She couldn't just let him catch her and drag her back to the camp....

But the sounds of her pursuers—for now there were at least two pairs of feet crashing through the underbrush behind her—were getting closer, and she was slowing. Her lungs were on fire, and a horrible, cramping pain knifed through her ribs—had she been shot? But no, she hadn't heard a report; it must be just a stitch in her side....

There were the three stones in the creek, just ahead! Splashing through the shallow water, she dared a glance over her shoulder and saw that the yellow-haired man was running in front of the half-breed and was within a few strides of seizing her. He had his hand outstretched to grab her flying braid....

Chapter Twenty

A gunshot from deep in the woods!

"Giddap, Toby!" Garrick shouted, smacking the brown gelding on the rump. *Did that shot mean he was already too late?*

In the distance, he could hear shouts and the sounds of someone crashing through the woods—then a second report, followed closely by a horse's terrified scream. Garrick urged Toby to greater speed, hearing hoofbeats pounding toward him over the rhythm of the gelding's galloping.

Then a roan horse burst onto the path in front of him, riderless and wild-eyed, and bolted past him, but not before Garrick saw the streak of crimson on the roan's rump. *Good Lord, had Maggie been riding that horse? Had the first shot he'd heard knocked her out of the saddle?* If whoever was shooting at Maggie had harmed one curly red hair on her beloved head, he was going to think hell was a lemonade social in comparison to what Garrick would make him suffer!

There she was! Just ahead, Maggie splashed across a shallow creek, with two men running right behind her! One of them, a white man with yellow hair, was just inches away....

Garrick raised his old Winchester to his shoulder, held his breath and fired.

The blast was deafening, but he thought he heard Maggie scream in the midst of it. He was barely aware of the yellow-haired man collapsing, clutching his knee, or of the dark-haired, copper-skinned man skidding to a halt, then turning and fleeing back the way he'd come.

All he could see was Maggie, running for all she was worth, her face white, her green eyes round with fear, her braid streaming out behind her.

"Maggie! Over here! Jump on back!" he shouted.

She saw him and changed her course slightly, and in the seconds it took her to reach Toby, Garrick sent another couple of rounds into the woods in case the other man was armed and felt tempted to shoot at them from cover. Garrick couldn't see anyone else coming through the woods, but that didn't mean they weren't there. The man he'd shot in the knee was no longer a threat, for he writhed on the ground, clutching his injured leg and moaning. Garrick was mighty tempted to send another, final slug his way—the man certainly deserved to die—but he had to help Maggie up behind him.

He shoved the rifle into its scabbard on the saddle. Pulling his left foot out of the stirrup, he wheeled Toby around so that the gelding's left side was toward Maggie.

"*Whoa*, Toby," he commanded. Then, to Maggie, he called, "Here! Take my hand!" Ignoring the agonized protest his shortened right leg made as he braced himself with it, he pulled her up behind him as soon as she had set her foot in his empty stirrup.

When she had snaked her arms around his waist, she vacated the stirrup and he replaced his left foot there. "*Hang on, Maggie!*" he shouted, feeling her face pressing against his back. Pulling his pistol from the holster, he cocked it and held it at the ready in case they were pursued, then drummed his heel into the gelding's ribs and flapped the reins. "Hyaaa, Toby!"

He kept expecting to hear the sounds of hoofbeats pounding behind them and bullets singing past them, but he never did. Nevertheless, several times during that wild ride back toward town, he glanced over his shoulder. No one pursued them, but he didn't pull up until they had drawn abreast of Cal and Livy's place on the outskirts of Gillespie Springs.

He didn't turn in there, though. Instead, he turned into the tree-lined park across the road.

Thank God, school must not have ended for the day, and the park was empty. Garrick felt Maggie sit up straight, but she didn't say anything until he reined Toby into a shady grove hidden from the road by crepe myrtle bushes.

"Shouldn't we go to the jail and tell Cal, Garrick? He's got to know where the raiders' camp is, so he can go capture them before they escape—"

"So that's who was chasing you. I figured as much. Dismount," he commanded, shoving his foot out of the stirrup again so she could. "We need to talk."

"But—they'll get away...." she protested, even as she obeyed.

"I'd wager they're already hightailing it out of there," he told her grimly as he followed her to the ground. "Even if Cal could gather a posse in five minutes, they'd still be far away by the time they got there."

Maggie listened in silence, her eyes round and thoughtful in the shady isolation of the grove. She seemed to be waiting for him to say something more.

Garrick hurt so badly—his leg from the intense demands he'd just put on it, his heart because of the fear he'd just endured that he would find her dead or see her killed. For a long minute he could do nothing but look at her, his hands on his hips. He was shocked to se her dressed as a man, but what she'd been doing was so much worse!

"Garrick, how on earth did you know where to come and find me?" Maggie asked at last, then gave a shaky laugh. "Your note said you had gone target shooting, but you couldn't have arrived in a more timely fashion...."

"I read the directions you left up in your room."

"But I didn't leave them," she said in surprise, pulling a folded sheet of paper from her pocket.

"No, but something told me you were about to get into trouble, and I went looking for you in your room. I didn't find you, but I saw the impression your pencil had left in the paper. Sure enough, when I wiped some ink on a rag across them, your words came out nice and clear."

"Oh. How clever of you! Well, I'm glad—"

"Miss Harper, are all Yankee women so totally lacking in a sense of self-preservation?" he cried, all his fear for her rushing out in an angry torrent of words. "What on earth made you do such a foolhardy thing as to go spy on a nest of rattlers like that? Don't you have any more wisdom than God gave a jackass?"

Garrick saw her mouth fall open and tears well up in the brilliant green eyes. He started to tell her he was shouting because he had been terrified for her, but she was already speaking.

"No one is more aware than I am...that my going out there was a f-foolish thing to do," she said, her voice choking and a flush of color suffusing her cheeks. "But I think you should be the first to know that I saw your *good friend* Zeke Barbee among the outlaws in the camp, still wearing that damned raggedy gray jacket."

Garrick closed his eyes. Hadn't he always known deep inside that she was right about Zeke?

"He's the same man who surprised me in the office last night, after you'd gone to the meeting," she continued, a bitter look of satisfaction in her tear-filled eyes. "He was up to no good, and he wasn't going to take no for an answer. If it hadn't been for Eureka's intervention…" She let the words hang in the air between them.

A suffocating sensation tightened his throat at the image her words had conveyed.

"Damnation, woman! You should have informed me about that first thing this morning! All right, you told me so—Zeke Barbee's an outlaw and I was wrong about him— but don't try and change the subject! Did you have *no* idea how I'd feel about you putting yourself in such needless jeopardy? If not me, couldn't you imagine how my son would feel if anything had happened to you?" He threw the questions at her like sharp knives.

Her face took on a scornful look. "You men—you pompous, all-knowing, all-managing men! You think you're the only ones who can do anything the least bit brave! It *wasn't* needless—"

She stopped abruptly, her eyes looking as if they possessed all the secrets of the universe.

"What is it?" he asked, suspicious of her sudden serenity.

The smile she revealed now was radiant. "Garrick," she breathed, taking a step forward, "do you realize what you were admitting, a moment ago?"

He had no idea what she was talking about. "Admitting? What in tarnation are you saying, Maggie?"

"Well, no, you didn't exactly come right out and *say* it, so I will. No matter how hard you try not to, and think you shouldn't, you *care* about me."

"*Care* about you? If that isn't just like a damn fool Yankee to pussyfoot around a feeling," he snapped. "I don't *care* about you, I *love* you, you Yankee carpetbagger! And I don't expect you to love me back—I don't even *want* you to," he insisted before she could say anything to the contrary, "but couldn't you please be a little more careful for *my* sake, if not your own, and not take such stupid chances?"

Her eyes shining, she advanced on him, and the next thing he knew, she was throwing her arms about him. "But I *do* love you, like it or not," she said, her lips inches from his, "and I'm not going to listen to any more talk of how I shouldn't 'throw myself away on a cripple,' do you hear me?" Then she pulled his head down to hers and kissed him so thoroughly he thought he'd died and gone to heaven.

For perhaps five minutes they kissed and touched and hugged, until both of them were breathless.

"Maggie..." Garrick had absolutely no idea what he was going to say next. He wanted her, he wanted her right now, he wanted her forever. But there was still some part of him that knew she would be repelled by that part of him that was no longer whole.

Then the sound of a boy whistling to his dog from the other side of the trees interrupted the spell that had been cast between them.

Regretfully, Garrick let his arms fall away from her and said, "School must have let out for the day. In another few minutes the park will be crawling with young'uns coming for a dip in the creek, as warm as it's been. I...I hadn't realized how late it was getting."

"You need to be getting home," she said for him.

He nodded, his eyes never leaving her face. "But this conversation isn't over, Maggie, not by a long shot. When...?"

"Can we...meet later tonight? Go for a walk or something?"

He stared down at her. "Jovita will be at the house, so Johnny won't be alone.... Yes, I'll come to the *Gazette* later, after Johnny is asleep...."

They went to Cal after that. He quickly deputized a half-dozen men, and with Garrick to show the way, rode out with them to the campsite. Just as Garrick had predicted, though, they returned to town at suppertime empty-handed.

Cal and Garrick stopped outside the *Gazette* office, and Maggie, who had been trying in vain to work on an article about her experiences today, ran outside. The outlaws were long gone, Garrick reported. Nothing was left at the campsite but some empty whiskey bottles and a few smoldering coals to mark that the outlaws had ever been there. Their tracks split up in different directions a mile or so south of the camp.

"But...but Garrick wounded one of them," Maggie told Cal. "In the knee, I think."

"Well, maybe he won't get too far before he has to hole up somewhere and get some doctorin'," Cal responded. "Before I go home I'm gonna have Hank Sweeney send a telegram to the towns around here to be on the lookout for all of them, especially the wounded man. Maybe he'll try to find a sawbones a few miles from here, and if we could just capture him I'm sure we could *persuade* him to lead us to the others."

"If he even knows where they went," Garrick said, his face dubious.

Cal shrugged. "We'll just have to wait and see. Meanwhile, I want your promise, Miss Maggie, not to take any more foolish chances." His face was stern.

Garrick had put him up to this, Maggie thought as her

gaze went from Cal's face to Garrick's. She couldn't find it in her to mind—it was just more evidence of Garrick's caring.

"I promise," she said to Cal, but her eyes were locked with Garrick's.

"And I think you'd better move your things down to our house, Miss Maggie," Cal added. "Garrick told me about you findin' that polecat Barbee waitin' for you here last night. Livy and I have a spare room, and I know she'd love to have you there."

Maggie was touched by the lawman's kindness, but dismayed. If she moved down to Cal and Livy's, she and Garrick wouldn't take that walk tonight, and then who knew how long it would take Garrick to... "Oh, no, thank you, Cal, but I couldn't do that. I—I wouldn't want to intrude on your privacy—"

"It ain't safe for you to be stayin' alone here at night, Miss Maggie, not after what happened."

Garrick was looking down at the ground. "Maybe you should do it, Maggie. I wouldn't want anything to happen to you."

"Garrick, even Barbee wouldn't be bold enough to return to Gillespie Springs now that it's known he's one of the outlaws," she said, hoping reason would dissuade them. She turned back to Cal. "Anyway, I'll make sure the office is locked—front and back—and I have a stout lock on the door to my room upstairs, too. I appreciate the offer, Cal, truly I do, but I'm just too used to working on articles and print jobs late into the night, if the fancy takes me."

"Miss Maggie—" Cal protested.

"I told you she wouldn't do it," Garrick muttered. "Damn fool stubborn Yankee women. Okay then, here," he added, handing Maggie the pistol he'd taken with him. "I want you to promise me you'll carry this with you at all times when no one else is around the office. Take it with you even when you go over to the hotel to eat.''

"All right," Maggie said, giving in gracefully, and relieved that neither man was going to insist. "Now both of you men, shoo! Go on home and have your suppers! Garrick, I'll see—''

"What?"

She felt her face redden, for Cal was still there, and with her mind on the upcoming night, she had been about to tell Garrick, *I'll see you later.*

"Oh, nothing..." she said airily, and turned and went inside before the pink turned to crimson.

Chapter Twenty-One

The next few hours seemed endless to Maggie. She lingered over her supper at the hotel, totally unaware of what she was eating, until the cook finally brought her out of her reverie by asking what it was about her beef stew that was making Maggie all moony-eyed.

"Nothing, Bessie," she said hastily. "I...I was just thinking about a story I was going to write."

"Huh," responded the black woman skeptically, her hands on her ample hips. "No story makes a girl look like that. Only story goin' on right now's the one you're givin' me."

Was she so transparent? Maggie thanked the cook for her supper, signed the ticket that enabled her to pay for her meals on a monthly basis, and left, feeling the unaccustomed weight of the pistol in her reticule.

Maggie didn't go straight back to her little room over the *Gazette* office, however. Instead, she walked across the street to the bathhouse.

She'd mostly been making do with sponge baths from water she hauled in a bucket from the pump in the center of town, but tonight nothing would do but a genuine bath in warm, scented water, with plenty of fresh water left over to wash her hair.

She told the startled attendant she wanted a bath, a bath in the facility's one private room, of course.

"All right, but that'll be—"

"I know, a quarter extra." The bathhouse currently was empty, but she wasn't about to use one of the row of tubs in the common room, where several cowboys might bathe at once on Saturday nights. Then, while the attendant began to bring in bucket after bucket of hot water from the boiler over the fire out back, Maggie took the precaution of plugging the knothole in the door with her handkerchief. The only man she wanted seeing her body was Garrick Devlin.

"Will there be anything else, miss?" the attendant wheezed, after plopping a couple of well-worn towels and a bar of soap down on the stand by the tub. He frowned as he saw the handkerchief-blocked hole, but she knew he wouldn't dare say anything or remove it.

"No, thank you," she said, walking him to the door and locking it firmly behind her. Then she poured the bottle of rosewater she had brought in her reticule into the water and brought out the bar of rose-scented soap. No ordinary lye soap for her tonight!

Savoring the flowery fragrance, she sank chest deep into the water. For once her hands would not smell of turpentine and her fingernails wouldn't be stained with ink!

He was just coming to see her to talk, she told herself. To complete their conversation from this afternoon. Perhaps they would finish it while walking through the darkened streets of Gillespie Springs, or perhaps Garrick would not be eager to walk after the hard riding he'd done today, and they'd talk in the office, by his desk.

No matter how their conversation ended, she knew that nothing would be the same afterward for them.

Lord, was she really doing the right thing by trusting Garrick with her heart? She knew the difference now between a man who *appeared* good and honorable, as Richard Burke had, and a man such as Garrick, who really possessed those characteristics. He'd said he loved her. But Garrick had been deeply hurt—was it possible that his soul had been so damaged that his love would not last if he discovered she had once foolishly given herself to another?

Then he must never find out, a voice inside her whispered.

You must tell him, another voice insisted. *You can be no less good and honorable than Garrick is. It would be dishonest to do otherwise.*

But would unburdening your soul merely burden his with something he doesn't need to know? the first voice retorted. Richard Burke had gone back to Washington and his wife; Maggie's mistake with him need never tarnish her and Garrick's love for each other. Besides, Garrick might not even be *expecting* her to be a virgin! Might his assumptions about Yankee working women have led him to think that she already had some sexual experience?

Undecided about what to do, she sighed and leaned back in the water.

Nervous as she was about what she hoped would happen between herself and Garrick, Maggie supposed she owed Richard Burke a certain amount of gratitude.

For all the fact that he had possessed no more honor than a skunk, Burke had shorn her of much of the ignorance that was imposed on gentlewomen from girlhood—and the fear that was a natural consequence of that ignorance. She already knew what happened between men and women in the bedroom, so she would not be afraid of what Garrick Devlin would do to her whenever they first made love.

What Burke had lacked in honor, he had made up in

lovemaking skill. He had taught her what her body craved, how it responded to this type of caress or that type of kiss.

She wished she could have placed her innocence as a gift at Garrick's feet. However, she reminded herself that what passed between herself and Garrick would be all new. And she need never encounter Burke again. He was in her past, and there he would stay.

Maggie thought she had dallied in the warm water a long time, but when she left the bathhouse, her hair still hanging in damp ringlets down her back, she could see from the big clock in the bank window that it was only seven.

Twilight was just beginning. No doubt even a small child like Johnny resisted falling asleep while the sun lingered above the horizon, so it might be hours yet before she would see Garrick. That was good, she insisted to her eager heart. She would have plenty of time to dry her hair and decide what to wear for this most important evening.

Upon reaching the *Gazette,* she didn't linger below in the office, but went directly up the stairs to her room. As she unlocked the door and went inside, she brushed past the lace-trimmed nightgown and wrapper that hadn't left the hook on the back of her door since she'd arrived.

Normally she wore an ordinary gown of white cotton to bed. The lovely, French-made lacy one been an impulsive purchase for her trousseau, back when she had thought to soon be Mrs. Richard Burke. She hadn't even understood why she'd brought it with her from Austin.

There was but one dress Garrick had never seen her wear before, a leaf-sprigged foulard, and like the creamy nightgown, she had never taken it off its hanger since arriving in Gillespie Springs. Maggie savored the smooth, silky feel of the fabric as she settled the folds of the dress around her hips. Mmm, it had been too long since she'd put on something that made her feel purely *female,* as this dress did. She hoped Garrick would find her beautiful in it.

Moving her chair in front of the window that looked out over the alley, she took advantage of the gentle evening breeze to further dry her curly hair, until it lay like a dark red cloud over her neck and shoulders.

"Jovita, I've...I've got something to take care of at the office," Garrick said as he passed the old Mexican woman, who was sitting in the kitchen, knitting by the light of the kerosene lamp. "I'll probably be late." He knew he could just as easily have told her the truth—that he was going to see Maggie and that he wasn't coming back until...until when? He hardly dared say it, even to himself.

"*Sí,* Señor Devlin," Jovita Mendez said imperturbably as he made his way toward the door—but there was a knowing twinkle in his housekeeper's obsidian eyes, as if she was adding up the things that made it unlikely he was telling the whole truth. Things such as his asking her to help him haul hot water up to the hip bath in his room, shaving for the second time today and changing his shirt for no apparent reason. He'd wager the wise old woman knew exactly what he had to "take care of" at the *Gazette* office—and approved!

Nothing got past Jovita, he thought with amused exasperation. She probably already had a wedding date picked out for himself and Maggie, and all their future children named.

Nevertheless, Garrick's heart hammered in his chest as he made his way down the darkened side street to the *Gazette* office and let himself in the back entrance.

The office was dark. He'd been sure that Maggie would meet him downstairs, ready to go for a walk or have their talk right there, where they worked every day. Had she been thinking about what it would really mean to love him, to be intimate with a man whose right leg ended above the knee? Had she reconsidered? The creak of the floorboards told him she was moving about in her room above. Would he find her throwing clothes into her bags, getting ready to leave?

No, he told himself. Maggie wouldn't do that. She had said, *You are not your leg.* The thought gave him the courage he needed to climb her stairs, then lift his hand to knock.

But before he could even do so, she was opening the door. "Oh! I—I was just coming downstairs! I'm afraid the time got away from me while I was getting dressed and drying my hair.... I wasn't sure when you would be able to come."

She was so lovely that for a moment he couldn't get his breath. Gone was the matter-of-fact Yankee woman in her practical work dress and her hair sensibly coiled at the nape of her neck, with her fingers ink stained and smelling of turpentine. In her place, smelling of roses, was a belle in a green patterned dress, her auburn hair curling in riotous glory around her shoulders.

He took refuge in gruffness. "You shouldn't have just opened the door, Maggie. What if it hadn't been me? You should have waited to hear my voice as I knocked."

Her lips—those kissable, full lips he had fantasized about ever since he'd kissed her this afternoon—curved upward in an amused, womanly smile at his rebuke.

"I know your step, Garrick," she said, her green eyes shining.

"I'd have been here sooner, but little boys never want to go right to sleep when their papas really want them to," he told her with a rueful shake of his head, wishing his heart would settle down. "It took two stories tonight, instead of just one."

"I see...."

He'd never seen her hair down when it wasn't in a thick braid. He couldn't take his eyes off of it, thinking it was a shame that such fiery glory need ever be confined. He wanted to bury himself in it, to tie himself up in it so completely that he could never be free of her.

"Your hair is beautiful," he said, his voice suddenly raspy, like a rusty key turning in a rusty lock. "May I...?" He had to touch it, had to convince himself that he could bury his hands in it and not be burned.

Her eyes gave him permission.

He propped his cane against the wall. "Maggie," he breathed, sinking his fingers into the silky, curly strands, and while he held her head gently, he lowered his mouth to hers.

She kissed him with a hunger that belied her outward calm, and the kiss went singing through his veins, igniting him. His hands left her hair and pulled her close to him, and he could feel her trembling, eager for more. But from the pounding of her heart against his chest, he thought she was afraid, too.

Perhaps he could set that fear to rest. And his own fear. He raised his lips from hers, resting his forehead against hers for a moment, then lifted his head and looked her in the eye. "Maggie, I know we talked about going for a walk, and I know I ought to lead up to this gradually and gently, but I can't wait any longer. I have to know, 'cause there isn't any point in going further until I do. Will you marry me, Maggie? I want you to be my wife—but only if you understand what that means—to share my bed and all. I— I'll understand if that isn't what you want, and I want you to know you needn't fear.... You can keep your job, if you decide against it...."

"Garrick, shut up!" she exclaimed, putting a finger against his lips.

"Pardon me?" he said in surprise, his voice muffled by that firm fingertip.

"I said shut up. You just proposed to me, Garrick Devlin, and now you won't stop talking long enough for me to say yes!"

"Yes?" he echoed, hardly able to believe his ears. "Just like that, yes?"

"Yes, just like that! This afternoon you said you loved me. I said I loved you. And now that you've asked me to marry you, I'm not going to pretend to need to be persuaded, or that I'm worried about my job—"

An earsplitting yell of triumph erupted from Garrick's throat, the rebel yell he hadn't given since that last charge at the Yankees. Bracing himself, he slid his hands down to his very own Yankee's tiny waist, picking her up and twirling her around on the landing while she giggled in his ear.

"We're going to be married, Maggie! How about tomorrow?" he said, putting her down so he could cup her heart-shaped face in his hands.

She just laughed at him. "Garrick, have you forgotten? Celebration Day is tomorrow, and the preacher's going to be much too busy judging pies to be marrying anyone! And besides, I'd like to give my father time to come from Austin. Oh, you'll *like* him, Garrick, I'm sure you will! The two of you will get along famously, talking about newspapering! And I'd like to have a special dress...."

He sighed, but couldn't find it in his heart to deny her these things that women always wanted. Couldn't deny himself, either, the sight of her in a wedding dress.

"All right, we'll have a regular wedding with all the

frills and furbelows," he said, grinning down at her. "But…"

"But what?" she said, her eyes dancing as she gazed into his.

"That doesn't mean we have to say good-night *now*, does it? I'd like some more of your kisses to…ah, seal the deal, as it were," he told her.

"To seal the deal?" she echoed teasingly. "Ever the Southern businessman, aren't you?"

"Giving me a dose of my own medicine, are you, woman?" he said, remembering when he'd accused her of being "ever the Yankee businesswoman."

"Yes," she admitted. "Now shut up and kiss me, Garrick."

He growled and pulled her against him, determined to kiss the sass right out of her.

He succeeded only too well. Within minutes they were clinging to one another, afire with need. They'd kissed and touched and stroked until he couldn't imagine how he was going to manage to let her go and wait the week or two it would take to bring her father here and arrange for their marriage.

And then he heard her whispering in his ear. "Garrick, darling, make love to me, please?"

Again he wasn't sure he could be hearing her right. He stared at her, his pulse pounding in his ears. "Maggie? Are you sure?"

The smile she gave him was all-woman. "I've never been surer of anything since I came to Texas," she said. "We can wait for the wedding if you'd rather, but I want you so much, Garrick…. If that's too bold, you can pretend you didn't hear it, but—"

Now it was his turn to put a finger over her lips. He said, "I'll pretend no such thing! I'm discovering I like—no,

love—a bold, pushy Yankee woman. This one, anyway.''
He swung her door open and picked up his cane. "Come
on then, my sweet Yankee Maggie.''

A kerosene lamp and a candle by the bedside cast flick-
ering illumination in the tiny, spartan room. The furniture
consisted of a table, a chair, a bed, and a chest of drawers
with a pitcher and washbasin on it. One could cross from
one wall to the other in a few short strides. He had known
the room was small, but that hadn't mattered when he'd
pictured some bachelor pressman sleeping in it. He hadn't
fretted too much over the fact when "that Yankee
woman,'' as he'd first thought of Maggie, had stubbornly
insisted on living there.

Now that he loved Maggie, though, Garrick was ashamed
that he had let her remain in such stark quarters. It would
have to change—tomorrow! But for tonight the tiny room
would provide the privacy necessary for their first coming
together.

Garrick could see she had enlivened the plain room with
her own personal touches—an earthenware jug holding
wildflowers, a rainbow-colored quilt on her bed, a half-
dozen books she had apparently brought from home arrayed
on the shelf. He spied a frayed tintype tacked to the wall
and went closer, seeing that it was a picture of an older
man in spectacles.

"My father,'' she said, following his gaze.

Yes, he could see the resemblance—the same stubborn
chin; the same eyes, both challenging and kind; the same
generous mouth.

I love your daughter, Mr. Harper, he told the photo silently. *Your daughter deserves a lot better than me, but I
promise I'll never hurt her. And I'll protect her with my
life.*

He felt her eyes on him and knew that she had to be

wondering why he was staring so long at her father's portrait. He also knew that he wanted her every bit as much as he loved her, and that he was scared—so scared he was going to disappoint her.

"Garrick..." she murmured, and he heard the unsure note in her voice. "What are you thinking?"

He turned around then, not wanting her to believe that his hesitation was her fault.

"About how much I love you, honey," he said, "and how much I want to hold you...." Garrick still hesitated, hating to seem as if he was rushing her, but knowing he wouldn't be able to move very gracefully once he had laid his cane down. Praying she would understand, he limped over to the bed and opened his arms to her.

Maggie did understand, or at least his action didn't scare her. She went into his arms easily and gladly.

Lord, she isn't wearing a corset, he thought, and the soft, womanly feel of her went to his head faster than the best whiskey he'd ever drunk, intoxicating him, making him feel there was nothing that mattered beyond kissing her, touching her, feeling her arms around his neck, her fingers in his hair....

She opened her mouth to him before he even realized he'd wanted her to, and then he was kissing her deeply, her eager response drawing him onward. She moaned as his hand closed over her breast, stroking it, feeling the nipple harden, so close to his questing fingers, just a couple of layers of cloth away.... In some dim corner of his brain Garrick realized he could touch her bare skin if he could just find the buttons that held her inside this dress. But doing so meant his hand had to leave her warm, full breast, and for several long minutes he couldn't bring himself to give that up.

He'd been aroused, but now he was hard as a rock. He

wanted to pull her down, push her skirts up and bury himself in her. Her hands strayed down his back and he felt her urging him closer to her, closer, the feel of her hips against his threatening to drive all rational, civilized thought from his head. Damn, but it had been a long time...*too* long. He thought he was going to explode with the fire building so hotly within him....

"Garrick..." she breathed, and the sweet sound of his name on her lips reminded him that this wasn't some camp follower he could take in a few selfish thrusts, this was *Maggie*. And he wasn't the randy young soldier he had been, purchasing the services of camp whores who didn't care if he spent his lust within them up against a wall or on the bare ground, in seconds and without preliminaries. He wanted this night to be the most wonderful one Maggie had ever known.

He wasn't the same man physically as that randy young soldier, either, dammit, he thought when he felt a twinge of phantom pain streaking down his right leg.

To distract himself, he made his hands leave her breasts and find the buttons that extended down her spine like a regiment marching in single file. He saw her close her eyes and lean into him as each button forced out of its loop revealed another inch of skin and then the lacy camisole beneath. When he had the dress fully opened down to her waist, he pulled it off over her head and gazed at the proud beauty of her breasts straining against the thin, ribbon-trimmed cotton beneath.

Garrick fumbled for the fastening of her petticoat, but he'd never been any good at finding tiny buttons among all the folds and flounces of that female garment, and this time was no different. At last Maggie took pity on him and found them for him; then, as the creamy white cloth sagged around her hips, she pulled it down and stepped out of it.

"Now you," she urged, as he stared at her, clad in just a thin camisole and drawers. She reached out, her fingers liberating the buttons on his shirtfront with nimble efficiency, pulling the fabric out of his waistband and pushing the shirt off his chest and arms until it puddled at his heels.

"Maggie," he murmured, "I need to—"

"Yes," she interrupted, her emerald eyes glowing. "Me, too. Take me, Garrick."

He wished he could do just that without another thought, without any more of the deliberate thinking ahead that a handicapped man must employ.

"Honey, first I have to..." he began. "My leg...you understand, don't you, that it's necessary..." He couldn't bring himself to say the words *I have to take it off.* "Blow out the lamp, please?"

Making it more difficult to see her was the last thing he wanted to do, but he had to shield her as much as he could from the less-than-lovely reality of what he must do next.

Garrick blessed the shadows that closed around him as she complied. Careful not to look at her, he unfastened his trousers and pushed them down, stepping out of them just as she had shed her petticoat. Still wearing his union suit, which was cut off above the end of his right leg, he sank down on the bed, his hands moving to the straps that bound the wooden appendage to him.

Then he felt the mattress sag slightly as she sat down on the other side of the bed.

His hands froze above the straps, and he felt his confidence slipping.... "Maggie," he whispered hoarsely, looking at her over his shoulder. "Do you...*can* you...really want this? Want me? We can stop now, you know. I'll still love you, you know that—it's just—"

"Hush!" she whispered back, reaching over to lay a gentle finger on his lips. "Do what you have to do to be ready for me, love.'' He heard the corn shuck mattress rustle, and saw her sink back on the pillows.

Resolutely Garrick turned around, his mind filled with the sight of her hair spread out over the pillow and her eyes gleaming with mysterious secrets. His fingers struggled to undo the straps, and at last he was free. Carefully, he pushed the wooden leg under the bed, where it was out of sight but still within reach. Then he began to unwind the wrappings that padded his stump and protected it as much as possible from the friction of the wood socket.

He felt the cool evening breeze caress the sore, irritated flesh, and for a moment he just rubbed the aching limb, anticipating the moment he must turn around and see her eyes on him. On his leg.

''Garrick...I need you....''

Chapter Twenty-Two

Maggie was aware, of course, that Garrick was nervous, that he was fearful of being rejected as he had been by his wife, simply because of his altered body.

She put her heart into her voice. "Garrick, I need you," she said again. Praying he wouldn't think she was a shameless hussy, she raised herself up, pulled off her camisole, then knelt behind him and began to unbutton his unionsuit, kissing his neck and the side of his cheek as she did so.

As her naked breasts brushed his back, he groaned, leaning on his extended arms, his eyes closed, until she had pulled the one-piece undergarment off his shoulders and down to his waist. Then he yanked it impatiently the rest of the way off.

He turned around, then stopped still, obviously aware that even the single candle flame revealed the reality of his body. His eyes dared her—no, *commanded* her to look.

Maggie lowered her eyes, finding nothing so awful about the leg that ended just above the knee joint, any more than she had before, the day he had returned with the posse. Nothing that should have made Cecilia, if she had really loved him, treat him as she had.

"I love you, Garrick," Maggie said. "Please, make love to me."

Triumph—and relief, too—flared fiercely in his eyes. Uttering a growl of pure male arousal, he pulled her down with him so that they were lying side by side, her soft breasts flattened against the hard, muscular planes of his chest, his hands cupping her buttocks, pulling her up against his manhood, which was once more throbbing and ready. He lowered his mouth to hers, shattering what was left of her control with the hunger of his kisses, until at last he raised his head.

"One of us," he rasped, tugging meaningfully at the drawers she had forgotten about, "still has too many clothes on."

Maggie quite agreed, and obligingly untied the tapes that held the garment around her waist so it could join his union suit on the floor.

He sank back beside her, but not to kiss her mouth again. Instead, he took one of her nipples between his lips, caressing it with his tongue, then drawing it deeper into his mouth, suckling until she arched wildly against him. The riveting sensations his mouth produced within her rocketed straight from her breast to her abdomen, making it feel heavy and tingly. Somewhere in the room, a voice called Garrick's name over and over like a litany, a voice that seemed disembodied from her.

"Ah, Maggie, *my* Maggie," he growled. "You make me feel so good, woman…won't you let me make *you* feel good?"

He was asking for permission to go further, she knew, but the truth was she positively ached for more of his touch. She kissed him in answer and was rewarded with the feel of his hand straying down between her legs, parting the curls there and stroking her until all she could do was moan and writhe against him while her own fingers tangled in his hair.

They were still lying on their sides. Garrick's breathing was as harsh and uneven as hers, and she could feel his arousal, hard and throbbing, pushing against her.

"Maggie, I...it's been a long time, love...." he whispered. "I don't know how much longer I can wait...I don't want to hurt you, honey...." His eyes were full of loving concern.

"Don't you worry about that," Maggie told him. "Garrick, please...I want you—I want you *now*...."

Her words, plus her hands on his backside, urging him closer, were enough, and with a single thrust, he was inside her.

She'd been so anxious that his discovery of her lack of virginity would cause him to stop at this point—and he filled her so quickly and completely—that his penetration did cause her to flinch. Instantly he was still, studying her face with concern.

"I'm sorry, honey, but it won't hurt again, I swear," he said in that drawl she'd come to love.

"It's stopped hurting already," she told him with a smile, and to encourage him to continue, she rotated her hips against him.

It was all the assurance he needed. He began to move against her again, slowly, in and out, his manhood stroking her womanly center until at last she cried out for release.

He gave it to her, and, gasping from the sweet agony of it, she drowned in a flood tide of bursting heat and light. And then he took his own release, and lay beside her.

"Now you can't get out of marrying me—you know that, don't you?" Garrick said some time later, after they had roused from an exhausted doze. He was grinning teasingly.

Maggie grinned back, thinking she had never been so happy in her life. "You sho' you want to marry a *Yankee* woman, *Mistah* Garrick?" she teased with an exaggerated Southern accent. "Why, she cain't possahbly be a *lady*—a lady's place is in the home."

"Anyone who thinks you're not a lady will have me to contend with," Garrick growled. Then he cleared his throat. "Now, on another subject... Maggie, honey, ever since I fell in love with you, I haven't felt comfortable about you living up here in this cramped little room. I must admit," he confessed with a wolfish smile, "it was mighty handy having someplace we could be alone tonight. But now I want you living in my house—tomorrow!"

"But I can't come live with you tomorrow," she said, smiling at his eagerness. "The town would be scandalized—and what about Johnny? That's not a good example—"

"No, it's not, and of course I have no intention of ruining your good name that way," he agreed. "But can't we get married tomorrow, after all? I'm not sure I can go back to being a gentleman around you anymore, either, not now that I know what's under that starchy dark dress," he continued, with a meaningful caress of the bare breast nearest his hand. "I'll even wait until the preacher's done judging his darn pies."

She laughed. "Garrick, I'd like for us to have a proper ceremony, with both our families present, so the folks of Gillespie Springs won't think 'that Yankee woman' caught you in a moment of poor judgment."

He groaned, sinking back against the pillow. "Sticking to your guns, huh? I'm just afraid if I give you time to think, you'll have sense enough to change your mind."

"No chance of that, love. And think of how darling it

will be if Johnny is our ring bearer! Do you think he'd be
willing to do that?''

"Johnny adores you. He'd hop and skip all the way up
to the altar," Garrick told her. "All right, if you really want
a formal wedding, that's what we'll do. But I want you to
agree to move over to Cal and Livy's. Once it's known
we're engaged, you won't be able to keep living up here."

"Why?" she asked, though she already knew what he
would say.

"Honey, this is a very small town. People will talk—
and you can bet they'll start watching to see when I leave
here in the evenings—and if I come back."

"Did anyone see you tonight?"

He shrugged. "I don't think so."

"Then we shall have to be very, very clever, won't we?"
she said, running a fingernail down his taut abdomen, feeling him tense, and seeing his manhood begin to firm again.
"Because I have *no* intention of giving this up until the
wedding, now that you've given me a taste, Mr. Garrick
Devlin. Yankee women can be so insatiable, you know...."
To demonstrate her point, she lowered her head and flicked
her tongue against his nipple.

"No," he said in mock disbelief. "Show me."

His eyes, blue and fierce and glowing, dared her, and she
answered the dare by extending one leg over his hip and
pulling herself atop him, sliding down with maddening
slowness on his newly revived manhood.

"Dear Maggie," he said, sinking back into the pillows
and circling her nipples with his thumbs. "If you are any
example of Northern womanhood, the generals should have
let you Yankee women do the fighting. I swear we would
have surrendered sooner."

Maggie could hear the stir among those already present
at Gillespie Springs Park when she and Garrick, accom-

panied by a capering, excited Johnny, arrived together. They were not touching, for Garrick had insisted on carrying the picnic basket under one arm, while the other hand held his cane, but evidently something—perhaps the way neither could take their eyes off each other, or the radiant smiles they wore—alerted those watching that *something had changed.*

"Well, if y'all don't look like the cat that swallowed the canary, both of you," called Olivia Devlin, ensconced in the shade of a tall cottonwood on the bank of the spring, her husband, Cal, by her side. Mayor Long and the saloon keeper, accompanied by their spouses, were also sitting nearby, as were Phoebe Stone, the preacher and his wife. Eureka Jones and his sister, Bessie, with Jovita Mendez and her son and daughter-in-law, and a flock of black-and brown-skinned children, were sitting under another cottonwood, close enough to hear.

Johnny left Garrick and Maggie to run up to his aunt Olivia. "My daddy ain't no cat! Miss Maggie ain't neither!" he protested.

"Isn't, not ain't, Johnny," Garrick corrected gently, still smiling as he and Maggie reached his brother and sister-in-law. "And Aunt Livy just means we look like we have a secret. Good morning, Livy, Cal."

"Isn't," Johnny repeated obediently. "They do have a secret! The secret is my daddy is getting married! To Miss Maggie! She's gonna be my new ma!"

Maggie felt herself blushing as Garrick put his arm about her waist and drew her near while pleased exclamations and shouts of congratulation echoed around them—and an audible gasp from Phoebe, who looked as if *she* had swallowed something very unpleasant.

"I knew something was comin'!" Maggie heard Bessie

announce. "That girl sure had her mind on anything but her supper last night, and now we know what! And I know why you were lookin' like you knew somethin' no one else did, Miz Jovita!"

"I'm so pleased for you, Maggie," Olivia said, taking her by the hand and urging her over to where an extra quilt lay spread out for them. Garrick followed as soon as Cal and the rest of the men were done with their backslapping and telling him Maggie was much too good for him.

"Oh, won't your mother be pleased, Cal?" Livy said. "Have y'all picked a date? I hope it's soon! Oh, wouldn't our yard be perfect for the reception, Cal?"

"Now just hold your horses, Livy!" Cal said, grinning. "My brother and his prospective bride might have ideas of their own!"

Maggie, feeling as if she were in the midst of a wondrous dream that she had no desire to wake up from, heard Garrick say something to the effect that while they hadn't had time to pick a date yet, he wasn't going to allow Maggie too much time to change her mind. She heard herself murmur something in agreement.

When she had awakened this morning, she'd been alone, for she and Garrick had agreed he would leave well before dawn so as to preserve her reputation. Dimly she remembered Garrick kissing her goodbye sometime during the night, after the last time they had made love. But he had arrived back at the office just as she was coming down the stairs, and together they had walked to Garrick's home on South Street and told Johnny and Jovita the happy news over breakfast.

Maggie stole a look at her fiancé as the others continued to tease and pepper them with questions and comments. On the day she'd first arrived in Gillespie Springs, she had thought Garrick Devlin a good-looking man in a stern, austere sort of way. Now, however, with the lines of chronic bitterness and suspicion erased as if by magic, he was truly handsome. Someone had just said something humorous, and Garrick had responded with an irresistibly devastating grin.

She felt a tugging at her hand. "Miss Maggie, I'm hungry," said Johnny. "Help me find a jelly sam'wich in that basket?"

"I sure will, honey," she said, reaching for the wicker basket Jovita had packed. *Dear Lord, I don't deserve this second chance for happiness, but please don't let me ever disappoint this wonderful man and his son.*

"Well, if everyone is done billing and cooing," Phoebe Stone groused, "I think it's time the reverend did the pie judging. My strawberry supreme will soon be wilted in this heat...." She stopped as the sounds of hoofbeats, the creaking of leather and a metallic jingling became audible.

"What's that?" queried someone.

"Sounds like a whole passel of riders comin' from town."

A minute later, an entire company of blue-coated federal troops rode into Gillespie Springs Park.

Chapter Twenty-Three

Garrick found himself automatically tensing at the sight of the blue uniforms. He had to consciously remind himself that the war was over and had been for three years. Texas was still under federal military rule, but everyone in the park was a law-abiding citizen and so had nothing to fear. Still, he couldn't stop the churning in his gut—or the throbbing of his absent leg—at the sight of the soldiers in their dark blue.

"Papa, who are they?" Johnny, round-eyed, queried, pointing at the mounted newcomers.

Garrick put his arm around the little boy's waist. "Soldiers, son," he explained in a low voice, seeing out of the corner of his eye that Cal was the first to step forward.

"Why?"

Garrick knew the boy meant why had they come? He shrugged. He wished he knew the answer; he had a feeling it wasn't good.

Cal drew near to the officer in charge, a dark-haired, mustachioed fellow who looked as if he probably cut a dashing figure at army social affairs.

"Afternoon, Captain," Cal said, touching the brim of his hat.

"Well! I must say I'm relieved to find some people! We came through town, and I'd begun to think it was deserted!" said the man atop the restive bay. "So this is where everyone's hiding!"

"Hiding?" Cal drew the word out. "Not at all, sir. It's Celebration Day, and I reckon everyone in town is here. I'm Sheriff Devlin. Anything I can do for you? If you're lookin' to water your horses, this creek is about the finest water you'll find for miles, but there's a better approach downstream about fifty yards." He pointed the way.

"Captain Richard Burke, sir," the officer said with a curt nod. "Yes, we'll water the horses—it's been a long ride from San Antonio. But that's not all we've come for." His dark eyes scrutinized the crowd, as if wanting to assure himself he had everyone's attention.

"Well, we'll render any assistance possible, if you'll let us know what you need," Cal prompted.

"I hope you still feel that way after you've heard me out, Sheriff," Captain Burke said with a cynical twist of his lips. "You could say my orders are twofold, sir," he added, "though it's my opinion that the two items are entwined. My company has been sent to investigate reports of raiding marauders—"

"Well, thank God for that," Mayor Long interrupted, starting forward. "Cal, sounds like your prayers for help have been heeded at last, no doubt thanks to the good offices of your brother here—" he nodded to Garrick "—in publicizing the reports of their depredations—"

Captain Burke held up a gauntleted hand. "As I was saying, we're here to investigate the reports of outlaw raids, *and we will stop them.*"

"Hallelujah!" cried Reverend Poole. "It's about time!"

Captain Burke allowed himself a cold smile that didn't reach his eyes.

"And the other matter?" Cal prompted, just as Garrick became aware that Maggie's face had drained of color and looked a sickly green.

"What's the matter, sweetheart?" he asked, only to have her make a hushing gesture and turn her face away.

"It's come to the attention of army headquarters that Gillespie Springs has become a hotbed of Confederate resistance," Burke was saying to Cal. "Would you be the same Devlin who edits the newspaper? The *Gillespie Springs Gazette,* I believe the rag is called?"

Garrick saw Cal shoot him a warning glance.

"Now, hold on, Captain," Cal said, tight-lipped. "What call do you have to be criticizing our newspaper like that?"

Burke's voice was a whiplash. "Just answer the question, Sheriff. *I said, are you the Devlin who edits the newspaper?*"

Garrick stood, unable to remain silent any longer. "'Hotbed of Confederate resistance?'" he mocked. "Horsefeathers! And I'd use a blunter term if there weren't ladies present, Captain. What's the basis for making such a ridiculous claim?"

"And you are—?"

"Garrick Devlin, owner and editor of the *Gillespie Springs Gazette,* the town's newspaper."

Captain Burke's smile took on a truly nasty quality. "Well now. What basis, you ask? This one, sir." Reaching into his breast pocket, he pulled out a folded paper. When he opened it, Garrick could see the masthead of the *Gazette.*

"This seditious rag is what has led headquarters to draw such a conclusion," snapped Captain Burke, shaking the paper like a dog would shake a rat. "In this paper you print constant, unremitting and libelous criticism of the army and the military government, as well as the government in Washington. Do you deny it?"

"I do not, sir," Garrick growled. "The last time I heard, we believed in a free press in this country. And I haven't printed a thing that wasn't either provable or a matter of opinion—*my* opinion—or aren't Southerners free to have opinions anymore?"

"Southerners," the captain retorted, "would be wise to remember who were the conquerors and who the conquered, especially if they ever hope to be received back into the United States of America. Remember what befell Atlanta and Vicksburg, all of you—such ravaging could still be repeated anywhere in the secessionist states, if conditions warrant. And to help the people of this town remember, I am hereby arresting you and impounding your printing press, so that the flood of inflammatory material will cease. Take him, men."

Four of the soldiers near Burke dismounted and started toward Garrick, their pistols drawn.

"Captain, no! You can't do that!" The cry was Maggie's, and Garrick looked back in time to see her streak toward the captain's horse, her flaming hair streaming out behind her, her pale face awash in tears.

He would have tried to stop her, but just as Maggie made her outburst, Johnny ran forward, too. His little hands clenched into fists, he screamed, "No! You can't take my papa! Don't you touch him!" Terrified that the nervous bay would rear and bring its hoofs down on Johnny's head, Garrick grabbed his son by his shirttail and hauled him up short.

Immediately he and his son were surrounded by men in blue. Garrick raised his hands in surrender.

Maggie, meanwhile, had reached the officer's side and was pulling at his gauntlet. Just as Garrick had feared, her sudden action did cause the bay to rear, but Maggie quickly jumped out of harm's way.

"Whoa!" Burke snapped, sawing ruthlessly at the bit until the horse returned its forelegs to the ground. Then he turned to Maggie, snapping, "Madam, don't you have any sense at all? You might have been killed! I—" He stared at her, and all of a sudden Garrick saw Burke's face metamorphose from stern to jovial.

"Why, Miss Margaret Harper, as I live and breathe!" he said, eyeing her with hot avidity. "Whatever are you doing in this Texas backwater? This is indeed a pleasant surprise! Why, I had no idea you had left Austin."

Garrick couldn't see Maggie's face, but he could hear the dead, expressionless quality of her voice. "And I thought you were still in Washington, Captain Burke. What am I doing here? I work for the *Gazette,* and I'm telling you you have no grounds to arrest Garrick Devlin! Every word that's been printed has been typeset by me, and I know my employer's rights! Garrick might not be exactly complimentary of the military and federal government, but he's written nothing that would qualify as sedition! You cannot lawfully arrest him and you know it! Nor can you impound his printing press!"

Captain Richard Burke sat back in the saddle, his face one big smirk that Garrick longed to wipe off with his bare knuckles. "Maggie mine, that fire and passion are what I always loved about you," he continued in amused, caressing tones.

Garrick's heart gave a painful, sickening lurch as he saw the captain touch a gloved finger to Maggie's cheek, a feeling that didn't subside when he saw her retreat backward, out of his reach.

"Papa, what is he talkin' 'bout? Tell them to go away!" Johnny demanded, his little face screwed up in anger and worry.

"Hush, Johnny."

"Why, Maggie," Burke said in his oily voice, "you're defending this seditious rebel? *And* calling him by his first name? My, my…what's been happening since you came to this little one-horse town? Can it be that you've found happiness in *another* man's arms, after what we had together? *Tsk, tsk,* my dear, to have forgotten me so completely!" He made no attempt to lower his voice.

Garrick couldn't believe his ears, and he was agonizingly aware that the curious townspeople were listening avidly. Some of them had even inched closer as Burke spoke.

"What I've been doing is really none of your affair, Captain," she said coolly, her voice pitched low enough that only Burke, Garrick and a few soldiers could hear it.

Burke's eyes went from Maggie to Garrick and back again. He was clearly enjoying himself.

"No, my dear, it's none of *my* affair. Regrettably, the days of *our* affair are over. I no longer hold the place in your, ah—*affections,* shall we say?—that I once did."

"You misbegotten son of a—" With a total disregard for the armed soldiers surrounding him, Garrick lunged at the man, intending to pull him off his horse and beat his face into a bloody pulp.

He hadn't gone three feet before he was pinioned by two of the soldiers, while the other two leveled their pistols at his head. Johnny shrieked *"Papa!"* and grabbed his trouser leg. The mounted remainder of the company raised and cocked their rifles.

Maggie screamed. Running forward, she grabbed Johnny, dislodging his frantic hold on Garrick, and carried him over to Livy.

"Hold your fire!" Burke shouted over Maggie's screams and the frightened cries of the child. Once again the clamor had agitated Burke's horse, and he had to fight to control the bay.

"Garrick! Don't move! And for God's sake, keep quiet!" Cal pleaded. "You can't defend Maggie if you're shot!"

Maggie stared at him, her eyes huge and frightened in her white face. Then she turned back to Burke, who had regained control of the bay. "Captain Burke, call them off!" she cried, pointing at the soldiers holding Garrick. "Can't you see you've frightened his poor little boy half to death?"

Burke, red faced now, his officer's hat a muddy, trampled remnant on the ground, swiped a hand through the hair that had fallen over his eyes, raking it out of the way.

"Why, Maggie, I do believe you care a great deal for this sorry remnant of a man," he sneered, ignoring her reference to the child as his contemptuous gaze raked over Garrick. "What is the nature of your relationship, may I ask?"

Maggie met his rudeness in stony silence, her green eyes blazing.

"Now, Maggie, this is no time for discretion," Burke admonished in his silky, insinuating voice. "You might well save your lover a great deal of grief!"

Her face as red as her hair, Maggie said between clenched teeth, "Damn you, Richard Burke! Garrick Devlin and I are engaged to marry."

"Ah…" He drew out the syllable, his dark eyes dancing with malice. "I see, Maggie mine."

"Don't call me that!" she cried. "You're less to me than what your horse just dropped," she said, pointing to the malodorous pile the bay had deposited on the grass.

His face flushing with fury at her words, Burke nevertheless managed to wag a gloved finger at Maggie. "Uh-uh, Maggie mine, let there be no nastiness between us who were once so…*close*," he said. Then, looking around to make sure he still had the townspeople's undivided attention, he added, "And as a favor to you, my dear—for old time's sake—I'm willing to cancel your crippled sweetheart's arrest, providing you will vouch for him."

"I've already done so, damn you!" Maggie hissed.

Burke ignored her curse, smiling urbanely. "Release him, men."

Garrick felt the soldiers' steely grips fall away, though the other two kept their pistols at the ready.

"And as a further gesture of goodwill," Burke continued, "I'll cancel my order to impound his printing press, providing that no seditious words are printed while we are—ahem!—visiting the fair town of Gillespie Springs." He turned to Garrick, who had been assisted back to his feet by his brother. "All copy is to be shown to me, Devlin, before our beauteous Maggie prints so much as a word, agreed?"

Garrick snapped, "I'll see you in hell first, you Yankee sidewinder! I'll be damned if I'll agree to censorship!"

Cal stepped between Garrick and the captain, saying, "My brother will cooperate fully, for the hopefully short period of your stay. May I suggest you make your camp right here in the park? There's plenty of space, water...you'll be free to concentrate on the main reason you came here, the outlaws. You've got nothing to fear from my brother, who's as law-abiding as they come."

"Don't I?" Burke retorted. "If looks could kill, I'd be on the way to the undertaker now, Sheriff. And don't worry, we'll get around to finding the outlaws, just as soon as I've satisfied myself your brother and the whole town aren't plotting an insurrection! So while I thank you for your suggestion, sir, I'm going to have to pass up this lovely park as our headquarters. It's too far beyond the center of town for me to keep an eye on this firebrand brother of yours, and those who may be in cahoots with him. My company will be pleased to take up residence in the lovely hotel we passed on our way out here, so we can be right in the middle of things, so to speak.''

Mayor Long, sputtering in indignation, started forward. ''In my hotel? But that's my business, sir! How am I to make a living, let alone provide shelter to travelers, if your troops are occupying every room, no doubt wearing their spurs to bed and burning holes in the mattresses?''

Burke grinned. ''Why, are you implying my men are anything but complete gentlemen, sir? You'll be reimbursed handsomely by the government, sir, someday....'' His voice was drowned out by his men's hearty guffaws. Then he barked an order, and the soldiers wheeled their mounts and trotted downstream to water their horses.

Chapter Twenty-Four

Gillespie Springs' Celebration Day was clearly ruined.

"Now what am I to do with all these pies?" Phoebe Stone fumed to no one in particular. Not a soul answered her, for they were too busy packing up their picnic baskets and blankets, looking everywhere but at Garrick and Maggie.

"Papa, why's everybody leavin'?" Johnny questioned. "What about the picnic?"

"Shh, son, I'll tell you about it later," Garrick said. *Once I figure it out.*

Within minutes the park had cleared, leaving only Garrick, Maggie, Cal, Livy, Jovita Mendez and Johnny.

None of the adults seemed to know what to say. Finally Jovita cleared her throat. "I weel take Johnny home, Señor Devlin. You and Señorita Maggie weel want to talk."

Talk? That was the last thing Garrick wanted to do, especially with Maggie. He wanted—needed—to be alone.

"Thank you, Jovita. Johnny, you go with her. Papa'll be along home in a while," Garrick said, his hand on his son's shoulder. He waited till they were several yards away before adding, "Cal, I'd be obliged if you and Livy would see Maggie back to the office—and would you mind taking my basket, too? I'll get it later."

He saw Maggie flinch as if from a physical blow. But he couldn't comfort her, for he was in too much pain himself.

"But..." Livy began, then her voice trailed off. She went to Maggie, putting her arm around her, murmuring something comforting and drawing her away from Garrick and Cal in the direction of their house across the road.

Hesitantly, Cal put his hand on Garrick's shoulder. "Now don't go and let your pride make you do something foolish, big brother. It doesn't matter what happened between Maggie and some other man before. What matters is the love you have between you now. She's hurting, Garrick. She's been publicly humiliated by that arrogant fool."

She's been humiliated? Garrick wanted to shout. What about me? I've been given back my press and my freedom by my fiancée's former paramour! But he didn't want to take a chance that Maggie might hear him.

His jaw set, he said, "I'll talk to her, Cal. I don't know when. Please, just do as I asked and take her back to the office."

Cal stared at him for a long moment, a muscle in his temple twitching. He looked as if he wanted to say something more, but he didn't. He just walked away, following Livy and Maggie out of the park.

"Maggie, honey, don't you worry, he'll come around," Livy was saying as they walked onto her porch, her arm around Maggie's shoulders. "Men are funny creatures, full of pride—*especially* my dear brother-in-law. But he'll calm down, and when he does, he'll realize that he still loves you, and that's much more important than the lies that man told—"

"But they weren't lies, not really," Maggie said woodenly, swiping at her tear-blinded eyes. "I...we...Burke and I..." She stopped and took a deep breath, then blurted, "We were lov—no, that's not accurate. He never loved me, I know that now. He just used me. What a fool I was, what an innocent fool! He ruined my good name in Austin, and then went on his merry way. Oh, Lord, Livy, I feel so dirty, so ashamed!"

They were inside now, and Livy ushered her over to a rocking chair in the parlor and knelt beside her.

"Now, none of that. You're *not* dirty. You made a mistake, that's all. You were tricked by a skillful seducer. It's happened to plenty of women, God knows. But Garrick's a good man, and he'll—"

Maggie interrupted her. "Poor Garrick. How I must remind him of his late wife. Jovita told me about her, you know. I...I have to leave," she said, starting to rise as the tears began again. "I have to pack my things...go somewhere...."

"You'll do no such thing," Livy said firmly, putting a hand on Maggie's shoulder as if she would hold her there by physical force if necessary. "Cal, tell her she's not to think of leaving town," she implored, just as her husband came into the parlor.

Cal nodded, looking awkward as he saw Maggie's tear-drenched face. Reaching inside his pocket, he handed her a handkerchief. "That's right, Miss Maggie. Give Garrick some time. I know my brother. He can be a hothead, but he'll settle down, you'll see."

Maggie shook her head. "No. Everyone will always know. They'll look at me and think, *that wanton hussy.* And Garrick—I can't expect him to want to have anything to do with me, not after what Burke told the whole town, not after what Garrick already endured at Cecilia's hands.

Oh, I knew it was a mistake to think I could start over...."
She buried her face in Cal's handkerchief and felt Livy
gather her into her arms. For long minutes she could do
nothing but sob.

Finally, the tears ran out, and she raised her head from
where it had been resting against Livy's bosom. Cal looked
ill-at-ease, but he had remained. "Livy, honey, maybe you
should tell her..." he began in that deep, rumbling drawl
of his.

Livy exchanged glances with her husband, then turned
back to Maggie. "Now you listen to me, Maggie Harper.
You're going to survive this, and folks here will go on to
other gossip. I should know, honey, for I lived down a
similar scandal," she said, "with Cal's help." Once again,
husband and wife exchanged loving, intimate looks.

Under other circumstances, Maggie would have voiced
her curiosity about what Livy Devlin could have possibly
done to cause a scandal. She was so *good* that Maggie
couldn't imagine her saying "damn," let alone causing
gossip. But that secret would have to remain between Livy
and her husband, at least for now.

Garrick wasn't Cal, and he wouldn't get over the damning revelation about a woman he had come to trust and
love, thought Maggie. His ability to trust had been badly
damaged before she'd come, and now it would be gone
forever.

"Why don't I put a pot of water on to boil and make us
some chamomile tea?" Livy said in encouraging tones.
"That always makes me feel better. And then you can go
up in the guest room and lie down for a while, Maggie,
and sleep. I just know things won't look so bleak after
you've had a rest."

Maggie choked back a bitter laugh. If only tea and a nap
could wipe out shame! "Thanks, Livy, you've been very

kind," she said, taking the other woman's hand and giving it a squeeze. "But I...I think I'd better go back to my room at the *Gazette*."

Livy must have sensed her determination, for she shrugged. "All right, honey, but you know we're here if you need us. *Anytime.* Don't you dare just leave town! Cal, you walk her back to the *Gazette*," she said, turning to her husband, "and don't you let anyone say anything...unpleasant to her."

Once he had been left alone at the park, Garrick made his way to the creek and lowered himself to its bank, staring at the clear water flowing over the stones in the creekbed, but seeing only Maggie's distraught face. He couldn't hear the happy gurgling of the spring, either, only Burke's damning words: *You've found happiness in another man's arms....*

Another. Which meant he, Garrick, had not been the first man to make love to Maggie Harper.

Well, he'd accepted that possibility from the first moment he'd thought seriously about falling in love with her. A beautiful working woman, far from home, might very well have had a lover before.

Garrick had been so full of passionate love for Maggie last night when they'd come together in her bed that he hadn't spared a thought for her lack of maidenly shyness or the absence of virginal blood on the sheets. It hadn't matter then. Whether he was her first lover or not, by God, he was going to be her husband, and they would love one another, Johnny and any babies they might have together until the end of time. Maybe he should even be grateful to that first man, whoever he was, for Maggie had come to him eagerly, open about her desire and able to give and receive pleasure in his arms. Garrick liked to think the man had been a soldier, killed in the war before he could return and marry the girl he'd made a woman.

He hadn't ever imagined *meeting* a previous lover, let alone having Maggie's seducer taunt him in front of the whole town and uncover her secret shame as if he were publicly stripping away her clothes.

Now the face he saw in the crystal depths of the spring was not Maggie's, but Cecilia's.

I couldn't bear the sight of you, you deformed cripple. Everyone knew I was too disgusted to remain your wife, to share your bed, to let you touch me! Yes, I hung horns on you with Will Prentice, a whole man! And now here you are, shamed again, 'cause everyone knows you fell in love with a Yankee woman who's no better than she should be! Fool!

How could Maggie have given herself to that pretentious, arrogant Yankee? Richard Burke had kissed her, had run his greedy hands all over her, had touched her in deep, intimate places....

No! Garrick couldn't think of that! That way lay insanity. But it was all he *could* think of, and he drew his good knee up against his forehead and wept for the first time since he had lost his right leg.

He doubted the spring was deep enough to drown him. It was a damn shame, he thought. And he certainly didn't have a pistol on him, worse luck, or even a whittling knife or a rope.

Finally he raised his head, exhausted. *You can't take the coward's way out,* he reminded himself. *You have a child.* Sure, Cal and Livy would take care of Johnny, but how would the little boy survive if a second parent died and left him? And besides, Garrick was a Devlin, and Devlins weren't quitters.

All right, so he had to go on. But he didn't know how

he was going to explain to Johnny why the announcement he and Maggie had made this morning wasn't true any longer. There would be no wedding, and Maggie wouldn't become Johnny's mother. Garrick was certainly glad that a three-year-old child wouldn't have understood the slanderous things Burke had said about Maggie, but how was he going to explain it to him?

And he had another thought, less important, but nonetheless painful—how was he going to be able to walk back into town, knowing that everyone was talking about him, that everyone knew his most personal, private business? He could imagine what they'd whisper when they saw him: *That's Garrick Devlin, poor man. Lost his leg in the war, then his wife left him, and when she died everyone found out she'd committed bigamy, but that Devlin was the father of her son! And the next woman he picked turned out to have a past.... Why, my dear, what did he expect, picking some strange Yankee woman who just arrived in town? And then the Yankee woman's fancy man returned and told everyone he'd had known her—'known her' in the biblical sense, naturally. Unlucky in love, poor Garrick Devlin, but he had a little boy from his slut of a first wife, so he had to just go on and raise him. He never trusted a female again, however, and remained a bitter old bachelor for the rest of his life, clumping around with that wooden leg....*

No, he *wouldn't* trust a woman ever again, by God.

He really ought to be getting home, he thought, struggling clumsily to his feet. Jovita'd be worried about him, and Johnny would be plaguing her with questions she couldn't answer.

But first he'd better go by the *Gazette* and see if Maggie was there, he thought, making his way toward the road that led into town. He wasn't able to explain, even to himself, why he didn't just put off until tomorrow what was likely to be a very uncomfortable meeting. He just knew he had to do it. Get it over with.

He didn't even know what he was going to say. The Garrick Devlin he had been since coming home from the war would have fired Maggie without a reference and made sure she was on the next stage out of Gillespie Springs, no matter where it was going. The sooner she left, the sooner he could get on with his life, even if there was a gaping, raw wound where his heart had been.

With Eureka Jones's help, he'd get along until he could hire another pressman—and this time he'd make damn sure to specify that the applicant be male. At the moment printing the newspaper seemed less than important, however. He couldn't even think offhand when the paper was next due to be published.

But he wasn't that same man he'd been when he first came home from the war. The arrival of little Johnny in his life had begun to thaw the ice that had grown around Garrick Devlin's heart, and the coming of Maggie had ushered in the spring. Now, even though his romance with Maggie Harper was a thing of the past, Garrick didn't know if he *could* go back to the bleakness of winter.

As much as he hurt now, he couldn't imagine never seeing Maggie again.

You don't have to decide today, he reminded himself. He'd never been an impulsive man—Sam had all the impulsiveness in the family. Cal had the tender heart. Garrick had always been the careful planner, the one who made decisions with his head, not his feelings. He'd just go and see Maggie, and maybe that would help him make his decision.

Idiot. He was thinking of this as if he was the only one who had a vote. Maybe Maggie would already have decided she couldn't survive in Gillespie Springs, not when everyone knew what she had done.

He remembered when Livy—she'd been Livy Gillespie then—had been publicly disgraced, getting pregnant when everyone knew her late husband couldn't have been the father. She had miscarried, but that hadn't stopped the town from treating Livy like a scarlet woman. It hadn't even been her fault—she had been raped—but she'd endured months of being a pariah until the truth had come out.

Maggie had no ties to Gillespie Springs as Livy had had. She had no reason to want to stay here, other than her job. And good pressmen were needed everywhere.

The thought quickened his pace.

Reaching the *Gazette* office at last, he went inside, but before his eyes could adjust to the gloom of the office interior, a voice spoke out of the darkness, startling him. "She's upstairs, Mr. Devlin. She's packin'. You aren't gonna let her go, are you?"

Once his eyes could make out the shadowy form of Eureka Jones, he saw that the black man sitting in the rear of the office had out his carving knife and was holding a block of wood, but as near as Garrick could tell, he wasn't carving a form. It looked as if he was just aimlessly whittling.

"I…I don't know, Eureka. That'll be up to Miss Harper, I imagine."

The black man stood and walked forward, his eyes entreating. "I know it isn't my place to give you advice, Mr. Devlin, but don't let your lady go. It doesn't matter what that devil did to her a long time ago, it just matters what y'all are to each other now."

No, it wasn't Eureka Jones's business, and Garrick had already had the same counsel from Cal.

He bit his lip to cut off the caustic retort he'd started to make. "We'll have to see, Eureka. But I'm going to need you to work for me, no matter what happens between Miss Maggie and myself.''

He'd expected to see relief flare in the dark eyes, but he didn't. "I know—that isn't why I said it, Mr. Devlin,'' Eureka said, and resumed his seat and his whittling.

Chapter Twenty-Five

Maggie was intent on folding her green-patterned dress just so, as if it wouldn't be a wrinkled mess when she arrived back in Austin regardless of how well she folded it!

It would be good to see Papa again, she thought, taking the picture down from the wall and wrapping it in an old *Gazette* to protect it. She felt her eyes sting a little at the prospect of having to tell him she had failed again. She'd already written him about her growing feelings for Garrick, so it wasn't as if she could pretend she was returning merely because she hadn't liked her job here. Once her father took a good look at her, he'd know the truth, anyway, even if she didn't say a word.

Then came the knock on her door, startling her so badly that she dropped the pair of slippers she was about to pack. Her heart began to thud against the restraints of her corset, and her knees felt as if they couldn't hold her up.

"Mag—Miss Harper?" she heard Garrick call through the door.

He'd come to give her her severance pay, she thought. To tell her he expected her to leave as soon as she could arrange it. Perhaps he also wanted to tell her exactly what he thought of her, and she couldn't find it in her heart to blame him. After all, she'd gotten on her high horse just as soon as she'd arrived over his assuming she couldn't be a *lady* if she was a working woman. And he'd been right, hadn't he? She wasn't a lady. A lady didn't pass herself off as innocent and lily-white when she wasn't, she thought, moving to open the door.

She invited him in with a gesture and backed up so he could enter. His face was drawn and haggard, his eyes expressionless. His gaze dropped from her face to the coppery brown traveling dress she'd donned.

"Eureka says you're leaving," he said, his voice rasping like dried sticks rubbing together.

She nodded, unable to take her eyes from him, unable to find her voice.

"You don't have to leave, Miss Harper. I still need you to print my paper."

Even if I don't need you as my bride, she finished for him silently. "There are lots of men who can do that," she said aloud. "You'll find someone. Eureka can help you till then, if you'll be sure and write legibly enough that he can translate your script. I can't possibly stay. You must be able to see that."

She could tell he could see that. He looked down for a moment, and then his eyes, still shuttered, but steady, met hers again. "But the paper..." he said quickly. "Surely you wouldn't leave me high and dry like that."

She started to tell him his damned newspaper was the least of her problems, but caught herself. "But the paper just came out yesterday, Mr. Devlin, remember? You have plenty of time to put a new one together, even without me."

He didn't look convinced. "But the soldiers have come, and that's a big story. I think there needs to be a special edition."

The thought of how Garrick Devlin would be apt to cover a federal army occupation of a Texas town made her worry for him in spite of herself. "You be careful, Garrick Devlin, or you'll end up in jail, after all, with your precious Washington press melted down into a useless lump of scrap metal," she cautioned.

"Then you'd better stay at least long enough to make sure that doesn't happen, hadn't you?" he asked her.

She couldn't interpret his expression, and decided he'd meant that in the worst possible way. She felt herself stiffening with rekindled anger—and shame.

"You mean, so I can keep influencing Captain Burke?" she said, her hands clenched on the mate to the slipper she had dropped. "Would you like me to go over to his hotel room now and offer myself? I think you'd better leave, Garrick. I'll be gone as soon as I can."

He started forward, a hand upheld. "You mistook my meaning, Maggie. I just meant so you can proofread what I'm writing and temper my hotheadedness."

I'm the hotheaded one, she thought. "I—I'm sorry. I thought you meant...but never mind. But I'd imagine having your very own Yankee censor would be the last thing you'd want."

"I don't know what I want right now," he admitted. "I just wish you wouldn't leave...at least for an issue or two. Then if you still want to..."

"Garrick, you don't know what you're asking," she told him frankly. "Can you imagine what it will be like for me to live in this town for even that long? Especially with Richard Burke right across the street at the hotel?"

Garrick's shoulders sagged. "I guess I hadn't thought of it that way," he said. "I suppose I *am* asking quite a lot. Okay, I'll have Bessie bring over your meals, if you'd prefer. Or Jovita. Or you can move in with Cal and Livy, as I suggested before.''

''Speaking of Richard Burke, Garrick, I need to tell Cal that I think I saw him at the outlaw camp! He—or a man that looked an awful lot like him—was standing with the horses when I was spying on them, before they nearly caught me. He wasn't wearing a uniform, but... '' She stopped as another thought struck her. ''Garrick, he was currying a bay horse! The same bay horse he was riding today!''

Garrick frowned. ''Maggie, that's impossible. How could he have been with the outlaws, wearing civilian clothes, two days ago, and riding with his company into Gillespie Springs today? No, as much as I'd like to see the son of a bi—'' he stopped himself ''—the *scoundrel* jailed, you likely saw a man that looked like Burke, not Burke himself. But back to what you're going to do, Maggie—what about staying, at least for a while?''

She sighed. ''I really shouldn't even consider it,'' she said, and saw the flare of something—it was too dim to be hope—in his blue eyes. ''But I will, though I'm not about to hide up here as if I were under house arrest. I'll go take my meals as usual.'' She held up her hand when she saw he was about to protest. ''And I'm not staying because I want to be your censor, either. I'll stay because I still believe it *was* Burke among the outlaws.''

''Maggie, if you're thinking of going to look for the outlaws again—''

''No, don't worry,'' she said, touched that Garrick still cared enough that he didn't want to see her harmed. ''I mean I'd like to see him found out for the snake he is.''

''Hell hath no fury...'' he mocked her, but gently.

''Like a woman scorned,'' she finished for him. ''I'll show you it's more than that. But please...just let me say this—Garrick. I'm so sorry I wasn't…honest with you. You deserved that much, at least. I—"

He held up his hand and headed for the door. "Don't say any more, Maggie, not right now.…"

Maggie deliberately waited until twilight to cross the street to the hotel to fetch her supper, hoping the soldiers had eaten by now and settled themselves in the saloon to drink the evening away. The dining room had just closed, but Bessie probably would have saved her something, just as she had on other occasions when Maggie had worked late and had nearly forgotten to eat. She would take whatever Bessie had wrapped up for her back to her room and eat it there.

Sure enough, the cook had set aside a roast beef sandwich and a big slice of peach pie for her. "Here, honey," Bessie said, pulling her big hands out of the soapy water and drying them on a towel before handing her the paper-wrapped food. "I was gonna bring this over if I didn't see you. Now you eat it all up. A body has to eat, I always say. And don't you be frettin' about Mr. Devlin—he'll come around. Don't you be leavin', either. Eureka told me you were ponderin' about it and Mr. Devlin talked you out of it. See, that means he don't wanna lose you."

Maggie felt tears sting her eyes at the black woman's soothing voice. "Thank you, Bessie. I—I think he's already…we've already lost each other. But I appreciate your kindness."

Bessie didn't look convinced. "And you watch out for those soldier boys when you walk back to the *Gazette,* Miss Maggie," she warned. "A mess of 'em were just whoopin' it up in the bathhouse, and I reckon they'll head for the cribs next. You go straight in the front entrance of the *Gazette,* don't cut up that side street to the back entrance, hear? In fact, I'll come out and watch you cross the street, just in case.''

"That's good advice, Bessie, but you don't have to do that. You already have enough to do," Maggie said, pointing at the mountain of dirty dishes the cook had to wash before she went home for the night. "I'll go in the front, and I'll be all right."

When she stepped out into the warm darkness, however, it seemed Bess's fretting had been for naught. No one was about.

She was fitting her key to the lock on the *Gazette*'s front door, however, when Richard Burke stepped out of the shadows at the side of the building, startling her so much that she dropped her reticule.

"I couldn't believe my good fortune when I saw you sitting among all those rebels today, Maggie mine," he said, taking a step or two toward her.

"They aren't rebels, and your good fortune has nothing to do with me anymore, Richard," she retorted. "You left me, remember? At the time, I didn't know how fortunate *I* was."

"Leave you?" He shook his head. "Maggie, I was perfectly willing to continue as we had. I said as much, didn't I? And wouldn't you like to come give me a kiss for old time's sake? Maybe more? Invite me up to your room—I could show you the magic all over again, Maggie mine," he said persuasively.

The seductive, husky invitation that once would have thrilled her innocent heart now only filled her with disgust. "The only magic you ever possessed was your skill in pulling the wool over my eyes, Richard. Are you this good at deceiving Beatrice, or does she know exactly what her husband is like? Where *is* Mrs. Burke, anyway? Back in Washington?''

For a moment he looked blank, then he actually laughed. "Beatrice? There is no Beatrice. She's just a phantom I invoke when…" His tone changed, became coaxing. "That is, I made her up when I was getting close to losing my heart to you."

Now it was Maggie's turn to laugh, but there was no mirth in it. "Heart? You don't have one, Richard. Now go away. I want nothing to do with you."

"Ah, still angry with me for spoiling your love affair with the cripple, eh?" Burke needled. "That's all right—I love to kiss a woman when she's angry, then make her want me…."

With a move too quick for her to follow in the shadowy darkness, his hands shot out to her, yanking her against him; then, as she struggled, she felt him forcing her up against the side of the building.

Panic warred with fury as his hand squeezed her breast, while his other hand clamped over her mouth, preventing her from screaming.

"Remember how it was, Maggie?" he whispered, his breath harsh and whiskey laden. "I'd stroke you, and you'd moan…."

Bile rose in her throat, but she fought it down, clenched her hands into fists and boxed his ears.

"Damn it, you bitch!" he said, releasing her.

She took a step backward, until she could retrieve her reticule from the plank walkway where she had dropped it. Pulling it open, she drew out the pistol Garrick had lent her.

She cocked it. "You conniving snake," she said. "Now you're not only trying to pull the wool over my eyes again, you're trying to pull it over the army's eyes. They don't know about your double game, do they?"

His eyes became wary. "What the hell are you talking about, Maggie?"

"I saw you among the outlaws that day I found their camp. That *was* you, wasn't it? Even if you were out of uniform, I'd recognize you anywhere. And you were riding the same bay horse you rode in on today. They're going to catch you, you know. And I'm going to enjoy seeing it."

Burke's eyes had narrowed and were glittering with hatred. She felt a surge of triumph, knowing she had been right. But his carefree, sensual face had hardened. Her discovery—and his knowledge of it—had gained her an implacable enemy.

"You don't know what you're talking about, Maggie mine," he said. "And even if you were right, no one's going to believe *you* now, are they? No one believes a slut. Now put down the gun, Maggie, and come show me how sorry you are," he hissed.

"You come any closer and I'll blow you to hell," Maggie promised him. "I'd enjoy doing it, too."

"Would you enjoy hanging for it?" he taunted her, taking another step closer. "Not that I seriously believe you could hit the broad side of a barn, but my boys'd lynch you this same night."

"You take another step toward the lady, Yankee," warned a deep voice from behind Burke, "and I'll save Miss Maggie the trouble of killing you."

Maggie recognized Eureka's voice, even as the barrel of the black man's shotgun prodded Richard Burke's back. Maggie could see her friend now, his white teeth shining in the darkness as he grinned at her.

She sagged with relief.

Burke raised his hands in surrender. "I'd think twice about threatening a United States army officer with a firearm, darky," he said.

" 'Darky?' " Eureka echoed, then clucked at Burke, "My, my, is that any way for a Yankee to talk after fightin' a war to get us 'darkies' freed? Oh, I did think twice, sir. Three times, in fact. And I still purely wanted to put lead into your heart for botherin' a lady nice as Miss Maggie. Now, you get on back to whatever rock you crawled out from, and don't let me hear about you botherin' her again."

"You'll be sorry you interfered," snarled Burke, his arms still reaching skyward. "The next time I see you, I'll—"

"But you won't see me," Eureka told him, clearly unruffled by the threat. "I'll see you first. Now *git!*"

Chapter Twenty-Six

Rain woke Garrick the next morning, a steady downpour that seemed perfectly in tune with his mood. His leg ached so badly that he swore he could feel each absent toe.

He wished he could just stay in bed today, staring at the ceiling in his room, seeing no one. He didn't feel at all inclined to encounter the pitying looks directed at him by the well-intentioned townspeople, or to deflect their curiosity disguised as concern.

He wondered if Maggie had slept. He'd lain awake most of the night, only to fall into a fitful doze at dawn that had lasted until the rain thrumming on the roof roused him. He went downstairs, finding Jovita and Johnny already eating breakfast.

Johnny looked up, and the sight of his swollen eyes wrenched Garrick's heart. He had had a long talk with the boy yesterday, but he was pretty sure Johnny still didn't understand why there was no longer going to be a wedding for his papa and Miss Maggie.

"Reckon I overslept," Garrick said. "Guess that makes me a lazy dog, huh, Johnny? I'm lucky y'all saved me any bacon."

Johnny tried to smile, but it wasn't a successful attempt.

"You are your own boss," Jovita remarked. "There ees no need for you to rush. Eet ees not press day, no?"

"No...well, actually, Jovita, I've got to get over to the *Gazette*—we're going to put out a special edition. I'll probably be there till suppertime."

Belatedly he remembered that Jovita had said something about helping her son's wife today, but she seemed untroubled. "You go, Señor Devlin. I weel take Johnny to my son's, yes? He can play with the *niños, sí?*"

"*Sí.* Thanks, Jovita."

When he arrived, Eureka was carving a woodcut of a soldier on horseback carrying the United States flag to run along with Garrick's article. Maggie had already composed and typeset a headline for the front-page story: Federal Troops Arrive to Capture Raiders—Celebration Day Postponed.

"That's fine, Maggie," Garrick said, wishing his heart didn't feel so much better at the sight of her. "It isn't as pithy a headline as I'd like to write, but it should keep me out of jail," he said wryly. "Perhaps you'd like to write a companion piece about the latest depredations of the raiders while you're waiting to set up what I'm going to write?"

Her manner briskly businesslike, she nodded, moving without further comment over to the desk she used in the back. Lord, how long would it take before his hands stopped aching to hold her, if only to touch her shoulder in passing?

"'Scuse me, ma'am," said a male voice, startling Maggie, who was just leaving the hotel after dinner. She had been glancing in the other direction at a pair of soldiers lounging in front of the saloon, wondering if they would make catcalls at her as she walked past them on her way to talk to Cal in the jail.

She turned to see a blue-coated sergeant whom she would have collided with if she had continued on her way.

"Oh! I'm sorry...I'm afraid I wasn't looking where I was going!" she said.

"That's all right, ma'am," he said, tipping his forage cap and stepping politely off the plank walkway to let her by.

Over the last two weeks, blue-coated soldiers had become a familiar sight in Gillespie Springs, walking in pairs along the streets, eating in the hotel, drinking in the saloon.

The occupation of Gillespie Springs was going more smoothly than anyone living there, especially Maggie, had expected. Despite the soldiers' nightly whiskey consumption, there hadn't been any disagreeable incidents between them and the civilians. The soldiers offered no discourtesy to the ladies of the town, confining their attentions to the trio of women who worked in the cribs, and the latter seemed perfectly content with the arrangement. The soldiers picked no fights with the men of the town, either in the saloon or elsewhere.

Every few days they rode out, either as a company or in groups of three or four, to patrol the area. Apparently, they had met with no success, for they were still here, but after the way Burke had publicly shamed her, Maggie had not dared to approach any of them for a comment.

She started to continue on toward the jail, but the sergeant spoke just then. "Ma'am, I...maybe this isn't my place, but I just wanted to say I'm sorry...about the way my captain spoke to ya...that day we come. He was outa line, ma'am, no matter what...no matter what happened between the two of ya. Most of us feel that way, but..."

"But he's your captain. I understand, Sergeant."

"Yes, ma'am." He seemed uncomfortable, but determined to say his piece. "I kin see you're a lady, and I imagine it ain't been easy for ya, after he said what he did. I'd just like ya to feel free to call on me if he or any of the enlisted men offer you any more disrespect, ma'am.'' He fingered the brim of his cap, which he held with both hands at his waist. ''Sergeant O'Reilly is my name, Brendan Aloysius O'Reilly.''

Yes, he had the look of the Irish about him, with his black hair and blue eyes. A normal woman with an intact heart might well have felt some stirring of attraction to the sergeant. Her own heart felt dead within her, but she *was* grateful for his kindness.

''Thank you, Sergeant, but I'm glad to report the captain has ignored my existence.'' After that night he had accosted her outside the *Gazette,* anyway, but the sergeant need not know about that, since there had been no repetition. ''Your men have not bothered me, and as for Burke, he's been a lot more of a thorn in my employer's side than mine.'' And Eureka's, Maggie thought. The black man had insisted on escorting Maggie to and from dinner every night, and sleeping down in the *Gazette* office by the back door, just to make sure Burke didn't try to molest her again. They never spoke of it to Garrick, and Eureka always left before dawn, but Maggie hated to have him give up all his free time in the cause of protecting her.

Captain Burke, accompanied by an enlisted man, had made weekly visits to the *Gazette* on Tuesdays to look over the handwritten articles before they were typeset and printed. Each time he'd come, Maggie had excused herself and sought refuge in her room until he was gone.

She listened at her keyhole, of course. It was possible to hear most of what was said between the two men. Burke had not found anything to object to in the articles, but he never failed to make needling remarks designed to goad

Garrick into a hotheaded response. So far, however, Garrick had kept iron control of his temper.

"Yes, ma'am," Sergeant O'Reilly agreed, a rueful look on his face. "I reckon we'll be moving out just as soon as we catch those outlaws. My captain hasn't found anything he could jail Mr. Devlin for."

"You haven't found any trace of the outlaws, either?" Maggie asked, since the sergeant seemed eager to talk. Maybe he'd tell her something that would be encouraging to Garrick. Garrick's face was a grim mask these days, but maybe she would hear something that would coax a smile from him.

"No, ma'am, I'm sorry to say...so far it's downright spooky—they seem to know we're coming, and skeedaddle before we can get there, even if we split up and ride in different patrols."

Which would make sense if Burke was somehow connected to the outlaws, Maggie reasoned. The raids had continued, almost unabated, since the army company had occupied Gillespie Springs.

"I see. Good day to you, Sergeant. And my thanks for your kindness."

It would certainly ease Garrick's and Eureka's lives when the army departed, as well as that of Mayor Long, whose hotel was totally occupied by the soldiers. But once the soldiers had left, it would be time for Maggie to leave, too. It was breaking her heart to be around Garrick Devlin every day, to be in his presence but not *with* him.

How Burke had the nerve to show his face in a church was beyond him, Garrick fumed, as the Yankee captain seated himself in the pew behind where he and Johnny were sitting, waiting for Reverend Poole to start the service. Garrick knew instinctively that Burke had chosen to sit there simply to annoy him.

Johnny turned around and stared at Burke with all the bright-eyed intensity a child could muster. "Papa, why is that man sitting there?"

"Johnny, turn around," Garrick said sternly, tugging on the boy's shirtsleeve. "It's not polite to stare at other people." Even if those other people were no more welcome there than a polecat, Garrick thought.

"Don't like him," the boy announced with a child's brutal honesty. "He made Miss Maggie cry."

"*Johnny, hush,*" Garrick commanded, letting his son see from his face that he meant business.

Johnny was quiet for a minute, though he fidgeted with the buttons on his freshly starched shirt. "Papa, I miss Miss Maggie. She don't even come to church no more," he said.

"She *doesn't* come to church *any* more," Garrick corrected mechanically. "And I'm afraid that's none of our concern, son," he added with gentle firmness. He was suddenly glad Maggie wasn't present, for as much as he longed to steal glances at her, all dressed up in her Sunday best, he knew she would have been acutely uncomfortable in the same room as the Yankee captain.

Garrick was uncomfortable enough, knowing that Burke had overheard their conversation. He didn't want that slimy bastard knowing anything about him or his family. Maybe it wasn't Christian, but he hated Richard Burke as much as he'd ever hated anyone in his whole life.

If he ever found out that Burke had offered Maggie the minutest additional disrespect, he'd kill him. He knew—even though Maggie and Eureka didn't think he knew—that Eureka had been keeping overnight vigils in the office, for Cal had spotted him coming and going a couple of times.

He guessed that there had been some incident to cause the black man to stand guard. He also knew Eureka wouldn't tell him what it was—probably at Maggie's request. Did she think it was no longer any of Garrick's concern? Or did she worry that, if some small part of him still did care about her welfare, his anger at Burke would provoke him into doing something foolish?

Garrick was grateful to Eureka for watching over Maggie, even though he knew Eureka would be uncomfortable if he mentioned it. So he hadn't. But he kept his eyes open.

Chapter Twenty-Seven

"Señor Garrick! Señorita Maggie!" cried Jovita, showing glimpses of thick brown legs as she ran into the *Gazette* office. She apparently didn't notice Maggie crossing the street from the hotel after eating her midday meal.

Maggie had heard the Mexican woman yelling all the way from South Street. Alarm skittered down her spine; Jovita was normally the calmest woman Maggie had ever met, so something dreadful must have happened!

Picking up her skirts, she flew across the street and ran in behind the Mexican housekeeper. "Jovita, what is it? What's happened?" she asked, finding the woman standing in the middle of the empty office, her chest heaving. She was wringing her hands, her eyes wildly darting about.

When she saw Maggie, she fell upon her, looking frantically behind Maggie's skirts as if she expected to find something—or someone—there.

"Ees Johnny weeth you? I cannot find heem! He ees *perdido*, lost!"

"Lost?" Maggie repeated. "When did you last see him?"

"He was not weeth you? Oh, I hoped he had come to

find you, like that other time!'' Jovita cried, her shoulders sagging with disappointment.

''No, I haven't seen him. I was eating dinner over at the hotel…. When did you last see him?'' It wasn't like Jovita to be neglectful. Maggie knew she watched over the child like a hen with one chick. But Maggie also knew it took only a minute for a child to slip away, as he had before.

''One moment he ees playing in the backyard weeth his kitten. I am snapping peas on the porch, and I see heem walking toward the barn. He likes to go and see Toby sometime. I go inside a moment to set down the peas, and there ees some man at the door, saying he weel chop wood for food, but I tell heem we don't need that. Then, when I come back out, I do not see Johnny. I go een the barn, and he ees not there!''

''Maybe he was in the stall with Toby,'' suggested Maggie, feeling Jovita's panic catch hold of her heart, too. ''He knows he's not supposed to be, when Garrick's not there, but maybe—''

''No, I look! He ees not there! He ees nowhere! I call heem, and he does not come! I tell you, he ees meesing! *Ay de mí*, I must tell Señor Garrick! Where ees he?''

''He went to Cal and Livy's for dinner—''

Jovita was out the door before the last words had left Maggie's lips, but Maggie ran after her, crying, ''Jovita, stop! I'm younger—I can run faster! Let me run down to Cal and Livy's, while you start looking around town! We'll find him! He's just a little boy—he can't have gotten far!''

But even as she said the words, desperately wanting to believe them herself, she knew it was false reassurance. Some sixth sense told her there was more to Johnny Devlin's disappearance than just a little boy's tendency to wander away.

Fortunately, the older woman saw the logic in what Maggie was saying. "Okay, I weel look all over the town!" she cried, heading the other way. "You go tell Garrick!"

"Go get Eureka!" Maggie called over her shoulder as she set off down the street. "He'll help you!"

An hour later, Gillespie Springs had been thoroughly searched. Even off-duty soldiers had volunteered to help. But Johnny had not been found, nor any trace of him.

"Where's your captain?" Garrick demanded of Sergeant O'Reilly. Garrick stood by his saddled gelding as a mounted search party gathered outside the *Gazette* office.

"He rode out this mornin', sir," Sergeant O'Reilly answered. "Said he wanted to ride alone over some ground we'd been over, lookin' for some sign we might've missed. He thinks it's possible the outlaws might double back to an area we already scouted. I expect he'll be back in town by this afternoon."

"You tell him if we don't find the boy, I'll need his help," Cal said, already mounted on his own horse.

"Yessir." O'Reilly was quietly respectful. "Of course. Meanwhile, we'll keep looking, Sheriff."

"Much obliged, Sergeant."

Garrick suddenly looked like an old man, his face haggard and gray. Maggie's heart went out to him, and she longed to run a comforting hand along his rigid back, but she knew he wouldn't thank her for it. He'd been like a man demented ever since she'd told him about Johnny.

He mounted, then caught her eye. "Maggie..."

"Yes?" She was already stepping over to the horse, her heart in her throat, wondering what he was about to say.

"You—you've you've already checked your room? Maybe Johnny went up there looking for you."

She sighed. "Yes, of course. First thing after I told you, even though I knew I'd locked the door to my room before

I went over to dinner.'' She'd been locking her door whenever she was out of the office, just to keep from being surprised there by vermin such as Burke or Barbee, since Garrick never locked the *Gazette*'s front door during the day.

''Garrick—''

He turned back impatiently, clearly more than ready to be off.

''We'll find him, Garrick. He'll be all right,'' she promised. *Oh, God, let it be true.*

''I pray you're right,'' he said. ''If anything happens to that little boy...'' His voice trailed off and he looked away, but not before she saw the tears standing in his eyes.

Maggie turned and went inside, intending to seek the privacy of her room for a few minutes before rejoining the search around town. She had to cry—it was that or break into little, hysterical pieces. While she was up there, she intended to spend some time on her knees in prayer, too. She'd promise God anything, if only he'd restore Johnny Devlin to his father's arms.

She was blinded by tears before she ever reached the top of the stairs, and had thought she would have difficulty seeing well enough to unlock the door, but to her surprise, it was slightly ajar. She must not have locked it as she had thought. Maybe Johnny *was* here! She swiped at her eyes with the back of a hand, not wanting to frighten the child with her tears.

But no little boy was waiting in the room for her, just a folded sheet of paper lying on the bed with ''Maggie'' written on the front of it.

She recognized the bold, ostentatious script immediately. It had been written by the same hand that had once written her love letters, messages that had propelled her to the heights of passion, only to send her to the depths of despair when she found that they'd been written by a liar—Richard Burke.

With shaking fingers she unfolded the paper, blinking to clear the rest of the tears from her eyes.

> Maggie mine, we have the boy. He is safe and will be released, but only if you come and exchange yourself for him. Ride out of town toward Austin, and we will find you. Come alone and unarmed, and don't tell anyone. Be there by nightfall, or the boy dies. If anyone else comes, he'll die and so will the boy.
>
> The others look forward to seeing that I have not exaggerated your considerable charms. Especially Zeke Barbee. I fear you were less than nice to him, Maggie, so he may be less than gentlemanly with you. Once we reach Mexico, however, you will be mine alone. Come soon, Maggie.
>
> R.B.

Maggie stared at the letter, her heart thudding against her breastbone. She had been right all along; Richard Burke was in league with the outlaws. In all likelihood he was their leader. She marveled at how he had managed to lead two such opposite lives. An officer had a lot of personal freedom to go and come at his own discretion, but to be an outlaw and a captain in the United States Army at the same time!

It was entirely in character for him, though. Burke was a despoiler in the guise of a gentleman. Just as he'd taken her innocence, then wanted nothing more to do with her, he probably loved destroying the lives and property of other innocent people.

Burke knew she wanted nothing more to do with him, but what she wanted was of no importance to him. In fact, her disgust for him made it all the more exciting to demand that she be the sacrificial lamb by which Johnny's safety was purchased. And once she was in his power, Burke intended to pass her around to everyone else in the band, including the despicable Zeke Barbee.

She shuddered, thinking of having to submit to all those bloodstained, dirty hands pawing her, and worse. Dear God, was she even capable of making such a sacrifice? She could tear up the note, pretend she had never received it and stay safe in Gillespie Springs.

And watch Garrick Devlin grieve when his son's lifeless body was found, knowing she could have spared him such a tragedy.

There was no choice. She couldn't let a child die, especially Garrick's child, not when it was in her power to save him. Woodenly, Maggie stuffed a few things into her reticule. A brush and comb, a change of underwear. What else did a woman need when going to live with outlaws? She looked long and hard at the pistol in the drawstring bag, hoping she would be able to keep it hidden there till Johnny had been freed. Should she then turn it on herself to save herself from a fate worse than death? Surely that was what a Southern lady would do! She twisted her mouth at the thought. To hell with what a Southern lady would do! She'd use it on as many outlaws as she could before she was overpowered, and hopefully, Richard Burke and Zeke Barbee would be the first two to die!

Before she left the *Gazette,* she lingered in front of the California typecases, her hand moving quickly with the type stick to leave Garrick a last message he would find after Johnny had been returned to him. He wouldn't be looking around the *Gazette* office until then.

My dearest Garrick,
I have gone to trade myself for Johnny, who is being

held by the outlaws. Don't try to follow. I will love
you always.

Maggie Harper

"Ride out of town toward Austin," the letter had directed her. That meant west, past the church and the livery
stable on the edge of town. But she couldn't very well *ride*
out of town if there wasn't anything to ride *on,* could she?
Every horse in Gillespie Springs, including those at the
livery, were being used by the search party. Eureka would
be on Bessie's mule.

And so Maggie walked out of Gillespie Springs, heading
west.

Just as Burke had promised, the outlaws found her, not
the other way around, surrounding her on the tree-lined trail
with their guns drawn. There were three of them—Burke,
the half-breed Indian and the black man. Burke, Maggie
noticed absently, had shed his army blue in favor of an
everyday shirt and denim pants. Without the uniform, he
looked so...*ordinary.*

"I was beginning to wonder about you, Maggie mine,"
he said, grinning down at her. "Now I see what took you
so long. Didn't figure you'd have to ride shank's mare out
here. You mean that crippled lover of yours hasn't bought
you your very own little mare yet? My, my, he must not
have loved you as much as I thought."

"I'm not here to talk about Garrick," she snapped, darting glances at the half-breed and the black man on the other
two horses. "Where's the boy, Richard? If you've harmed
so much as a hair on his head, damn you—"

Her flash of temper didn't discomfit Burke in the least.
"Oh, the brat's safe enough, back at our hideout. Ol' Zeke
is tendin' him."

The thought of the despicable Zeke Barbee being in charge of Garrick's precious son was almost more than Maggie could bear. *Keep your temper, Maggie.*

"And what are *you* doing with the likes of Zeke Barbee, anyway?" she needled. "Isn't he a little...*below* an officer and a 'gentleman' like you, Richard? Not to mention a rebel." She wanted to include the other outlaws who accompanied Burke now, but didn't quite dare.

Burke just laughed. "Ol' Zeke is a bit *coarse,* I grant you, but he has his uses. He can take orders, for one. It's a skill you ought to cultivate, Maggie mine."

She ignored the gibe. "How do I know Johnny's safe? Will I see him...before the exchange is made?"

Burke chuckled. "Fond of the brat, are you? Yeah, you'll see him. Meanwhile, I think you better hand that bag you're carryin' over to the 'breed to be searched."

Her heart sank. She wasn't going to get a chance to use the gun. A moment later, the renegade half-breed whooped, and his hand came up holding the pistol.

"Naughty Maggie," Burke reproved. "Did you really think you'd get to keep that? And now I've got to blindfold you, then I'll put you up on my horse and we'll ride double back to our hideout. Actually, I'm real glad you didn't have a horse t'ride," he said, dismounting and pulling off his bandanna, folding it until it formed a band and tying it around her eyes.

"Oh?" she said, hating being blind in front of these lawless men, but determined not to show her fear.

"Sure," he said, and she felt his hand unbuttoning her blouse and reaching down the front of her corset, casually pinching her nipple.

She stiffened, and acid swirled in her stomach, but she held her tongue. He wanted her to object, so she wouldn't.

"Mmm, I'd purely forgotten how good you felt, Maggie.

You'll have to ride behind me, holdin' on to me, and I'll feel those soft tits rubbin' up against me all the way back— like a foretaste of heaven, right, boys?''

She heard snickers from the other two.

''They're gonna give *you* a foretaste of hell, though— they're still pretty riled that your lover shot their pard. He's dead, Maggie mine, died of gangrene from bein' shot in the leg. So they ain't too happy.''

She closed her eyes beneath the bandage, hoping for the strength to make it through this ordeal.

''And you don't even dare fuss, 'cause you know if you do the boy'll die. Here now, reach your foot into this stir-rup, and push yourself up....'' She shuddered as she felt his hands on her derriere, propelling her upward.

''Damn you,'' she whispered, even as she moved to obey. She felt him settling himself in front of her.

''*Whoa,*'' he ordered the bay, which sidestepped at the additional weight. ''Put your arms around my waist, Maggie,'' he ordered, and when she complied, she felt him tying them together with a length of rawhide. ''Now I reckon you won't be going anywhere without me,'' he said, chuckling again as he kicked the horse into a lurching trot, then a lope. Soon other hoofbeats joined that of Burke's bay on either side of her. Maggie, forced by her bonds to lean against her captor, felt tears of helpless fury and despair slide out from under her blindfold.

''Why, Richard?'' Maggie asked, after they'd been riding for a few minutes.

''Why what?''

''Why are you leading this double life? Why would you endanger your army career like this, trying to be an officer and an outlaw at the same time?''

''I'm not *trying* to be both, I'm succeeding! And is that all you think I want out of life, making the next promotion and retiring a full colonel, if not a general? No, no, Maggie mine, there's more to life than that! Life has...well, it's been just damn boring, now that the war's been over so long and there are no more rebs to kill.''

Once, the idea of killing ''rebs'' in the war would not have chilled her heart, but now it did, because she loved a man who had once been a rebel. ''You like being an outlaw—killing and destroying—because it's more *exciting* than being an honorable officer in the United States Army?''

He chuckled. ''That's about the size of it, Maggie.''

They rode for perhaps half an hour—in what direction, Maggie couldn't tell—before Burke reined in his horse, saying, ''We're here, Maggie mine.'' She felt him undoing her bonds, and then he dismounted, pulling her down after him while she was still rubbing at her wrists to bring the circulation back.

''Where's Johnny?'' she demanded.

''Bring out the boy, Barbee,'' Maggie heard Burke order, even as his fingers fumbled at the knot holding the blindfold on.

Before he had even succeeded in loosening the knot, she heard Johnny's voice crying ''Miss Maggie! *Miss Maggie!*'' and felt the little boy throwing his arms around her legs. A second later, the cloth fell away from her eyes, and she was kneeling and holding a teary-eyed, white-faced Johnny Devlin.

Hugging him tightly, smoothing his hair and breathing a silent thanks that he was thus far just scared, not harmed physically, Maggie looked around her. The ''hideout'' consisted of a dugout in the side of a hill, which was reached by a narrow trail with steep banks lining the path on either side. The outlaws had chosen their location well. As long as one of them stood guard on the hill, it would be difficult to sneak up on them here, and impossible for more than one man on horseback to approach the dugout at a time.

"Lovely accommodations," she said, trying to drawl her words in the same lazy rhythm Garrick used.

"It's not much, but it's home—for the moment. We've kept on the move a lot, as I'm sure you've guessed. But we'll have a palace in Mexico, Maggie mine."

She forbore from comment.

"Now ain't that a purty picture," Zeke Barbee said, coming up behind the boy. "Almost as purty a picture as it's gonna be watchin' Garrick Devlin ride in here to his death."

Maggie whirled around, facing Burke. "But you said—"

"I said Johnny would be all right, and he will. I'll drop off the brat at the edge of town when it's safe. He'll make it back to town, and I reckon that sheriff an' his lady'll take care of him, the kid being kin and all. I didn't promise anything about your cripple livin' through this, did I? The more I thought about it, the more I didn't like the idea of you moonin' about some man we left behind. I figure you'll get over him faster if he's dead."

Chapter Twenty-Eight

"If he's dead..." repeated Maggie numbly. "You're expecting Garrick to ride here? But he's off with the search party."

"They won't find us here, and they've got to go back to town sometime. He'll find the note then."

"How did you leave those notes, anyway? Your sergeant said you'd ridden out of town earlier. And I could swear I'd left the door to my room locked."

"You did. But the lock hasn't been made that the 'breed can't pick," he said, nodding at the renegade. "He isn't half-Comanche for nothing. He can slip in and out of a place in broad daylight like a ghost. It was simple to plant the notes while you and the Mex housekeeper and everyone else were running around like chickens with their heads cut off."

Maggie saw the half-breed grinning from ear to ear, and longed to smash her fist into his face. She could imagine Garrick arriving home, heartsick at not finding his son, with his leg likely making him miserable with pain, and seeing that note.

"You all think you're so cleverly hidden, but the search party will find us before they go back to town," she taunted, clutching Johnny closer to her. The boy had begun to cry. Maybe he hadn't understood all of Burke's threat, but he had understood enough.

Burke uttered a short, ugly bark of laughter, and the others hooted.

"It ain't likely, missus," said the black man. "They ain't found us all the time we bin raidin', has they?"

"And we're ready for them if they do," added the renegade, shaking the rifle in his hand meaningfully.

"But they won't," Barbee concluded. "And my ol' pard Devlin will come riding in jest as soon as he gets his marchin' orders, thinkin' he's gonna get to take his son home with him."

"And meanwhile—?" She had to know. *God, please don't let them attack me in front of the boy,* Maggie prayed.

"We wait."

"I know how we can pass the time," Zeke Barbee said, licking his lips and eyeing Maggie.

"There'll be none of that till Devlin's dead and we're miles away from here," Richard Burke snapped. "You don't want to get caught with your pants down, do you, Barbee?" he inquired with a nasty smile. "It's going to take all of us staying alert to make sure this ends up the way we want it to."

Barbee's piglike eyes narrowed. "Awright, awright, but I'm pokin' her first."

Burke's mouth tightened to a thin line. "We'll draw lots. Meanwhile, keep your trousers buttoned."

It was dusk when the search party returned to Gillespie Springs, empty-handed, and against Garrick Devlin's strenuous objections. He wanted to keep looking, all night if necessary, widening the radius around Gillespie Springs and beyond.

"Garrick, most of us will be perfectly willing to ride back out—there's a full moon tonight, which will help if it stays clear—but what if the boy's been found in the meantime?" Cal argued. "He'll be wanting to see his papa."

"He hasn't been," Garrick insisted stubbornly. He hit his chest with his clenched fist. "I'd know *here*. He hasn't been found."

"Well, if he isn't, we'll go back out, right, men?" Most of the rest of the party nodded in agreement. "But we'll be able to look longer if the horses are rested and watered first. You men ride back to your homes. Eat some supper. See to your mounts. If the boy's been found, or I need you sooner, I'll have the preacher toll the church bell. If not, those of you who can, meet back here at nine-thirty."

Garrick thought about going to the *Gazette* office first. He was so certain that Johnny was still missing that he felt there was little purpose in going to his house. He needed to see Maggie, to bury his face against her soft breast and weep, and feel her cool hands comforting him.

He'd been a fool, he knew that now. Nothing mattered besides love—his love for Johnny, his love for her. Nothing anyone said about her mattered, nothing she'd done. If God granted him another chance, and he could regain his child and the woman he loved, he wouldn't let anything or anyone stand in his way.

He rode slowly past the *Gazette* office, but saw no one standing in the doorway, watching for him, so he forced himself to keep going. He'd tell Jovita they hadn't found the boy, she'd tell him the same and *then* he'd go find Maggie before it was time to ride out again.

Jovita, however, *was* waiting for him, practically jumping up and down in her impatience. Her face was gray beneath its brown complexion, her dark eyes ringed with white.

"Señor Devlin—the keednappers, outlaws—they leave a *mensaje*, a message!" she cried, her agitation thickening her accent so he could hardly understand her. She waved a piece of paper at him.

"'Keednappers?' What are you talking about, woman?" he said, snatching the note from her before he even dismounted.

"He has been taken, your son! Keednapped! Mees Maggie, too!"

"But that's impossible—about Maggie, at least! She was at the *Gazette* office when we rode out of here," he said, feeling the cold sweat break out on his forehead all over again.

"She ees not there now, I check! She ees meesing, too!" Jovita insisted.

The full implication of her words struck him as he unfolded the paper, and for a moment the script swam in front of his eyes. Terror gripped his heart as he imagined the three-year-old boy and the woman he loved being roughly seized by strangers.

He read through the note, which confirmed what Jovita had said.

We have your boy and your woman. Ride north out of town when you get this. Carry a lantern if it's dark. We'll find you. Bring a thousand dollars. Come alone, or you'll never see them alive again.

"And how did you make sense of this, Jovita? I thought you didn't read or write."

"She brought it to me, Garrick," another woman's voice said. He looked up to see Olivia framed in his doorway. "I read it to her. Oh, Garrick, what are you going to do?"

"But how could they have Maggie?" he said aloud.

"They can't. *I left her here, dammit!*" Not willing to stay here talking when he could be proving to himself that Maggie was just fine at the *Gazette,* he whirled Toby around and, spurring him into a gallop, headed back the way he'd come.

But when he ran into the office and called her name, she wasn't there, of course. Livy had followed him from his house, and somewhere between there and the *Gazette,* Cal had joined her, so that by the time Garrick was walking down the stairs from Maggie's empty room, his brother and sister-in-law were waiting for him at the bottom of the stairs. Eureka was standing there, too, a worried expression on his dark face.

"Livy told me about the note," Cal said, before Garrick had to explain. "We've got five hundred dollars in the bank that you're welcome to. Do you have any money, brother?"

"About fifty," Garrick said with a bitter laugh. "Starting up the newspaper didn't leave me with much. But that's only five hundred fifty. Where am I going to get the rest before they get tired of waiting and kill my child and Maggie?"

"You'll have it, if I have to hold up the bank myself," Cal said, and without another word walked out the door.

Eureka had been striding around the office, looking at everything, almost as if he expected to find Maggie hiding under a ream of paper. In Garrick's agitated frame of mind, the black man's pacing was getting on his already-frayed nerves. He was just about to tell him to stand still or get out when Eureka stopped dead in front of the table next to the Washington press, peering at something.

"Mr. Devlin, you ought to read this," he said, holding up the heavy bed of a typeset page.

"Later, Eureka," he said, figuring Maggie had been passing the time typesetting copy while she had been waiting for the search party's return. Had the kidnappers been bold enough to come *here* and seize her right in the *Gazette* office? "Articles for the newspaper just don't matter right now."

"It's hard to read backward, but I don't think that's what this is," Eureka said, nodding toward the typeset page. "Let me print this out. It'll just take a minute."

Down the street, a bell began to toll. Garrick watched without interest as the black man smoothed the tympan, fastened the frisket with the metal tongues, set the bed of type in the holder and rolled it under the platen. Garrick walked away, gazing down the street at the gathering crowd in front of the church, but heard the thump as Eureka pulled on the devil's tail.

A moment later, Eureka shouted, "Mr. Devlin, come look! I was right! It's a note from Miss Maggie to you!" He handed it to Garrick, who took it over to the door where he could read it by the fast-failing light.

"She wasn't taken, she went there of her own free will," he said, feeling hollow inside. "She says she went there to trade herself for Johnny. Dear God, she thought they'd let Johnny go if she went. She didn't know they were going to leave me a message, too! Maggie was *safe,* and she went there to free Johnny!" Suddenly his legs—his good one *and* the wooden one—wouldn't hold him up, even with the cane. He managed to make it to the chair at his desk before slumping down in a heap.

"Mr. Devlin, I'll ride out with you," Eureka promised. "We'll kill every one of those outlaws!"

"No, you can't," Garrick said, his voice echoing dully in his own ears. "They'll kill Maggie and Johnny if I don't come alone."

"But you can't go alone!" Livy said, startling him. He'd forgotten she had remained behind when Cal left.

He was about to reiterate what the note had said when Cal ran back in. "We've got the money," he announced, holding out a full burlap sack.

"What?" Cal's words made no sense.

"The rest of the thousand dollars," Cal explained. "The bank manager opened up the bank at my request, and I told the folks that came in response what we were up against. They all went in and withdrew whatever they could."

"They...they did? God bless them." After what Burke had said about Maggie in front of all of them, it was nothing short of a miracle. They must have been doing it for his innocent child's sake.

As if he could read Garrick's mind, Cal said, "There's a lot more sympathy for Maggie out there than you think, brother, after what Burke said. Folks said they didn't cotton to some Yankee coming to their town and shaming a lady. Some of the soldiers showed up and gave money from their pockets, too."

Garrick blinked at that news. "What'd their damned captain have to say about that?"

"He wasn't there. They haven't seen hide nor hair of him since early this morning. Sergeant O'Reilly is of the opinion the bastard—has deserted."

"So Maggie was right."

"Right? Right about what?"

"He's gone to the outlaws. He's one of them. Maggie said when she spied on the outlaws' camp that she'd seen a man that looked like Burke among them. She'd thought he was in Washington at the time, so she didn't really think it could be him—not until he showed up in town just a day later. I—I didn't believe her, Cal. The day she told me was the day Burke had said those things, and I...I reckon I thought she was just trying to distract me from that. That's why I didn't mention it to you. God, what a fool I am!"

Burke had to have been the one who had written the note Jovita found in his house. It was written by someone who'd had some education, not by a half-breed or an ex-slave, or an ignorant cracker like Barbee. *Why hadn't he believed her? He could have been watching that slippery bastard, Burke....*

"Don't be so hard on yourself. We had no proof. Who'd have thought he'd kidnap a child, or Maggie? The important thing is we're going to get her back."

"No, *we're* not, brother. *I* am. The note said to come alone, or they'd die. I'll give them the money, and then we'll ride out of there. You tell those good people I'll pay every penny of it back. I don't know how, yet, but—"

"To hell with the money!" Cal shouted, startling everyone, for as a former preacher, he didn't often cuss. "Don't you see it's a trap? They'll kill you! They can't let you go once you know what all of them look like, especially now that you know one of their names."

"Two," Garrick mumbled, and reminded Cal about Zeke Barbee being in the camp.

"Two, then. They'll keep the money and Maggie, and who knows what they'll do about Johnny?"

Garrick felt an icy spear of dread go through his heart at the thought that they might kill his son, simply because they found his presence inconvenient.

"I have to go alone!" he persisted. "If they see more than me coming, they'll kill them anyway. Don't follow me, Cal—or let anyone else. If you do, and that gets them killed..."

Cal held up his hands in surrender. "All right, all right. I won't. *We* won't. But I think you should wait until morning."

Garrick stared at his brother as if he'd just started spouting Greek. "Are you loco? Leave Maggie and my son with the outlaws overnight? Do you know what they might do if they have a woman like Maggie to toy with all night?''

Cal looked down at his boots, then back at his brother. ''If you carry a lantern like the note said, it'll outline you like a target. It'll be too easy for them to ambush you.''

''That's a chance I'll have to take,'' Garrick retorted. ''I'm not leaving Johnny or Maggie a moment longer than I have to,'' he told Cal. ''I'm heading out, and don't any of you try to follow me.''

Chapter Twenty-Nine

"All right, if you're bound and determined to be pig-headed, I guess I can't stop you," Cal responded. "But you might as well go armed to the teeth."

Garrick shrugged. "They're going to make me drop any guns I'm wearing."

"So you give 'em the weapons they can see. You keep some back they can't see. Livy, Eureka, you might as well go on home...." His arm around his wife's waist, he steered her out the door. Eureka followed.

Garrick watched out the window as Cal kissed his wife on the cheek, then said a few words to the black man. He saw Eureka seem to listen intently, nod, then both he and Livy walked away.

"What were you jawing about with Eureka?" he asked suspiciously when Cal returned.

"Oh, I just asked him to walk Livy home," Cal said, his tone casual. "Anyway, as I was saying..." He walked back into the jail and motioned toward the rack on the wall that held a number of rifles and pistols. "Take this Winchester, and a boot gun—" he handed him a derringer "—and a knife for the other boot. And here's a pair of pistols and a holster. You can wear one in the holster, tuck the other inside your waistband.''

His brother was giving in mighty easily about him going alone, Garrick thought as Cal handed him the weapons. But maybe after a lifetime of being related to him, Cal recognized that Garrick meant just what he said.

''All right, I reckon I'm ready to go,'' he said, once the weapons were loaded and on him, and after he had fetched the lantern from the back of the office.

''Not yet, you're not. First, we're going to your house and change your shirt.''

''Now what kinda nonsense—'' Garrick began, exasperated at the thought of delaying his departure any longer. Johnny and Maggie were in danger, and his brother was worried about what he *wore?*

''You might as well be wearin' a bulls-eye as that white shirt,'' Cal interrupted. ''You have a dark shirt at home, don't you? It'll only take a few minutes to go put it on, Garrick. Just humor me, will you?''

He could hear the brotherly love and concern in Cal's voice. And it would be easier to just go along with Cal's request than to stand here arguing with him, so he shrugged. ''Okay, come on.''

Garrick rode north for perhaps half an hour. Clouds that had dotted the evening sky had thickened, obscuring the moonlight. Now Garrick was glad of the lantern he'd been commanded to bring. He couldn't very well help Maggie and his child if he let Toby walk into a gopher hole along the way.

Once or twice he'd thought he'd heard something nearby—the rattle of one rock against another, a snapped twig—and had tensed, thinking it was the outlaws about to approach him. But when he'd reined in Toby, silence reigned. *Probably just an animal, you jumpy idiot.* He started forward again.

Several minutes later, a voice came out of the darkness. "Mister, just keep walkin' that horse the way you're goin'."

"Where are you?" Garrick strained to see the man in the inky shadows, but couldn't. The voice seemed to be coming from somewhere just off the trail amid the undergrowth.

"Oh, you don't have to see me," the man told him. "Just follow my voice. You're goin' the right way."

Garrick kept Toby moving a few minutes, then the voice directed him to turn left. At first Garrick didn't see a break in the trees, but then he spotted a narrow dirt path, little more than a deer track, that led between two rows of loblolly pines. The path sloped gradually downward, and Garrick's lantern revealed high, foliage-covered banks flanking the sides of the path. *A damn good place for an ambush.*

The voice spoke again. "Okay, I'm right behind you, mister. Keep goin', but don't try anythin' funny. I got a rifle aimed right 'tween your shoulder blades."

"I hear 'em," Barbee muttered, rousing Maggie.

She jerked awake, amazed that she had managed to doze in her cramped, uncomfortable position, tied to a tree with Johnny asleep in her lap. How could she have slept, knowing that Garrick was going to be gunned down as he arrived? She strained against the gag that kept her from being able to call out a warning as soon as he came into sight.

Yes, she heard it now, the faint sound of hoofs, the creak of saddle leather.

Barbee kicked dirt over the small campfire, smothering it. Now the campsite was a place of silvery shadows.

The half-breed's voice came from above, just out of her

line of sight. "Yeah, there they come. Devlin's bein' driven right to us...."

"Like a lamb to the slaughter," Richard Burke concluded with a low chuckle. He stepped forward, into the faint circle of light that a break in the clouds provided. Nearby, Burke's bay whinnied, catching the scent of a strange horse.

Maggie could see Garrick now, thanks to the lantern he carried. Its light flickered over his white face, distorting it. With the dark clothes he wore, he looked like a frightening apocalyptic figure.

"Welcome to our little hideaway, Devlin. Thanks for accepting my invitation," Burke said in an urbane voice. "Why don't you dismount?"

Maggie could see the twin pistols Burke had trained on Garrick. In her lap, Johnny sighed in his sleep, unaware that his father was here. *Oh Lord, don't let him see his father die trying to save us....*

"The pleasure's all mine, I'm sure," Garrick drawled, dismounting and pulling his cane out of the strap that held it in back of the saddle. "Here's the money," he said, setting the bag down by his feet, but keeping the lantern. "Where're Maggie and my son?"

"Right over here, under this tree," called Barbee, standing up and coming forward. "Jes' waitin' to see ya. But first, I reckon we need to relieve ya of any firearms you may be packin', ol' pard. Put the lantern down and raise your hands in the air. Don't try anythin' funny—Burke ain't the only one with guns aimed at you. The half-breed's out there *somewhere*...." He guffawed.

Maggie could see Garrick turning his head slowly, peering through the darkness. She knew when his eyes found her and his son. He nodded slightly. She knew he wouldn't be able to see the renegade from his vantage point, though.

She could see Garrick frown, but he did as he was bidden, setting the lantern down and raising his arms. Barbee stepped forward, taking the Colt from its holster at Garrick's hip. Then he patted him down, pulling another pistol from the front of his waistband, *tsk*ing at Garrick like an old-maid schoolmarm. Garrick's face had smoothed out into an expressionless mask, as if losing his hidden gun mattered less than nothing.

"All right, now let me see them," Garrick said, his voice level. He ignored Barbee and spoke to Burke.

"I suppose we could do that."

Somewhere on the hill above them, there was a rustling of underbrush, a short, strangled cry, then silence.

"What was that?" Burke demanded, falling into a crouch, aiming his guns at the noise. "'Breed, you still up there?"

Silence.

"*Hey, 'Breed! Answer me!*" Burke ordered, his voice a little less assured now. Barbee looked downright nervous.

"You fellas are jumpy as cats on a skillet," the black man jeered. "That yelp was probably some critter gettin' caught by an owl or somethin'. The Injun probably just doesn't wanna give away his position."

Burke considered that. "I imagine you're right," he said. He gestured toward the tree where Maggie and Johnny were tied. "Go ahead over there, Devlin. See your brat—and your *whore*...."

Maggie froze, seeing Garrick stiffen. But then he calmly raised his lantern and started forward, his awkward, ungraceful gait as familiar and lovable to her as a caress. When he reached her side, the first thing he did was lean over and pull down her gag.

"Are you all right, honey?" he whispered hoarsely, his eyes studying her face before lowering to his sleeping son.

She nodded. "They haven't...done anything to me yet," she whispered back. "They've let me take care of Johnny. But Garrick, they mean to kill you!" She had to warn him, even if they shot her for it.

He didn't seem surprised. "Cal said as much.... I'm going to try and get us out of this, honey, if at all possible. If I succeed, we're getting married—if you'll have me. But no matter what happens, I love you, and that will never change." While the tears were forming in her eyes at his words, he leaned over and kissed her swiftly and hard. He kissed his sleeping son's head, also.

"And I love you—"

Burke interrupted, "That's enough of tha—"

Suddenly, behind Burke and to the left of Garrick and Zeke Barbee, something fell from the hill. Something large and long that landed with a sickening thud. A body!

Barbee lurched over, peering at it. "Jesus, it's the 'breed! He's got a knife in his back! Someone's gotta be up there!"

Everything seemed to happen at once. Garrick swept his cane in a downward arc, knocking over the lantern and smashing the glass, extinguishing the light. Then, while Barbee was still goggling from the loss of the lantern light, Garrick grabbed the man's pistol from the holster at his hip.

"Barbee, you fool, he's got your gun!" shouted Burke out of the darkness.

The black man's rifle spat from over by the horses, but his shot went wide.

Johnny awoke with a start, crying at the noise and confusion. Then he saw Garrick and began shrieking, "Papa, Papa!" He struggled to get loose, but the ropes that bound Maggie to the tree tethered him to her lap.

The black man fired again, and Garrick went down heavily. He was still alive, but she couldn't tell where he'd been hit. Before she could ask him, though, another shot rang out from above, and suddenly the black man collapsed like an empty grain sack.

Burke turned and fired up the hill, but there was no outcry, no thudding sound of a body falling.

The moon chose this moment to come out from behind the clouds, but Garrick had dragged himself into the shadows under the tree, where he knelt in front of Maggie and his son like a human shield. Barbee, however, was spotlighted by the silvery light as he turned and came at Garrick, drawing the pistol he'd taken from him.

The report exploded in Maggie's ears as Garrick raised Barbee's gun and fired, dropping his old comrade in one shot. Then, before he could shift his aim toward Burke, another shot rang out from the shadows atop the hill, striking Burke in the wrist. With a howl of pain, Burke dropped the gun he'd been holding in that hand.

"Drop the other gun and put your hands in the air, or you're a dead man, Burke!" ordered a familiar voice from atop the hill. Cal's voice.

Maggie held her breath.

Burke stared in the direction of the voice, seemingly weighing his options, then he dropped the other gun and raised his hands in surrender.

"Garrick, where are you hit?" she demanded.

"In my leg."

Her heart sank. Would he now have to lose his other leg?

He must have seen her somber expression. "No, Maggie, not in the good leg—in my damn wooden leg!" He started laughing then. "The slug hit like the kick of a mule and knocked me down, but it just hit wood!"

At that moment, Cal came slipping and sliding down the grassy hill, his face blackened by something smeared all over it. He was followed by another man—Eureka! At a nod from Cal, Eureka collected the pistols at Burke's feet, then pulled down one arm, then the other, prisoning the erstwhile captain's wrists in steel come-alongs.

"Richard Burke, you're under arrest," Cal announced. "You'll stand trial, but until you do, you make one false move and I'd purely love letting moonlight through your black heart."

Burke hung his head and said nothing. All the fight, all the bravado seemed to have gone out of him completely.

For a moment, no one spoke. Garrick, who had cut Maggie's bonds with the knife in his boot, was busy hugging both his son and Maggie at once. Then, his voice thick with emotion, he said, "Brother, I'm glad to see you, even if I did tell you to stay put in town."

"Papa, Unca Cal's face is all dirty!" Johnny crowed.

"Boot blacking," Cal explained. "I couldn't have someone spotting me up there. Eureka muffled the horses' hooves with old rags and we rode bareback, so you wouldn't be so likely to hear us following. We almost didn't get going in time to catch up, even though Eureka and Livy started readying the horses as soon as they left the *Gazette* office!" He was clearly very proud of himself and Eureka.

"I *thought* I heard someone behind me," Garrick admitted. "Which one of you killed the renegade?"

Eureka raised his hand.

"Much obliged," Garrick said evenly, but Maggie, lifting her head from Garrick's chest, saw that his eyes spoke volumes about his gratitude.

Eureka straightened after checking all three of the other outlaws lying on the ground. "They're all dead, Sheriff. Looks like you're going to be the only one left to step on the gallows, Burke."

Burke seemed not to have heard him, for he didn't move or speak.

"You okay, Maggie? And the boy?" Cal inquired. She assured him they were fine, and he turned his attention to Garrick.

"Eureka's going to have to do some woodcarving to patch up my leg, but other than that I'm fine," Garrick assured him, pushing up his trouser leg so Cal could see the damage done by the rifle slug to his "calf."

"I'll fix you up good, Mr. Devlin!" Eureka promised.

"All right, let's get this scoundrel tied onto a horse, and head back to town," Cal suggested.

Moments later, they started up the sloping trail and back onto the main road leading to Gillespie Springs, with Cal and Eureka riding on either side of the handcuffed Burke. Cal held Burke's mount's reins.

Garrick and Maggie rode behind them, Maggie on Toby, while Garrick, holding Johnny, rode one of the outlaws' mounts.

It wasn't long before the darkness, the rocking motion of the horse's movements and exhaustion put Johnny back to sleep. The moon had come out from behind the clouds again, making it easier for Maggie and Garrick to study each other's faces.

"I meant what I said back there, when I thought I might die trying to get you both out of there, Maggie," Garrick said. "I love you. I always will. I was a fool...because of what Cecilia—"

Maggie reached out a hand and laid a finger on his lips to stop him. "Don't. I understood how you felt. I wanted to die when he told you—"

Garrick shook his head. "Don't say that," he answered. "*I'd* have rather died than lose you. And as for what he said, it doesn't matter. It really doesn't, not now or ever again. I…I would have come to my senses in a day or so anyhow, I reckon, but the way it happened, I nearly lost you. Maggie, I'll believe what you say for the rest of my life. If you tell me the sky is full of flying cats, I'll believe it. I wouldn't blame you if you never wanted to set eyes on me again, though.''

"Ssh. Enough of that. I won't have you apologizing anymore. I love you, and that little boy you're holding. Now, let's see…if we sent Papa a telegram tomorrow, I think he could be in Gillespie Springs in a few days. If Livy will lend me her wedding dress, we could get married that much sooner.''

Garrick chuckled approvingly. ''That's my managing, meddling Yankee sweetheart,'' he said, reining in his horse. Maggie did the same, and carefully, without waking the sleeping child, each leaned over just enough to exchange a kiss of promise in the moonlight.

In his sleep, little Johnny Devlin smiled.

* * * * *

COMING NEXT MONTH FROM

HARLEQUIN HISTORICALS

- **TAMING THE LION**
  by **Suzanne Barclay**, author of PRIDE OF LIONS
  In a continuation of *The Sutherland Series,* a roguish knight
  plans to steal a clan's secret. What he doesn't plan for is falling
  in love with the clan's beautiful leader.
  HH #463 ISBN# 29063-2 $4.99 U.S./$5.99 CAN.

- **THE WEDDING GAMBLE**
  by **Julia Justiss**
  A penniless lady forced to marry a wicked baron is rescued at
  the last minute by the Marquess of Englemere, a wealthy
  widower, when he proposes a marriage of convenience.
  HH #464 ISBN# 29064-0 $4.99 U.S./$5.99 CAN.

- **THE MARRIAGE KNOT**
  by **Mary McBride**, author of STORMING PARADISE
  An older man dies and leaves his mansion to the local sheriff
  instead of his much younger widow, with the clear intent of
  matchmaking.
  HH #465 ISBN# 29065-9 $4.99 U.S./$5.99 CAN.

- **A COWBOY'S HEART**
  by **Liz Ireland**, author of PRIM AND IMPROPER
  A handsome cowboy falls in love with a tomboy who turns out
  to be a strong-willed and determined young woman.
  HH #466 ISBN# 29066-7 $4.99 U.S./$5.99 CAN.

DON'T MISS THESE FOUR GREAT TITLES AVAILABLE NOW:

HH #459 THE WELSHMAN'S BRIDE
Margaret Moore

HH #460 HUNTER OF MY HEART
Janet Kendall

HH #461 MAGGIE AND THE MAVERICK
Laurie Grant

HH #462 THE UNLIKELY WIFE
Cassandra Austin